POCKETFUL OF STARS

JULIETTE DOUGLAS

"When we walk in difficult places, God sends the strength and nourishment to face what comes our way, not all at once, but day by day." Sue Monk Kidd

On January 23, 2018, the community I love and live in suffered an unimaginable tragic event at our Marshall County High School in Benton, KY.

This book is dedicated to all who met this tragedy head on:

Our first responders: 911 dispatchers, local law enforcement agencies, EMTs, KSP, fire departments, rescue squad, fish and wildlife. The students, parents and relatives, school administration, teachers, hospital staff, nurses and doctors, local governments, our citizens along with the surrounding counties who all banded together when the unthinkable happened.

You all are awesome shining stars and heroes. Thank you.

Our hearts and souls were shredded that day, but through this darkness, God shone his light and we shall prevail.

Because WE ARE MARSHALL COUNTY STRONG!

"Now faith is being sure of what we hope for and certain of what we do not see." Hebrews 11, verse 1, Holy Bible NIV

PRAISE FOR JULIETTE DOUGLAS

All writers would like to have something nice said about them. It's the truth. There isn't a creative western writer in the world who doesn't like to feel acknowledged as a talent. Juliette Douglas is certainly one of those authors who needn't fear negativity. Her work speaks for itself as some of the finest in the Western world. A talented writer, a great storyteller and a fantastic talent. If you have already discovered her great books—you will already know what I mean. If you haven't—boy, have you been living up a tree? You need to grab this, and all other Douglas books, right away.

—*Robert Hanlon – number one bestselling author of "The Texan Avenger" Western series and many, many others*

For a writer to really please their audience, they must have the correct ingredients. A talent for writing, a talent for storytelling, a talent for creativity and a desire to spend long hours crafting a story. From what I have read of Juliette Douglas, and her outstanding work, I know that all Western readers would love her stories. I believe all Western writers could use her as an inspiration. Here is a writer who turns out story, after story, after story with all the ingredients needed for success.

—*M. Allen – bestselling Western author of the top twenty hit "The Rifleman" and many others.*

1

———————————

SPRING 1882

" *"All the cowboys I know are afraid of only two things...a decent woman and being set afoot..."*

— TEDDY BLUE ABBOTT: COWBOY 1882

"Pffftt," Carlie Anne Russell exhaled into the late spring air, "This is harder than I thought it would be," she mumbled to herself, sliding tiredly off Waldo.

Her bottom lip blew sweaty bangs off her forehead as she gazed at the herd. It didn't look like she had made much of a dent, even though she had been wrestling and branding calves for over a week. Carlie went, "Pffftt," again.

That is until a brilliant idea flashed through her brain. She decided to ride into the herd with the hot iron, sticking it to whatever part of the calf she could reach from horseback.

The results were brands burned into shoulders, necks, backs and ribs. Waldo had dumped her a couple of times too, trying to dodge those bodies bumping, bucking and hooves kicking as the critters reacted to the hot iron.

She ran her tongue across her dry lips wetting them as she

sighed. Taking off her hat and fanning herself with it, she tucked a loose strand of sun-bleached honey colored hair behind her ear. She blew again mumbling tiredly, "That wasn't such a bright idea after all." Crossing her feet, she plopped to the ground laying her battered beat up old hat to the side as she pulled a blade of grass and absentmindedly feathered it across her hand as she watched the mixed red herd.

She'd been out of kilter ever since her mama and daddy had died from the fever. Her small family had been close, including her grandparents. Now it was just her, and the way things were looking right now, it wasn't going to get any better any time soon. Just like her gramma used to say when someone had too much hard luck to handle. *Had a wagonload of lemons dumped on 'em and don't have 'nuff sugar to make lemonade.*

Just like me, Carlie Anne sighed sorrowfully, again.

Rising, she trudged back to Waldo, mounted and reined him around back toward the herd.

2

"I will not hire anyone, Harley," Carlie said crossly. "I don't trust them slimy, under-handed saddle bums, wandering around claiming to be looking for work when they ain't! They could rob me blind! Stealing my cattle or my horses!" She rattled on, her eyes flashing. "I'll not allow them to set up a maverick factory using my cows for their benefit," glaring at Harley. Then she pointed a finger in his face, "You got that, Harley?"

Harley Trimble was at wit's end with the girl. He knew the two of them couldn't take care of 800 cows this winter. *Hell, she may have mor'n that by now, hell,* he knew she had more than that by now. Half-pint was kind of unpredictable when it came to punching cows. Her mind always seemed to be flying off yonder way instead of concentrating on the task at hand. And that worried on Harley like a dog itching with its fleas. His ticker hadn't been acting exactly right; sometimes he'd have pain, but most of the time he didn't have the strength to do the simplest of chores being always short of breath. And that worried on him too, because Carlie Anne had no one to look after her except him. But he couldn't let her know that as it would just make her more determined to run *Three Pines* all by herself.

Carlie Anne had an itsy-bitsy frame, the spitting image of her grandma. Many a time Harley had felt spooked looking at a younger image of Rose Russell. From the top of her head to the tip of her toes, there was no denying it; Carlie Anne carried the blood of the Russell clan.

Carlie might have a woman's body, but in reality, she was still just a kid. What with her being spoiled rotten by love, making her even more childlike, seeing the world through rose-colored glasses.

Harley slowly shook his head; the girl wasn't even green-broke enough to run a spread, *a real shave-tail*. Even though she had shadowed her pop's and grand-pop's every move, idolizing the two men.

Nope. Carlie Anne is gonna need help, no matter how hard she fought and spit when he put the bit in her mouth. She might make it through one more year, but she wouldn't be able to tackle it alone in the long haul.

Harley sighed again. "Honey, you gotta lissen ta reason now..."

"...I told you no, Harley," Carlie interrupted, rising as she planted small fists on narrow hips and continued to glare at him.

"Why?"

"You know how many people have offered to buy this place since Mama and Daddy died...and only offering me a pittance of what it's worth? How can I trust any saddle tramp who comes in here, knowing in the back of my mind that they may create an accident, so no one could suspect that it was really murder. Or burn me out, or," Carlie paused, thinking then adding. "Capturing and selling off my horses, finding lost cows when they ain't even lost yet, claiming them for their own, just so they can get their hands on this land and the grazing leases!"

Harley blinked. *Where in the hell did she get that idea?*

"I wouldn't put it past Tom Riley to set me up like that," she rattled on. "He's already tried to skin me several times!" Carlie cried, stopping to heave in a big breath. "No. The only ones I'll trust are those friends of yours who've helped before," she finally finished.

Harley squinted tired eyes at the defiant girl. "Honey, I don't know where them boys is at, hain't seen them fer several years now," he said.

"That's fine, just real fine! I'll take care of those cows just like I have been," she crossly replied, spinning on her toes as she slammed the door on the way out.

Harley rose, stood gazing out the front window. *Girl's stubborn, blind and green.*

Racking his brain, he knew his health wasn't what it should be. Oh, he could help some, but not in the way Carlie Anne was going to need.

Seemed like all of a sudden Carlie Anne had become distrustful of folks. She had always been friendly, now she acted leery. Guess he could blame that on Tom Riley, sending his hired hands to scare the poor kid into selling out to him.

That's why he'd taught her how to cut the lead in those cartridges. It would give her a better advantage if she had to take pot shots at any more of Riley's hands threatening her.

Thinking again, he didn't know where Rube, Yancy, or Bushy was. The only one he'd heard from was Colt Rawlins. He knew the boy had been stationed at Fort James for a while. Rawlins was always good at dropping Harley a line or two over the years.

Slowly pushing himself up from the table, he shuffled over to an old writing desk. Pulling some paper out of a drawer, Harley angled the chair and sat to begin a letter to Colt Rawlins.

3

LATE SUMMER 1882

Colt Rawlins sat his bay, looking down the road from where he'd reined up and studied the town of Kaskaskia, Montana, remembering the last time he was here. It was nestled between the Bitterroot Range and the Rockies. With an overhang of clouds that were cloaking the mountains in their grey smoke and creating a cold, dark and dismal atmosphere, it suited Colt Rawlins' foul mood. Looking at the damp sky, his hand pulled his fur coat collar up tighter around his ears. The weather at this altitude could change in an instant: from warm sunny skies to cold and snowy. *Just wait five minutes*, he remembered Harley saying, *Hit keeps ya on yer toes...*

While he'd been stationed at Fort James as a scout, he'd received a letter from the old coot asking him to come here. Harley needed his help. That's all the letter had said, that Harley needed his help.

"Yep," Colt muttered. Kaskaskia, Montana had to be the only place he'd ever been that truly was five hundred miles north of nowhere. Why anyone wanted to settle this abrasive, unforgiving wilderness, they had to be out of their minds. *It's one hell of a lonesome piece of ground,* his mind repeated.

Colt retrieved the memories of the winter he had spent with Harley, Rube, Yancy, and Bushy up here five hundred miles north of nowhere. They had all done very well that year with the money stuffing their pockets from the furs they had trapped in these mountains. The rest of the time 'the girls' as Harley liked to call them, played chess or poker, and told some whopping tales as only woodsmen knew how to tell while they holed up out of winter's banshee call. The chilly dank day brought forth the memory of how really cold it got up here.

He couldn't believe that it was five years ago; it felt to him like it was just last year. Colt hadn't been back till now.

"Hup, son," he softly said, heels nudging ribs and moving the gelding into motion, heading down toward the little town that was five hundred miles north of nowhere.

4

As Rawlins entered the town limits, he gazed around, noting that most of the buildings were still the log structures he remembered from before. Not many folks made an appearance outside to ogle him as he and his bay traversed the still muddy street from the rains a few days ago. The silence seemed to echo around him as all he heard was the squishy sucking sounds from his bay's hooves. He sniffed. There were no discernable odors he could pick up either, just the sharp aroma of spruce and fir in the heavily moist, still air.

The town wasn't really a town, more of an outpost that had sprung up from the needs of the trappers during their hey-day. Then a few homesteaders trickled in after the war, wanting a place of solitude from the carnage that was left behind. A sheriff's office was seen to his right, nothing remarkable about it, and a few doors down, was the saloon advertising rooms and meals. The word *Saloon* was framed by at least a dozen racks of various sized antlers. His grey eyes caught a shingle hanging within his peripheral vision. Turning his head slightly, he read, *Dr. B. Caldwell*. The general store loomed on his left, and then a few buildings sat at the edge of town that looked to be a combination church-schoolhouse from the cross and rope swings in the front yard. Colt didn't remember seeing that five years ago. *Humm...* he thought. A livery across from that building and that was it; one street, a few log and clapboard structures, nothing else. This was Kaskaskia, Montana, five hundred miles north of nowhere. From the looks of it, nothing had really changed in the last five years.

Reining up in front of the general store, he dismounted into the mud. Colt noticed the door to the sheriff's office open and someone stepped out shutting the door behind him. The man continued to study him as he walked to the edge of the boardwalk, buttoning his multicolored wool coat, then sticking his hands in the large pockets down the side. Rawlins smiled faintly; he was used to the stares. Colt Rawlings had one of those tall, loosely jointed builds that created an unusual walk, and wide shoulders that didn't quite seem to fit with the rest of him. Brown hair that liked to curl when wet, and his most impressive feature, silver grey eyes in a square jawed face that was now covered with a good month's growth of stubble. A thick blue wool coat with a beaver fur collar covered his torso. Long muscular legs were encased in tan canvas britches.

Grabbing his war bag off the saddle horn, he turned and openly stared back at the sheriff before two fingers brushed along the brim of his battered hat acknowledging the lawman before stepping on the walk at the front of the store.

A bell dinged above his head when Rawlins opened the door. Stepping inside, the heat from a wood stove felt good as his eyes brushed the room. The store was well stocked, he realized. Tins and boxes of goods sat on the shelves behind the counter. Burlap sacks of flour, cornmeal, and oats along with feed were stacked on the floor to his left against the wall. Grey eyes flitted to his right taking in the items that were commonly sold within establishments such as this. Harnesses, collars, clothes and other things folks might need. Sewing notions, several sizes of shovels, metal pails, washtubs and a table that held pelts. Throwing his bag on the counter, it landed with a thump and a dull clink as the tin utensils inside were jostled. Rawlins waited.

A man emerged from an open doorway, "Oh…didn't hear the bell, I was way in the back…countin'…gotta git enough supplies in for winter hits and blocks the passage. What kin I do for ya?"

Colt turned hearing the man's comments about winter supplies. He remembered the supplies they had stored ahead of that long, cold winter he'd spent with Harley as he continued to study the proprietor. Ruddy, chubby cheeks, spectacles halfway down his nose with a snow-white thatch on top. He had a nondescript nose and a barrel body that was covered by a well-worn dirty canvas apron. His face supplied a toothy grin when the silence stretched out. "Mister? You need something?"

"Um…yeah. Need to replenish my trail supplies," Colt answered, handing over a list.

"Planning a long trip?" he asked, taking the piece of paper, adjusting his specs as he scanned and read the list.

"Don't know yet. Maybe you can give me some information?"

"I'll try," the proprietor replied, turning back around, adjusting his glasses again to scan the shelves, reaching here and there, beginning to gather up what was on the list.

"Um…you know a fella by the name of Harley Trimble?"

Turning, "Why…shor…real character, that Harley," he answered, glancing up hearing the bell ding again. "Howdy, Sheriff…" he greeted, then returned to filling the rest of the order.

"Sam…" the lawman acknowledged flicking his brown eyes to the lanky newcomer, letting them roam from his mud caked boots to finally settle on the lean weatherworn face.

Colt kept his face deadpan straight; he was used to being looked over, giving back his own scrutiny to the man beside him. He was about six feet in height, not stocky, not slim but looked like he could hold his own in a fight. Fingers of silver hair showed above his ears under his hat.

The sheriff moved closer and stuck out his hand and introduced himself. "Sheriff Ed Page. You passin' through...?"

"Rawlins, Colt Rawlins," he said, returning the firm shake the sheriff had given him. "Do'no...right yet..."

One eye squinted, recognizing the name, "I've heard of you..." he began.

Turning slowly, Colt's world-weary eyes gazed at Page, noting the not too friendly tone directed at him. "Sheriff...I'm a peaceable man. I don't go lookin' for trouble, but if backed into a corner I *will* defend myself."

Silence reigned, waiting to see who would speak first.

Sam butted into the quiet. "Mister Rawlins here, is asking 'bout Harley."

"Harley?"

"Mmm...yeah. You know Harley Trimble?"

"Sure...everyone knows that ol' skinflint."

Rawlins smiled at that.

"What business you got with Harley?" the sheriff asked.

Colt tapered his eyes. "He sent me a letter, saying he needed help. Is he in some sort of trouble?"

The sheriff and Sam cut a swift glance at each other before Ed answered.

"Could be, how well do you know Harley?"

"Good enough, we've worked together off and on over the years. Why...?" *The sheriff's being just a tad too nosy,* Colt thought. "...How come all the questions, Sheriff?"

"Just wondered is all," the sheriff answered, giving Sam another quick glance.

Ed explained, "We had a fever come through here about a year and a half ago. Pert near wiped us out, we're kinda locked in here as you probably noticed."

Colt nodded as he continued to listen, thinking, *Why is he telling me this?*

"Took ah lotta folks, mostly the older ones along with a few young ones; it wasn't pretty. Doc was overwhelmed, couldn't keep up. Harley and Carlie Anne stepped in to help, using some kind of Indian medicine they knew about. It worked, at least the fever quit spreading like wildfire..." Page said.

Nodding since he knew about Harley's medicines, then asked, "...And this concerns me...how?"

"I'm gittin' ta that..." he continued, "...Harley's been up to the Russell place helping Carlie run that spread of hers ever since she lost her folks from that fever." The sheriff paused, his eyes leveled at Rawlins. "And I guess Harley wants your help?"

Stuffing the supplies into his bag, Colt took his time answering. Red flags seemed to be nudging him between his shoulder blades.

"Do' no. He didn't say." Colt offered up, catching the quick look the two men gave each other again.

"I'll bet that's what Harley wants you to do...help them out. Carlie Anne Russell can be a real handful. Harley's not a drinker, but when she frustrates the hell out of him, he comes in here and has a few more than his usual..." he then added, "Harley told me to be watching for you..."

Registering surprise, Colt stated, "Now you tell me...after giving me what for?"

Page grinned, then shrugged, "Way-ell...gotta be careful nowadays..."

"I see...now where can I find Harley?"

"Depending how bad Carlie gets his ire up, which has been a lot here lately, he'll probably be in here tonight." The sheriff continued, "Saloon's got some empty rooms, stable is down the street." Pausing, as he leaned an elbow on the counter. "That is, effen you planning on staying?"

"I'm staying." Colt stated, picking up the gear bag, his boots leisurely thumping toward the door, leaving small cods of mud in passing. The bell dinged again when Rawlins let himself out the door, shutting it in his wake.

Sam and Ed looked at each other.

"This is gonna get mighty interesting...ain't it Ed?"

"Could be...Sam...could be."

Sam leaned on the counter as he said, "That Rawlins fella, don't look like he takes much guff from anyone."

"Nope," returned Ed.

"Carlie Anne ain't gonna like it, taking orders from someone like him," Sam said.

"Nope."

"Fur is gonna fly, and maybe enough sparks to set the woods afire," Sam added.

"Yep." Ed threw over his shoulder as he left the store.

Sam just grinned.

5

C arlie Anne poured Harley a cup of coffee that morning before she served him some breakfast.

"Good Gawd...girl! When you gonna learn ta make ah decent cup of coffee!" he spluttered. "Hit's strong enough ta dissolve an axe!"

She gave him a squirrely look. "When you teach me," she sassed back.

A moment later, Carlie placed a bowl in front of Harley. He looked at it, then flicked his eyes at Carlie. "What's this?"

"Oats."

"You sure?"

"That's what it said on the bag."

"And you made this how...?"

She shrugged, ignoring Harley's question as she spooned her own sticky, gooey mess into a bowl.

Harley sighed. That was one thing he was going to have to warn Colt about, if he actually showed up. Colt expected to eat, and he expected the woman to cook it for him. But in this case, he was the one who was going to have to do all the cooking.

Harley knew Colt liked spirited women up to a point. But he also knew Carlie Anne was going to turn Colt's notions of a woman upside down, real quick. Harley shook his head again, *Sparks were sure to fly...and maybe a little fur, too.*

Carlie watched Harley shake his head, prompting her to say, "It doesn't taste very good, does it?" after sampling it, then grimacing at her spoonful.

"Hit's filling," replied Harley, eating the goo that passed for breakfast. Even adding the sugar, milk and butter to it did not help. *Now...how 'n the hell can you ruin something as simple as oats...* he thought, then silently added to himself, *Carlie Anne can...* He sighed as he shifted his butt on the wooden seat then asked, "Young'un, you thought any more 'bout hiring some drovers ta hep ya out?"

"I told you, I'm not hiring anyone! 'Sides, I got you! You and I can do it," Carlie defended her plan.

"Honey, you know I cain't do that kinda work no more. Least-ways all them hours in the saddle, like you're proposing," Harley said.

"Why, Harley Trimble, you're fit as a fiddle! You're just trying to backslide on me!" Her eyes narrowed as she threw him a dirty look. Watching Harley manfully spoon the oats into his mouth without a word, her eyes softened as she gazed at her old family friend, "I just want to be left alone and in peace to work the land I love. Is that too much to ask for, Harley?" Carlie finished softly.

Harley glanced up quickly at her comment. "No, honey I guess not," he answered with a heavy sigh.

Carlie nodded.

COLT RAWLINS SAT on the porch outside the saloon. His long frame slouched down in a rocker, big feet crossed at the ankles and resting on the railing as he watched the town's early morning bustle. It was warmer out today with the sun providing the much-welcomed heat after the chill and heavy cloud cover of the day before. The street was drying out quickly except for a few places. His eyes kept skirting here and there, constantly moving and observing, waiting to see if Harley might come into town today.

A buckboard caught his interest from his side view; his eyes and head slowly turned and followed the team and wagon. At first glance, it appeared to be driven by a kid with a battered felt hat pulled low over the brow to shield the kid's eyes from the brilliant sunlight. He watched as a nice pair of mules pulled the buckboard up in front of the general store.

Colt was right. It was a kid and a young one at that. He continued to watch as the kid set the brake, wrapping the reins around it and swinging a leg over the side of the seat box and placed a booted foot on the wheel. The kid's foot suddenly slipped off the muddy metal rim, tumbling the kid into the mud and sending the scruffy hat flying.

Rawlins sat up, swearing softly, "I'll be damned...it's a girl..." but made no move to cross the street to help her.

Embarrassed, Carlie Anne quickly looked around to make sure that no one had seen her make a fool of herself. *Whew...* she thought, reaching for her hat and jamming it back on her head as she rose. Flicking the mud off her hands before wiping them down her corded britches, she walked to the three steps and skipped up them only to catch a toe on the ragged weather-beaten edge of board, landing hard on her knees. Groaning as she rose, Carlie muttered, "Sheesh..." while a dirty hand rubbed the sore spot as she briskly disappeared through the door of Sam's store.

Placing his feet back on the railing, Colt settled back, grinning as he rolled his eyes, thinking he'd just seen his entertainment for the day in this sleepy town. He turned his attention elsewhere.

The bell dinging made Sam look up from what he was doing. "Hey, Carlie Anne," Sam said.

"Sam," Carlie acknowledged. Paper crackled when she removed a list from her hip pocket. "Need this filled, please," she requested.

"Getting ready for winter?" he asked, his eyes scanning the list.

"Yeah, Harley and I will take the supplies up to the line shack probably sometime this week," she answered.

"We got a nice day today, but it's already been colder than usual this month," Sam said.

"I know," Carlie agreed, picking up a heavy sack of flour. Wobbling under its weight, she headed out the door to the wagon. Nearing the edge of the porch, her toe caught a nail, tripping the girl and the entire bag of flour pitched forward into the street. The sack hit the dirt first, causing it to split and Carlie's face and upper torso plopped into the now opened bag of flour.

Watching this scene unfold across the street, Colt shook his head as his eyes rolled once again at the awkward filly. This time, he felt obliged to help. Ambling over, he squatted down in front of her. "Graceful, ain't cha?" he said drily, taking an arm and pulling the girl to an upright position.

Unusual eyes snapped at him from a powder white face. "Oh, shut up, you big moose," she spurted, spraying flour onto his shirt while her hand continued to swipe at the white powder that covered her face.

Pulling a bandana out of his back pocket, Rawlins held out it to her and Carlie Anne quickly snatched it out of his hand. He continued observing the girl as she tried to wipe the flour off.

Carlie caught him watching her, his eyes merry at what a fool she'd just made of herself. "I didn't do that on purpose," she began, pointing at a nail sticking up out of the frayed and weather-beaten edge of a board.

Colt's eyes followed her finger.

"That nail tripped me and quit laughing at me, you half-wit," she bristled.

Still grinning, Colt asked, "Uh-huh, what else you got to load?"

"I don't need your help," Carlie shot back as she turned heading back to the steps. This time, she gingerly stepped up them. Going through the propped open door, she came out a few seconds later with a hammer in hand. Giving him a wicked glare first, she knelt and pounded the nail back into the board. The stranger was still watching her with a silly grin plastered on his face when Carlie rose and spun on her toes and disappeared inside again.

Shrugging at her lack of common courtesy, Colt sauntered back to his perch on the sun-warmed porch of the hotel.

Sam and Carlie both came out of the store this time. The proprietor had large sacks draped over his shoulders when he spied Colt. He called out, "Hey...Rawlins? Wanna give us a lift?"

Stopping at the voice, Colt turned and moseyed back, pointing, "Don't think she much wants my help..."

Sam grinned. "Aww...Half-pint is more bark than bite...she don' mean nuthin' by it..."

Carlie gasped. "Dang-it, Sam, I don't need nobody's help!"

"Now girlie...you jus' listen ta ol' Sam...here." He flicked his eyes at the lean figure watching with an amused look on his face, waiting. "Go ahead, Rawlins..."

Colt reached for the sack the girl was carrying; she spiraled away from him. The weight of the sack unbalanced her and caused her to sit down hard in the mud with the sack landing up in her lap. "Ugh..." Carlie Anne moaned.

Rawlins reached for the sack again.

Swatting at his hands, she growled. "I told you...I don't need no help!"

Ignoring the girl, he picked up the sack and flung it into the buckboard. Turning back to the young upstart, he offered his hand to pull her up. All he got was a scorching look as she angrily rolled away from him.

"Suit yourself..." Rawlins said, as he moved around her and helped Sam load the rest of the supplies into her wagon.

Rising, Carlie swatted at the caked mud on her wet backside. Staring at her grimy hands, she muttered, "Sheesh…I'm gonna have to take a bath when I get home…"

Sam grinned, eyeing the fur-flying going on between Carlie Anne Russell and this Rawlins fellow.

Rawlins kept casting quick glances every now and then at the girl as he and Sam finished the job. She stood with her arms folded in defiance and her lips in a tight thin line. Flour was still smudged across her face with white-crusted lashes framing her unusual colored eyes. Colt couldn't quite put a finger on what color they really were; they kept changing their hue with her mood.

"All right, Half-pint, guess yure ready for the winter," Sam told her, wiping his hands on his canvas apron. Steadying himself against a porch post, he began scraping the mud off his boots on the edge of the walk.

Carlie climbed gingerly back into the wagon; she didn't want to be embarrassed again with that big moose watching her. Unwrapping the reins from the brake, she released it. "Thanks, Sam," Carlie said. "Hup, Jack, Jill," she called out slapping the two mules' rumps with the reins. "Let's go home," she said, guiding the team around in the street.

Still standing next to Sam with his thumbs hooked in his back pockets, Colt observed the girl driving back the way she had come. *Didn't even bother to thank me, little squirt.* He heard her whistle and saw a big grey form appear out of the brush and begin following her.

Eyes going wide, Rawlins spoke to Sam. "That's a wolf," he exclaimed.

Finished with scraping the mud off his feet, Sam grinned, saying, "Yea-up. You just met Carlie Anne Russell and her pet wolf." Sam gave his toothy grin. "Won't find anyone quite like her within five hundred miles." He pointed his finger at Rawlins, "But she's got fire…I'll gaaruntee ya that, 'n iffen ya don't believe me...jus ast Harley..." he added, then disappeared back into his store.

Colt took two fingers and pushed his hat back from his fore-head, continuing to gaze at the disappearing speck of a girl driving the wagon, followed by a damn wolf.

6

Eating supper in the saloon, his eyes continued to roam and observe the patrons as he chewed his food. Colt was hoping Harley would show up tonight. The room contained a few cowhands, some trappers and the local trade totaling about ten in all, not counting the barkeep and himself. The hanging lanterns illuminated a suspended smoky haze in pockets above a few of the tables from the cigarettes and cheroots. A low murmur of voices reached his ears along with a chortle of laughter every now and again. The room's decor matched the sign outside; antlers hanging on the walls, a testament to the hunters who had bagged a big one.

Rawlins had been a scout for the Army when he had met Harley Trimble, becoming fast friends despite their age difference. They would occasionally run into each other over the years, working together again for a spell, then moving off in different directions.

Harley had once saved him from a bullet in the back when they had both worked as scouts. So, when Harley wrote him saying he needed Colt's help, Rawlins headed to Kaskaskia,

Montana. Friends were hard to find and even harder to keep out here, and he wanted to keep Harley as a friend for good.

Shoveling another bite of apple pie in his mouth he thought again, *If that thin strip of dried hide don't show up tonight, I'll have to go track him down and get to the bottom of what Harley wants from me.* From comments made by the sheriff and the store keep, Colt had a sneaky suspicion it had something to do with the kid.

SHUFFLING ALONG THE WALKWAY, Harley Trimble leaned back against the wall of the saloon and stopped to catch his breath. An hour ago, Ed had run into him and told him that the man he was looking for, Colt Rawlins, was in town staying over at the saloon. Resting gnarled hands on top of swinging doors, he peeked over them. Rheumy eyes traveled over the customers until they landed on the tall stranger sitting at a corner table with his back to the wall eating supper. A faint smile cracked weathered skin as he whispered, "Old habits die hard...don't they, son..." The boy sure looked good to Harley's tired old eyes. Expelling a sigh, he pushed open the doors and walked over to Colt Rawlins. "Howdy, son."

Colt looked up when he heard the raspy voice, then smiled wide. He stood, giving Harley's hand a solid shake. "You ol' bandy rooster, took you long enough to get here." Eyes scanned the old trapper's skinny frame. Harley always reminded him of a short, thin strip of dried buffalo hide with tuffs of hair sticking up on one end.

"Been busy," Harley lied.

Seeing Harley when he stepped into the saloon, Jake the barkeep called out. "You want yure usual, Harley?"

Harley glanced over at Jake, thought about it a few seconds then shook his head, saying, "Naw...just bring me a cup of coffee."

The barkeep's eyes popped. "You sick, Harley?" Jake asked,

filling a mug with stale black brew, walking around the bar and handing the cup to Harley.

Taking it, he nodded his thanks, answering, "Yeah," Harley grumped. "Sick in tha haid."

Jake grinned. "Half-pint giving ya a hard time again?"

"Don't she always?" Harley tersely replied.

"Let me know if you want something stronger," Jake said as he headed back to his post behind the bar.

"Yeah, yeah," Harley answered, giving a dismissive wave of his hand.

Fond memories of the old coot brought a softness to Colt's otherwise time-hardened features. "Well...you crusty old codger, how ya been? See you made it through another winter. How's the fur trade?"

"Tolerable..." Harley gruffly replied.

Colt leaned back in his chair while he patiently waited.

Staring into his cup, Harley finally looked across at the man who had become like a son to him. "How ye been?"

"Tolerable..." he repeated.

"Been working them scraggly cows?"

"Mostly..." Eyes of grey steel narrowed shrewdly, "All right, what's really on your mind? You brought me five hundred miles north of nowhere...why?"

Taking a deep breath, Harley plunged into his next statement. "I need ya ta show someone how ta run ah spread..." he trailed off, waiting on Colt's reaction.

"Why?"

Harley slammed his hand on the table so hard it made Colt's silverware jump and others in the room look their way. "...Cause yure a cowman, you got cow smarts! You know what them critters is thinking, even when they's asleep! And don't go getting obernoxious wit' me 'bout hit neither...I's need your hep!"

Colt gave Harley another crooked look.

"Aww…hell…damn it…Jake, bring me a double," Harley called over his shoulder to the barkeep then exhaled annoyingly.

Grinning, Jake picked up a bottle and two glasses and walked over to the table. The slight sound of glass tapping wood was heard when he set the tumbler down in front of Colt, gesturing with the bottle.

He placed a large palm over the glass and shook his head no.

Shrugging, the barkeep poured Harley a full glass, then handed it to him.

Harley nodded his thanks and put the rim to his lips.

Rawlins watched as Harley drank that straight down.

Harley swiped the bottle from the barkeep and set it down hard on the table.

Shrugging, Jake walked away.

Harley swallowed half of the liquid before he leaned back in his chair, swiping at his mouth and still not saying a word.

Grey eyes remained narrowed, as he'd watched his friend swill down the liquor. "What's got you so het up, Harley? You don't normally drink like that. What's going on, you old coot?"

"I need ya ta help someone winter some cows."

"And teach them how to run a spread," Rawlins added.

Harley gave Colt a sharp look. "I aw ready said that," he exhaled in irritation.

Rawlins raised the question. "This wouldn't have anything to do with the kid, now, would it?"

"What kid?"

"That Carlie Anne Russell?"

Surprised, Harley asked. "How'd you know?"

"Oh…we sorta crossed paths today when she came to town… she got a big grey wolf?"

Harley nodded.

"Kinda stubborn, sassy, hard-headed," Colt continued.

"Yeah, that'd be her," Harley heaved a tired sigh.

"She the one got you all bent and ready to tie on a twister?"

"Yep, that'd be her," Harley repeated.

Colt continued to grin. "She wouldn't be hard to handle."

"You say that now. I'll jus' let you deal with her Gawd awful hard haid!" Harley fired back.

Reaching across the table, Rawlins took a match out of the glass and stuck it in his mouth. He then proceeded to tilt the chair back on two legs and fold his arms while he contemplated what it was that Harley really wanted of him. "You want to start at the beginning and tell me what this is all about?" Colt prompted.

Harley looked up quickly and then nodded.

Allowing the chair back down on four legs, his tongue moved the match around in his mouth as he waited to hear what Harley would spin.

"They was five of them Russells ta come out this a way. Half-pint...uh...Carlie Anne was jus' a baby then, back in the mid-sixties, after the War. Her parents and grandparents said Kentucky got hit pretty hard, like most places did during the War and after. They wanted a place where's they could breathe, start over again..."

Colt nodded, shifting the matchstick to the other side of his mouth with his tongue. He knew the feeling; he'd run across many over the years carrying the same sentiments.

"...They'd brought some of the finest heads of those red and white-faced cows with 'em, said they's a new breed, built fer meat...gonna breed them with mavericks and see what came out..." He paused to catch his breath, and continued to rattle on, "...Kaskaskia was just a spit in the dust, but it was what they was looking for..." Harley explained.

Cutting a glance at the lean figure across from him, he swallowed the rest of the liquid in his glass. Swiping the back of his hand against his chin, Harley stated, "...Them Kentucky boys was smart, Cal and Jim started a small logging business. They built a water powered sawmill on their place north of town..."

Harley looked around the saloon before adding "...Most of this here town is built wit the wood from them and pretty soon they had enough money to buy some more of them red, white-faced stock and begin adding to their herd. We all looked at them like they was squirrelly, but they made hit work. We became fast friends…" Harley trailed off.

"And…"

Harley came back to earth at the sound of Colt's voice. Cutting him a quick glance, he went back to twirling the brown liquid, deep in thought as he said. "Half-pint…uh…Carlie Anne, believes she can run that spread all by herself. She did for a little while after her folks died. But you know and I know, she might be able to for the short haul, but not for the long haul, and that's what's got me so worried."

Harley finished that drink and reached for the bottle. A big palm gently closed itself over a gnarled one. Colt spoke softly. "I think that's enough for today, Harley," moving the bottle out of his reach.

Giving a shrug, Harley continued. "The young'un is smart, knows most of what ta do, following her Pop and Grand-Pops around like ah stray dog. Somehow, she's got hit in her head, she's got sumthin' to prove. But she's got 800 cows, maybe more, ta move from summer graze down ta the valleys for the winter. She might could handle a hundred or so, but not 800 plus!"

"Why you so interested in what happens? What's your stake in this?" Colt inquired.

Rheumy eyes bored a hole in Colt Rawlins as a knobby finger pointed at him. "You watch yure tongue, boy!" Harley said. His voice suddenly softened. "Nuthin', no stake, jus' a friend thet cares 'bout her…Half-pint is my godchild, lost my own Katydid, and our baby boy in childbirth," he said.

Colt blinked in surprise at the news. "I'm sorry, Harley. I didn't know you'd ever been married."

He nodded in response to Colt's comment. "Well…leastways, I

need ya ta hep her out fer a while. Branding needs ta be done, cows taken ta the railhead next summer," Harley said.

"Now you just hold on a minute, you old bandy rooster," Colt interrupted. "You're talking about me staying mor'n a year! I can't do that!"

"Why not? Ya got sumthin' special planned? Ya got ah girl waiting on ya?" Harley demanded.

"Well…no…but maybe I…"

Staring into his cup, Harley finally looked across at the man who had become like a son to him. "Then it's settled…I sure do need yure hep, bad," he stated.

Leaning forward again, Colt took a sip of his now cold coffee. His muscular forearms rested on the table, his hands wrapped around the earthenware mug. Colt let his gaze flick over the scruffy weather lined face to the watery eyes and then stopped at Harley's corkscrew bushy overhanging eyebrows. Resettling his look back on the old man's eyes beginning to grow cloudy with age. "Alright…what's going on…"

Harley peered into his cup, took a sip and swallowed. "Well…I hain't been doing so good here lately…think it's my ticker," he confessed.

"You seen the Doc?" Colt asked, voicing his concern.

Harley hissed the words, beady eyes glowing with fury. "What the hell's ah doctor gonna do? When hit's my time ta go…I'll go!"

Colt sighed and sipped more coffee as Harley poured more whiskey.

"Harley, you ain't gonna be able to walk out of here tonight," Colt observed.

Harley's watery eyes shone bright as he grinned. "Why…I'll jus' bunk wit' you son, be like ol' times, eh?"

7

C olt wasn't in any hurry to meet this Half-pint or rather Carlie Anne Russell again. He didn't like her attitude from what he'd experienced in front of Sam's store the other day. But well, he'd told Harley he'd see what he could do to help her out. When he gave his word, he kept it.

The road ended, just as Harley had said it would. Leaning on his saddle horn, Colt surveyed the layout of the yard. The corral was right in front of him. A solid barn built to last was on his right with a lean-to-shed attached. A buckboard sat underneath and had been backed in with a tarp covering the supplies he'd help load, he was pretty sure.

The big two-story log house stood to his left, as big as some of those adobe ranch houses he'd seen in the southwest. To the west and back, the land seemed to fall away into a small draw. Colt could hear water running.

With a southern exposure, the house had been built into a stand of fir and pines on the backside, cutting those cold northern and western winter winds.

Colt urged his bay forward, slipping easily off the leather at the house steps. Automatically he tied the bay to a porch post.

Turning, his eyes scanned the area. He heard no people sounds other than the two mules and a sorrel standing quietly staring at him chewing some hay thrown over the fence. The pile had not been eaten down and scattered from pawing, indicating someone had just turned them out and fed them recently. But the place had a vacant feel about it.

A few chickens scattered as he ambled over to the corral. Rawlins leaned on the top rail, and comfortably settled a boot on the bottom one. The mules and the one horse looked to be good hearty stock, their coats glistening in the sun.

Carlie had been cleaning the stalls one last time before heading to summer pasture. She stopped when Wolf had begun a low quiet growl. Peeking around the door, she spied a big saddle bum ogling her stock.

She did not like visitors for they came for one thing only, to see how they could steal her ranch away from her. Tom Riley had been the worst, sending different men in here, threatening her. She had wounded the last two, shooting at them from the barn loft. It was a wonder her barn or house hadn't gone up in flames in retaliation. The tall stranger was probably another hired gun of Riley's sent to threaten her further forcing her sell out to him.

Carlie had to admit staring at the broad back and shoulders of this one, Riley must be getting desperate hiring someone that big to try and convince her to sell quickly.

Harley had told her to always be observant and on guard, or one of these days she'd buy the farm. He'd also told her with her small size, the element of surprise was her best defense.

This man is big, he could easily make three of me. Carlie looked down at Wolf, patted his head, and raised a finger to her lips in a shushing motion.

Peeking around the door once again, the man still had his back to her. Carlie took a deep breath, exhaling as she tore out of the barn.

Colt heard a noise coming from his right, his head swiveled

only to have something hit him broadside, knocking both of them through the corral fence, catching him off guard.

Two arms were squeezing tight around his neck, two firm legs clamped around his waist. Rawlins couldn't seem to get any leverage to break the strangle holds the four limbs had on him. He levered himself and rolled hard onto his back, his muscular weight sending air whooshing from the body beneath him, releasing the grips the attacker had on him.

Rolling off the body, Colt rose smoothly. He grabbed a fistful of shirt with one hand and yanked up the body as an angry fist began to sail toward his attacker's face. Then he got his first look. He barely stopped his arm in time from landing a solid blow to Carlie Anne Russell's jaw. He lowered his tightly coiled hand, relaxing his hold on her shirt.

Defiant, angry eyes glared at him, small fists ready to defend herself. "You!" she spat, seeing the man who had laughed at her the other day in front of Sam's store.

Before Colt could answer, he saw the girl's eyes dance to his left with her mouth going into a big 'O'. He half turned to see pale eyes, fangs and a grey streak before it rose through the air and jaws clamped onto his arm.

Wolf's growls and human yells permeated the warm air as dust swirled in a fog around the three. The mules huddled with their ears laid flat against their heads, rumps plastered against the back of the corral not sure what to make of the disturbance.

Rawlins pulled his gun.

"No!" Carlie cried, as she jumped against him, knocking the three of them to the ground again. Colt's finger automatically pulled the trigger, but the pistol fired uselessly in the air. The shot echoed against the hills as the mules danced and brayed and the horse gave shrill nickers.

Rawlins had a teeth-gnashing wolf on one arm and a hellion on the other.

Carlie tried to wrestle the pistol from his hand, but he wouldn't let go. So, she bit him and bit him hard.

Colt yowled, dropping the weapon quickly.

Scrambling out of his reaching distance, Carlie hastily picked up his pistol as she rushed over and grabbed a handful of fur and tried to pull the animal off the man. "Down, Wolf, down!" she yelled.

Pulling Wolf several feet away, she tried to soothe the animal, "Good...boy...easy...now." But Wolf's jaws continued to snap as he growled, frenzied slobber dripping from his mouth.

Keeping her hand on her friend, Carlie glared at the intruder. His face took on the appearance of granite, eyes flashing in anger at her. Her heart thundering against her ribs was knocking the breath out as fast as she could suck it in. Drawing in air, her voice squeaked when she said, "Mighty quick with your weapon, Mister...you aint got no call to go off half-cocked...Tom Riley send you?" waggling his pistol at his chest for emphasis.

Colt Rawlins gritted his teeth as he tried to kneel, stopping abruptly at the mention of Tom Riley. "Huh?"

"Be still. I don't want to use your own gun on you," Carlie said. Eyes rapidly flicked over him for more weapons when she noticed his knife. Still sucking wind for her starved lungs, she exhaled the words, "Your knife, throw it over there and don't try any sudden moves or you're dead," she threatened.

Swearing under his breath at Harley, he did as he was told. The knife landed a good ten feet from the girl.

Hard grey steel bored down on her. *If his eyes could spit bullets... that's exactly what they would be doing,* she thought, making her even more rattled. *And I'd be dead...*

Glancing at Wolf, "Fetch," she said.

Wolf trotted to the knife, keeping an eye on the man kneeling in the dirt. He picked it up and trotted back to his mistress and dropped it at her feet. Carlie patted his head. "Good boy," she told him.

Forgetting she was to keep her eyes on the man, she gazed dismally at the busted corral. "Now...look at what you've gone and done...you busted my fence..."

Colt blinked in surprise. "Me? If you had been more civil and not slammed into me...you'd still have a fence..." he growled.

"I outta make you fix it..." she retorted.

"Like...hell...you caused it, you fix it!"

Carlie closed her eyes for a moment before picking up and tucking the knife in her hip pocket. She looked at the weapon in her left hand, sighing as she did so, then tilted her head and looked at the trespasser. "Tom Riley send you?"

"Who?" he gritted.

"Tom Riley..." She stared hard at him, "...He send you to threaten me into selling out to him?"

"What? No...I never heard of the man..." Colt lied.

Sighing woefully, "That's what they all say..."

So part of why Harley wants me here must be true...a land grab...he thought, still grimacing in pain.

Puckering lips, "I'm gonna check your arm. Just so's you know, I'm as good with my left as my right in shooting at something," she warned him.

Colt just nodded as he struggled into a more comfortable kneeling position. He could take the pistol away from her but didn't want the risk of being mauled by that damn wolf again.

He spoke harshly. "That damn thing got rabies or something," he gritted, staring at the drool still dripping from the beast's mouth along with intermittent warning growls.

Carlie threw a glance at Wolf. His head was buried between his shoulder blades with his mouth in a snarl, his legs spread and ready to pounce again at one signal from his mistress.

"No. He's just protecting me," she said, kneeling next to him.

"Protecting you? Hell...you can protect yourself! You don't need a damn wolf to help you!" Colt spit out through clinched teeth. His arm was on fire and his hand throbbed where she had bit him, *Damn kid even left teeth marks in my hand...*he thought looking at the marks she'd left.

Carlie raised her eyebrows at what he believed as she peeled his bloody fingers from his arm and gently pulled the embedded and shredded material from the wound.

"Well...Wolf did a good job."

"Ain't that the damned truth..."

"Aww...quit your fussing! I told you he was just protectin' me..."

Struggling into a standing position, Colt leaned threateningly towards her.

Carlie Anne reared back a tad at his infringement into her space.

Wolf's growls became more menacing and louder.

Ignoring the wolf ready to pounce again, Colt chewed the words out, "Like...hell..."

Frowning, she asked, "That all you can say...*like...hell?*"

"...You train that damn dog to kill?"

"He's not a dog...he's a bona fide wolf..."

"...He ought to be shot and skinned for the pelt..."

"He's my protector and my friend..." Tilting her head she gave him an impatient gaze. "Now...you 'bout done registering your complaints or you got any more?"

Colt just stared at the kid.

"I need to tend to that wound..."

Who in their right mind would have a wolf for a pet... was the only thing he could think of at the moment. He remained silent.

"I've got medicine in the house. Think you can walk that far without keeling over in a dead faint?" she chided him.

Harley, you gonna have hell to pay next time I see you! Colt thought, *You didn't tell me she had an attack wolf, ya old skinflint!* his mind bellowed. He followed the girl towards the house.

Carlie led him into the kitchen and pulled out a chair and gestured for him to take a seat.

He sank gratefully onto the wood, leaning against its sturdy back. He was still gripping his arm, the blood cooling and becoming sticky. He felt it throbbing in rhythm to his heartbeat. Suddenly, he felt exhausted. Colt closed his eyes. The adrenalin rush that came with the attack had left him drained and coupled with the pain from the gnashing teeth of the wolf, he felt as if he hadn't slept for days.

Bustling about the kitchen area, Carlie held the teakettle under the pump and pushed down hard on the handle, a rhythmic squeaking accompanied each downward thrust of the lever.

Colt opened his eyes at the sound as he concentrated on every move the girl made, further wondering about her. *Harley's wrong... she don't need anyone looking after her...*

Setting the kettle to the side on the cook stove and standing on her tiptoes, she reached for the lifter from a nail in the wall above and hooked it under the stove lid, removing it to stuff a few pieces of wood into the tender. The lid rattled back into place as she slid the kettle over the plate. The sound of metal screeching against metal seemed loud to Colt's ears. Afterwards, she dusted her hands off and disappeared into a storeroom to the right.

Colt twisted his head peering after her, taking in the short hallway with the door opening inward and a screen door that led onto another covered porch yielding a nice view from the back of the house showing the mountains beyond.

His eyes shifted when she came out a few moments later with a rag, bottle of something and a leather pouch. He watched as the girl placed his knife and pistol way at the other end of the scarred kitchen table making him smile briefly.

The girl turned towards him, a soft rosy hue rose from the open neck of her shirt clear to the roots of her hair, but her eyes remained steady on his face as she spoke, "Will you let me help you? I feel kinda bad about you getting hurt…"

"Embarrassed…are you? Well…you should be," he snarled.

"Ya don't got to be so nasty about it…" she retorted. Taking in a deep breath and exhaling, "I've had problems lately...I can't trust no one..." Surprised at herself for revealing something like that to a man she only saw once before. "Uh...take off your shirt..."

Doing so, Rawlins saw a familiar scar on her wrist as she helped him. His hand snaked out, his big palm engulfing her small wrist and turning it over.

Carlie gasped as she tried to pull loose from his tight grip, "Sheesh...Mister, you sure are quick," she said.

Giving her a hard look. "Where did you get that scar?" Rawlins asked.

"You're hurting me...let me go..."

He relented, releasing her wrist. "The scar...where did you get it?"

Looking at the marks his fingers had left on her wrist, she finally answered, "It's a long story..."

"I've got time," he replied.

Carlie inhaled a deep breath, "Uh...never mind..."

A brow cocked slightly at her sidestepping his question.

She'd seen a scar on his wrist too when he had grabbed her. Sitting next to him at the table, she noticed other older wounds on him. His right shoulder had a ragged scar and there was a small one under his left eye along with a long-healed gash on his right upper arm. "From the looks of it...you've been banged up some..."

"I've had my share..."

She kept staring at him, noticing the slight curl to his dark brown hair lying against his neck and those startling eyes. They were a pale grey with a darker line outlining the color at the edge. Interesting, intelligent eyes she noted that were framed by dark brown lashes. Mentally shaking herself, she rose from the table to give herself some breathing room. Carlie Anne wasn't sure why she was so interested in him. *He's just another saddle tramp looking to steal from me...*her mind buzzed.

Retrieving a bowl from the cabinet, she filled it with the now hot water from the kettle. Turning, Carlie noticed how tight his jaw was clinched. "You in pain?"

"Naw," he gritted. "I just get chewed up by wolves on a daily basis, I'm used to it by now," he added sarcastically.

Rolling her eyes, Carlie Anne smarted right back, "It was your own fault…" sitting the bowl of steaming water on the table, she sat again and dipped the rag to begin gently cleaning his wound.

Colt had allowed his gaze to wander over the kitchen area. It had the large scarred top table that he sat at and enough chairs to seat six people. A sink area with a window that showed a view of mountains in the distance he noticed as his eyes continued to take in the room. Cupboards above and to the sides of the sink, shelves built alongside the cook stove with a tender keeper box filled with kindling shoved against the wall before the little hallway.

As his eyes resettled on the girl's face, he noticed the tip of her tongue sticking out and brow puckered as she concentrated on his wound. Watching her he felt that she had a gentle touch, as soft as the first spring breezes blowing across your skin with the promise of warmer days ahead, and the biggest eyes he'd ever seen with gold and brown flakes scattered through the green. Her oval face had been kissed by the sun with just a smattering of freckles crossing her cheeks with a little turned up nose. She also had a determined but delicate chin. The sun had touched her ridiculously long lashes, turning them from dark brown to blonde on the tips. A long thick braid hung halfway down her back that looked like golden wheat had been woven through the strands from the sun.

Crinkles at the corners from squinting into the sun too often framed her eyes. But there was a sadness he saw in those eyes, too. Her hands were tan, work rough, but gentle.

This Carlie Anne Russell is obviously a walking contradiction, he thought. She could become a she-devil one minute, soft as a feather the next. And she was cute as a button, and as pretty as four aces setting in his hand during a high stakes poker game. Suddenly he realized that he was attracted to this little firebrand.

The girl spoke, drawing him out of his musings.

"Don't think that shirt will do you much good now," she said as she pushed the chair away from the table and stood.

Colt looked at her.

Embarrassed at him staring at her, Carlie whirled and bounded up the stairs. Returning a few moments later, she held out a shirt, offering, "That was my Granddaddy's, he was a big man like you."

Colt took the shirt and laid it on the table in front of him

Pouring the man a cup of coffee, Carlie set it down in front of him.

Rawlins took a sip and then spewed the bitter brew from his mouth after tasting it. His hand wiped his chin as he glared at her. "What the hell was that…you trying to kill me? First that damn wolf, now this!"

Surprised at his fury, Carlie cut him a squirrelly look. "It's just coffee," she responded.

His eyes became a darker grey. "Coffee? Hell…more like lye…" he said crossly, pushing the cup away.

Carlie frowned then rolled her eyes again in response while she turned and went back to her task of mixing herbs into pasty goo at the sink counter. Spinning, she walked over to the table, sat and scooted her chair closer. Carlie gently took his forearm laying it on the table, surprised at how heavy it seemed. Reaching behind her, she picked up the bowl of medicinal herbs and dipped her fingers into it; she began spreading the herbs on his wound.

Carlie heard him whistle in air, making her cut a sharp look in his direction. "Sorry…don't mean to hurt…" As she finished wrapping the bandage, she asked, "So…you a blood brother?"

*She saw mine, too…*he thought. "Uh-huh…Shoshone…"

Her head bounced in agreement. "We had Shoshone visitors a lot. They'd trade for beef. Then they moved to the Canadian territories, it was safer for them there...to avoid being sent to the reservations. It's a shame the government forced them to leave their ways and their beautiful homeland..." she stated quietly as she busied herself cleaning up the remains of doctoring the man's arm.

His brow cocked, he didn't hear favorable opinions of Indians very often. "That's nice to hear...I was raised by the Shoshone. I left when I was fifteen summers..." Rawlins offered.

"Whose lodge were you with?" she asked setting the bowl in the dishpan, working the pump to fill it with water.

Talking over the squeaking pump, "Grey Elk..."

Carlie's hands stilled as her heart suddenly jumped in her chest. *Lone Wolf...*her thoughts screamed as she stared out the window for a few moments trying to wrap her mind around that bit of news. She spun and charged him yelling, "Where are they?" Taking a handful of his hair she jerked his head back hard. "Are they near here...do you know?"

Caught off guard, Rawlins hit the girl with his injured arm, hard enough to send her spinning to the floor. He winced at the returning pain puncturing through his anger at her. He quickly jumped up and knocked the chair over in the process. Colt retreated allowing himself room as he waited. He'd be ready for her this time.

Carlie rose faster than a lightning bolt and grabbed the upside-down chair by the back and swung it at his chest.

He caught it in mid-air, ripping it out of her grasp.

She gasped at his strength even though he was wounded and watched as he threw the chair aside.

Eyes flashing cold steel as he gritted out. "I've 'bout had all the sass I'm gonna take off of you, what the hell's got into you?"

He could barely hear her words as her eyes canvassed his face looking for answers.

"Do you know where they are?"

"No!"

"I just…"

His voice bellowed when he butted in, "…How the hell should I know…I ain't seen them in years…"

"You dang saddle tramp! Get out!" She grabbed the spare shirt, his gun and knife and threw them at him, catching him by surprise. "Now git…" snarled Carlie as she pointed at the door.

"Don't mind if I do…" he snapped, his angry footsteps sounding hollow on the wood floor as he stormed out the front door.

"Damn fool kid! Harley…you just wait till I get my hands on you!" Colt muttered, slipping on the shirt and jerking his bay's reins from the hitch post before he mounted. He reined him around hard, heading north, his shirt flapping in the breeze. Riding around back of the house he pulled up on the reins, slowing the bay when he saw the four graves, two looking newer than the others. Rawlins hitched around in the saddle with his right palm resting on the cantle as he looked back at the house. The girl had come out the back door and stood on the porch staring hard at him. Her hands were stuck in her hip pockets as she continued giving him an evil glare. Colt jammed his heels in the bay's ribs making him bolt.

Carlie saw him stop by the graves. He looked back at her and their eyes connected. A few seconds later, he whirled his horse towards the rise. She watched until horse and rider disappeared.

Still fuming because the stranger had not given her any clues as to the whereabouts of her childhood friend Lone Wolf and his family, she whirled and kicked the doorjamb hard. Storming into the house and muttering out loud to the walls, "Who does he think he is anyway? Good riddance…ya two-bit saddle tramp!"

Carlie had a saying that she often repeated to herself, *Stay away from trouble*, not realizing trouble followed her like a honeybee to nectar.

8

C olt was still fuming several hours later. Men before had beaten him up, but never in his born days had a girl and a damn wolf taken him down. *Good thing no one was around to witness that disaster,* he thought. He wasn't small by any means and it had wounded his pride to be taken down by a tiny slip of a girl and her wolf.

"Damn you, Harley..." he muttered. "...You're on your own, you old coot!"

What Colt had just experienced further verified his thoughts, that women were nothing but a *saddlebag full of trouble!*

Later that evening Colt sat sipping coffee with his ears tuned to the night sounds. The cool night air continued to bathe the solitary man in a cloak of darkness as pleasant memories began to wash over him. They were also tinged with a bit of sadness too, remembering Grey Elk. His band must have been the ones who bought beef from this girl's family and the way she reacted they must have been close, but it still puzzled him. There had been a family and a little girl he vaguely remembered, but so much had happened in his life it was hard for him to pinpoint the memories. The time frame didn't match unless it had occurred long after he had left and after the Indian wars when the Army was rounding up the many tribes to send them to the reservations. He glanced up and around staring into the deep darkness while his memory pulled the rugged terrain forward in his mind. He could see how Grey Elk and his band could disappear into these mountains and not be found except by an experienced tracker.

Colt's eyes once again focused on the flames but they soon faded from his sight as an image of Grey Elk filled his vision. His adopted father had told him he could stay or go back to the white man's world when he was old enough. So, he had decided to venture back into the world that he was born into, but knew nothing about, not even his own white man's name.

He became blood brothers with the one who had raised him and who had taught him not only the ways of the Shoshone, but also about truth and honor. Grey Elk had passed on his own wisdom to the strapping youth and one particular bit of knowledge had stayed with him. *Make sure your word is good*, his father had told him. And Colt Rawlins had held the chief's words close to his heart as he had traveled the country taking odd jobs for a few pennies in his pocket. Never settling down in one place for very long, always itchy, always restless. For some reason he seemed to be searching for something, but what he didn't know. He stared at the two scars on his wrist, one bolder and overshadowing a thin scar line underneath it. He couldn't for the life of him remember where that one had come from. Giving himself a mental shrug, he tossed his coffee and settled down for the night. Tomorrow he would head towards Harley's place.

Cleaning up his campsite the next morning, Colt rode out. He was going to give that old skinflint a piece of his mind

9

A nger renewed itself as Colt Rawlins came in sight of
Harley's cabin. As far as he was concerned, his debt to
the old bandy rooster had been paid in full.

Colt dismounted, bellowing, "Harley! Harley, you in there?"

The boy is already here? "In here, son," Harley answered.

The door slammed open so hard it bounced off the wall.
Harley winced.

Colt strode into the room, his size filling the small interior of
the cabin, his anger seeming to bounce off the four walls.

Corkscrew brows rose as Harley felt the heat of the boy's
temper.

Colt took off his hat and slung it across the room where it too,
bounced off the wall.

Harley's eyes followed that hat sailing across the room, then
came back to rest on ones that were the color of cold .45 slugs.

Rawlins marched across the room slamming two big palms on
the table as he leaned across toward Harley. Through clenched
teeth he growled, "The deal's off, Harley!"

Two pairs of eyes sized each other up. One held stone cold

42

slate-grey ones on the grizzled man staring right back, not flinching a lick at Colt's fury.

"She got ta ya, huh? Bested ya? Wounded yure pride a little?"

Colt's mouth twisted into a hard, thin line. "She attacked me four times, Harley…" Colt informed him. "…Twice in the corral, she jumped me when my back was turned, bit me when I wanted to shoot that damn wolf…" His deep baritone rose to a peak in frustration. "…Who almost tore my arm off, and then…then she tried to hit me with a chair when we were in the house…" Colt finished.

Harley let loose with his trademark raspy laugh as he slapped his thigh. "That's my girl."

"It ain't funny…Harley!" Colt shouted. "And she ain't no girl! She's nuthin' but a snarling, spitting she-devil! She can take care of herself, she don't need no help," Rawlins responded angrily.

Half-pint must've wrapped a rattlesnake 'round his neck, 'cause days later the boy is still hopping mad… Harley figured.

Colt inhaled deeply, trying to calm himself. Turning he walked to the open door and leaned against the doorjamb as he stood staring into the distance. Raking his hands through his dark hair, he inhaled deeply again. It had been a long time since he had allowed his temper to get out of control like that. He did not like losing his temper: when that happened you lost control, you could get killed.

Harley saw Colt struggling with his emotions. He'd only seen that happen once or twice before to this degree. Colt always kept his emotions in check, veiled, close to his chest. It made him a good man to have around in a bad situation. So, she must've got to him pretty hard.

"Son, why don't cha take care of yure harse, bring yure gear in then we'll eat and talk," Harley stated softly.

The voice brought Colt back with a jerk. He looked at Harley, then down at his boots, nodded and walked out.

A half-hour later, Colt dumped his gear in a corner, walked over and sat down at the hand-built table with a sigh.

Harley poured him a cup of coffee.

He gratefully sipped the brew. "Tastes a hell'ava lot better than what that girl passed off for coffee," he admitted.

The old man chortled. "You got a taste of that wicked brew...eh?"

Nodding. "If I didn't know better, I would a thought she was trying to kill me. First that damn wolf, then her coffee..." Rawlins said.

Harley grinned. "Let's take a look-see at that arm. I'm sure it needs to be re-dressed."

Pulling the shirt out of his britches, Colt unbuttoned it and slid his arm out of the sleeve.

Harley cautiously unwrapped the bloodstained bandage. Cleaning the wound, he saw that the flesh was healing nicely, he asked. "What did Half-pint use?"

Colt shrugged. "Some kind of herbs..."

Harley nodded saying, "She used the right ones then...it's healing up real purty."

10

The team had been hitched to the loaded buckboard with Waldo tied on behind. Harley told her he had things he needed to get done before winter set in. Carlie scowled, she'd have to take the supplies up all by herself *again,* just like last year.

Walking around back of the main house, she stopped by the four graves and whispered, "I miss you so much, but I'll do my best to make you proud of me." Carlie stood in silence for a few moments, recalling happier times before finally pulling herself away and returning to the buckboard.

Driving the team toward the winter cabin with Wolf zigzagging in and out of the brush, Carlie again thought about the man she had bested. She suddenly realized that she had never asked him his name. *Oh...well...* and after Wolf chewed him up, she knew he'd never return. Besides, she had enough on her plate without a man interfering in her affairs. *I've got enough trouble as it is...* she admitted to herself.

❧

CARLIE'S STOMACH rumbled with hunger, she just couldn't eat the burnt beans. Forgetting about them on the campfire thinking of other things, they now tasted like some evil potion. She should have listened to her Mama and Gramma more when they wanted to teach her how to cook. Carlie had thought at the time that she had plenty of time to learn that kind of stuff, but now it was too late; they were both gone.

Carlie stared at the stars overhead. She spoke softly as a tear slid out of the corner of her eye and down her cheek. "I know I've had a wagon load of lemons dumped on me, Lord. But I'm trying real hard to make lemonade. Lord...please help me to make lemonade..." she sniffled, swiping at her wet cheek with her hand.

Wolf came and lay down beside her. Placing a hand on his back and with his slow rhythmic breathing relaxing her, Carlie drifted off.

11

Colt and Harley sat outside on the bench, leaning back against the wall of the cabin. Harley was puffing away on his pipe and Colt sat staring off into the distance. A comfortable silence that had been established long ago between the old man and the young one continued.

Cutting eyes to his right at the strong features of Colt Rawlins, "Well...son what are yure plans now?" Harley asked.

"Do' no..." Colt replied softly.

"You could stay wit' me this winter," Harley offered.

Shifting on his seat. "Maybe..." he replied.

"Or...you could go help Half-pint..." Harley slyly added.

"Uh...no..." Colt said firmly, fidgeting again.

"She needs you, don't know it yet, but she needs you. For being raised on a ranch, she's a real shave-tail," Harley said, taking the pipe and tapping out the burnt remains.

Leaning back again, Colt folded his arms across a wide expanse of chest and stretched his long legs out crossing his feet. "Do' no 'bout that Harley..." he said.

Sliding the pouch out of his pocket, Harley fiddled with the string opening the bag. "Well...she is and does, just hain't figured hit out yet," Harley replied, refilling his pipe. He struck a match on the wood seat and the phosphorous flared; sucking on the stem he lit the tobacco.

Sighing the word out, Colt said, "Maybe..."

"Son...you always liked punching cows' mor'n anything else you ever did."

"I know."

"Real talkative today, ain't cha?"

That brought a smile to the young man's face. "Maybe..."

"I get the feeling Half-pint is bothering you?"

"Some...a little, I guess."

"Uh-huh..." puffing some more, Harley grinned around the pipe stem staring off into the distance.

"Well...why isn't she married, so her husband could take over now and help her? Why, she's almost past marrying age," Colt said.

"See them mountains in front of us," Harley pointed with the stem of his pipe.

Colt nodded.

"They're wild and untamed, free spirited. Kinda like Half-pint, she's a real child of the mountains, a forest fairy. Them Irish, they call them the little people, leprechauns, or fairies way I heerd tell it," Harley paused, giving a glance to his right at Colt. "Oh...she could 've had anyone she wanted in town, but she jus' wasn't interested," he said. Tapping out the pipe again, he laid it on the seat next to him, and continued, "Never saw a female take to the land like Half-pint has, says it's her responsibility to take good care of the land, so it'll take care of her," Harley said.

"Indians believe that, too," Colt answered.

"Guess that's where she got that notion from. She and Lone Wolf were thick as ticks on an ole hound dog. He taught her Shoshone and she taught him the white man's tongue. Taught him how to write the white man's words, too," Harley finished.

When the old man said those words, he knew the puzzle was

falling into place. "This Lone Wolf...was he part of Grey Elk's tribe? Did they buy beeves from Carlie's family?"

"Uh-huh...Lone Wolf was his adopted son. Peers he rescued a young white boy from some Pawnee they wuz havin' a go round wit and raised him as his own."

"I see...I was raised by Grey Elk."

"You never told me that!" Harley said cutting a sharp glance at Colt.

Showing Harley his scar. "The girl had one, too. Was she and this Lone Wolf blood brothers, or ah...sister?"

Harley gave his rusty squeaky laugh. "Them two was always mimicking the adults, she caught hell from her Mama and Gramma for that stunt."

"Damn..." he whispered as more memories came flooding into his brain like a dam had burst. "Harley...I'm Lone Wolf..."

The old man liked to have fallen off the bench seat in surprise. "Wha...? Holy hell..." straightening himself and staring at Rawlins bug-eyed.

Colt grinned. "Took me a while to remember...too many miles and people tacked on to my hide..."

"Well...I'll be damned..." was all Harley could mutter.

"I tried to put them out of my mind...become white again. Though I honed the skills the Shoshone taught me, I forgot about the other..."

"Boy...Half-pint will shor be glad ta know yer Lone Wolf...her long lost friend..."

"May not tell her..."

"Why?"

"She don't like me..."

"Awww...she'll change her mind oncet she finds out..."

"Doubt it...she's still hardheaded..."

"Ain't that thuh dad-blamed truth!" Harley chuckled as he filled his piped and lit it, puffing away.

Enjoying the scent of fresh lit tobacco, Colt sat back against the logs once again, his hands laced across his stomach, as he re-crossed his feet. "I suppose you want me to have another go at helping her?" sending a hard look at the skinflint.

Harley smiled. "That'd be nice," he said.

"I'm not guaranteeing anything after what happened a week ago," Colt told him.

"I know," Harley agreed.

12

Colt was ready to move out of Harley's place. He had agreed to go back and try again with the little she-devil shave-tail. He took the gear bag Harley handed him, hooked it over the horn and faced the old bandy rooster. "Thanks for everything, Harley," Colt said, sticking out his hand.

Harley taking it. "Ya mind yure manners with my girl, ya hear me son?"

Leather creaked when he slipped easily into the seat. Colt flashed a smile. "Maybe you ought to write her a letter, telling her to mind *her* manners with me, you old coot!"

His feet shuffling in the dirt, Harley dropped his gaze.

As Colt began to rein the bay around, Harley looked up and spoke, "Son, iffen ya aim ta eat out there, yure gonna have ta do all the cooking…"

Quickly turning the bay back in next to the old man, Colt leaned into Harley's face, making him rear back. "What?"

"I said…ya gotta do all the cooking," he told Colt again.

"Why?"

"Half-pint…she cain't cook."

"What 'da mean she can't cook?"

"Jus' what I said. Hell…son, ya drunk her coffee! It gets worse, ya try eatin' her food," Harley spluttered. "Ya want ta make hit through the winter, yure jus' gonna have ta do all the cooking, that's all. Heavens knows her Mama and Gramma tried, but she wouldn't sit still long enough ta learn."

Harley's sun-stained and wrinkled face squinted up at the man in the saddle, he spoke quietly. "Hit's the truth, son."

Grey eyes bored into the dried buffalo hide with the corkscrew eyebrows. "What else have you neglected to tell me, Harley?"

"Well…" he began, dragging the word out, scratching his head. "Got more energy than a lightning strike," Harley finally admitted.

Straightening in his saddle, Rawlins asked, "Anything else you just might want to add…Harley?"

"See ya Christmas?"

"Take care of yourself, old man," he said fondly, reining the bay around and trotting out of Harley's place.

13

Carlie groaned seeing how large her herd had gotten and that wasn't even counting the strays that had wandered off into the brush.

Her elbow resting on the saddle horn with her chin in her hand, she blew sun-drenched bangs off her forehead as she surveyed the big job ahead of her.

"Maybe I should've listened to Harley and hired some stupid saddle tramp," she muttered out loud.

But she didn't want Harley to know that she was broke and didn't have the money to hire anyone. And after buying the winter supplies, well...that shopping spree had cost her everything she had and left only eighty-three cents in the Ranch's account. It was too late to get to the railhead in Moose Jaw, they'd get snowed in trying to cross the pass. She also didn't have any remounts ready to sell to the Army either. Carlie didn't know how the time seemed to slip away from her but it always did and now she was in a real pickle.

Well...let me get these cows south and see how they winter, then make the drive to Moose Jaw as soon as they fatten up next spring... Carlie decided.

Sighing, she reined her horse around and began flushing cattle out of the brush. Whistling for Wolf, she signaled for him to do the same.

Driving what she had found in the scrub into the rest of the herd a few hours later, she stopped to let the mule rest as Wolf sat nearby, his tongue dangling as he panted.

It was at least five more days' drive to the winter-feeding grounds, but she didn't mind. Carlie always felt that she became more alive when she was out here with the cattle and her horses. Signaling to Wolf, Carlie sent him after more strays while she went after the others.

Looking as she rode, the trees had bathed the mountainsides in bright color, earlier it seemed this year. *God was working over-time with his paint brush,* she thought. *Might be a long winter. Oh... well,* she had spent the last winter by herself and she could do it again. Thinking of the solitary months ahead, she realized then that she really didn't want to endure the long winter alone.

UNSADDLING WALDO, Carlie Anne dragged her saddle over to the old fire ring where she and her family had always set up camp and made up her bed. Straightening, she gazed over the herd settling down for the night. She realized then that she had to find Thor and his harem. She had always loved reading the stories of the Sultan chiefs and their harems when she was younger. Carlie smiled to herself as she gathered deadfall wood for the fire.

Later as Carlie's arm draped itself over Wolf's neck, she rested against the saddle, rubbing his thick fur and smoothing the black tipped ears. Her mind drifted back to when Lone Wolf had brought the pup to her, saying the mother died chewing its leg off that had been caught in a trap. Wolf had been by her side ever since.

Burying her face in his fur, she whispered, "It's just you and me Wolf, just you and me."

Lifting her head, everyone thought she was squirrelly keeping a wild creature. Her hand continued rubbing his ears as he nuzzled her cheek. Most wild animals in captivity sickened and died, but Wolf seemed to thrive under her firm but loving hand.

Carlie laid back against the saddle and closed her eyes, her hand never leaving Wolf's back as he settled down, too.

14

R iding a small ridge above the narrow valley, Colt Rawlins pulled up when he spotted the mustangs. Gazing over the herd, he noticed some nice stock. He let his eyes roam some more before they settled on a grouping of mares. They seemed to be fascinated with something in the middle, milling around whatever it was.

Colt blinked when the girl suddenly popped up and walked away from the mares.

Sticking two fingers in her mouth, Carlie Anne produced a shrill whistle.

Resting his forearm on the saddle horn, his eyes followed the direction the girl was facing. A few moments later, he saw the big stallion come racing out of the scrub in answer to her call. Colt's eyes popped open in surprise. That was one handsome horse.

Carlie patiently waited for Thor. As she gazed fondly at the stallion, she thought that he looked really good this fall. The stallion raced around her playfully, as she followed his graceful moves. When he trotted up to her, Carlie reached out and wrapped her arms around his neck hugging him. Then she rubbed between his ears, fingers combing his forelock and tangled mane.

Colt straightened in the saddle, not believing what he was seeing between a willow branch of a girl and a wild stallion. The next thing she did left him dumbfounded. He realized that Carlie and that damn stallion were playing tag. The girl would take off, turn, cut quickly to the left then the right, and take off running again. When the stallion would race close by, she would stand her ground and tag him on his flank or his withers. The girl and the wild horse repeated this scene several times to his amazement. Colt pushed his hat back on his head while he remained spellbound watching the two of them interact.

The girl's laughter tinkled frequently through the clear air reaching his ears. Her voice had a pleasant happy sound that made Colt smile.

Carlie stopped, color high in her face as she rubbed Thor's nose and neck. "Wanna go for a ride, boy?" she breathed softly into his ear.

Thor snorted and then seemed to bob his head yes to her question.

She grinned wide as she grabbed a handful of mane and flung herself up on the stallion's back. Settling her seat, she patted his neck. Taking two handfuls of his mane, she urged, "Let's go...big boy..."

Colt straightened up, watching horse and rider race around the valley floor, the mares watching from their huddle. The girl remained hunched over his neck with no bridle, no saddle, just riding and doing a *Damn fine job of it, too...*he thought. *Harley you're right,* Colt sat watching the pair thinking, *The kid really did have some kind of magic with animals.*

Watching the stallion run, he noted that this was no ordinary mustang. He'd seen some pretty nice mustang stallions in his time, and most were of Spanish origin. But this one had different blood running through his veins, a whole *lotta* different blood.

Rawlins watched as the stallion slowed to a lope and stared as the girl raised her face to the sun. Letting go of the mane she stretched her arms straight out from her body. The girl's smooth rhythm riding the stallion made it appear as if she was riding in slow motion. Colt sighed inwardly, *The girl sure as hell could ride.*

Finally coming to a standstill, Carlie slid off Thor and crooned to him. The stallion's nostrils flared even more picking up a scent. His ears pricked forward as he gazed at the lone figure sitting on his bay, high on the ridge above. He snorted loudly.

Carlie stopped whispering when Thor stiffened, focusing on the upper ridge in front of them. Following the horse's gaze, she saw a man setting his bay high on the ridge. Her gaze narrowed then widened as she recognized the man from a few weeks ago. "Fiddle sticks!" she whispered. Carlie watched as his hand rose doffing his hat to her, then resettled it back on his head when he turned and ambled back into the trees.

Carlie expelled the breath she had been holding. She had never expected to see that man again and then there he was watching her from the ridge. Carlie didn't like it, not one bit.

15

Carlie's stomach rumbled with hunger. She had burnt the beans again, even Wolf turned up his nose at them. She drank the black mud she called coffee just to put something in her stomach. One of these days she was going to have to do something about her cooking skills. *Or lack of them*, she thought wryly.

Wolf sprang up, growling and focusing into the darkness on her right. Listening carefully, Carlie thought she heard shod hooves ping on shale and footsteps crunching ground cover coming toward her. Reaching for her rifle, she rose as she cocked it, the metallic click sounding loud in the still night as she waited.

The same man whose arm she had bandaged a week ago and had seen on the ridge today strode into her sight. When he spotted her, he stopped and then walked a little further into the circle of firelight, then stopped again and waited.

Her eyes tapered as she scoped out his face again. Firelight danced across his rugged features with dark stubble beginning to fill in the recesses of his face. But his most startling feature, his light grey eyes, were studying her with such intensity that Carlie Anne gave herself a mental shake. "What are you doing here?"

"Jus' passin' through…" he lied.

"Sure…looking to rob me blind is what…"

"I could…you're wide open to cattle rustling…"

That stubborn chin with the cleft rose as her hands tightened on the rifle, her finger wrapping around the cool half-moon of the trigger and raising it threateningly. "Am not…Wolf and I can handle anything that comes our way…" she said with more bravado then she felt.

"That so? I doubt it…"

Carlie gave him a dirty look then eyeballed him as she tilted her head, allowing her eyes to start at his boots and track along his length. When she finally reached his face, she asked, "You still growing, mister?"

"Depends on what day of the week it is."

Carlie crooked one corner of her mouth in a scowl.

A low growl rumbled from Wolf's throat. Carlie silenced him. "Shush, it's just the saddle tramp who broke our fence and thinks he's an Indian," turning to him she said, "Why did you really come back…lookin' to steal my cows after you kill me for Tom Riley?" she challenged him.

"No…lookin' for a job…" he lied.

She glanced away for a brief moment, sighing inwardly thinking about her lack of funds before swinging her eyes back. "Ain't hiring…"

Ignoring her comment, he pointed his finger at the rifle. "You know how to use that thing?"

Carlie nodded saying, "Told ya that once before…"

Colt cocked a brow.

Still sizing him up, she tilted her head in the other direction as she stated, "My Granddaddy used to tell me stories about tall men like you. He said that if you looked real close, you just might see moss growing on the north side of them." Tapering her eyes further she bent forward, she scoped out his side as she asked seriously. "That true? You got moss growing on you, Mister?"

Moss, hell! Harley, what the dickens did you drag me into? Rawlins thought.

"You always believe everything your Granddaddy told you?"

Carlie nodded again. "Pretty much."

Looking at the girl from where he was standing, all he saw was a ragamuffin who called herself a girl. She sure didn't resemble the little girl who had taught him the white man's words long ago with her dirty face and her hair messy pulled out from that braid. The pocket on her overgrown coat was half ripped off, along with a seam under one arm split, showing the padding. Strings were hanging from frayed cuffs and one elbow was worn clear through. Suspenders were holding up baggie-corded britches. Well-worn, sodbuster boots peeked out from under frayed pants' legs. Either the girl didn't care about her appearance or couldn't sew. *Probably both,* Rawlins thought. Thinking some more, *It's gonna be a long winter, but I promised Harley.*

He broke the silence first. "Uh...we didn't exactly have time for proper introductions last time we met," he said, walking forward and sticking out his hand. "Name's Colt Rawlins," he offered up.

One eyebrow quirked up as Carlie took a few steps closer, too. She questioned, "Colt?"

"Uh-huh..."

"What kinda damn name is that? Your folks loco naming you after a foal?" she exclaimed.

"They didn't."

Carlie gave him a squirrelly look, jamming a hand in the good pocket on her coat. "Didn't what?"

"Name me..." Rawlins replied then waited on the girl's next comment while he eyed her face puckering up as she remained silent. "Remember..." he began, "...I was raised in an Indian camp. I was too little to remember my white man's name, so..."

Carlie butted in, "...So, you looked at a bunch of horses and decided to name yourself Colt."

"You don't mince words, do you?"

The girl lifted her face up in another stubborn stance, showing more clearly the dimple carved into her chin. "No." Giving him another crooked look while asking, "Well, you gonna tell me or not?"

"Tell you what?"

Carlie rolled her eyes. "Pffftt! I knew I was right."

Colt smiled slightly. "Not quite...got a job on a trail drive as a cook's swamper. They asked what my name was, so while I was studying on what to call myself I noticed the trail boss's pistol. He was wearing a Colt, so told them my name was Colt," he explained.

Carlie frowned. "Where'd Rawlins come from?"

"Ever hear of Rawlins, Wyoming?"

Carlie nodded.

Well, at least the girl wasn't too back woodsy... "Delivered a cattle drive there, thought it went nice with Colt..."

Carlie blinked then rolled her eyes again. She took a dirty hand and rubbed the end of her nose with it. She expelled air as she raked her dirty hand through her hair then tucked a stray tendril behind an ear as she looked at the ground, up and around before focusing back on him. His boots were placed as wide as his shoulders making him ooze self-assurance, something she wasn't used to seeing with the boys in town. The tilt of his head and those unusual eyes formed a curious expression that told her he was waiting on her answer.

Clearing her throat, she stepped forward and stuck out a dirty paw. "Name's Carlie Anne Russell, but most folks jus' call me Half-pint," she told him.

Colt stepped forward again. Engulfing the dirty little hand in his, squeezing it.

Carlie's eyes grew round as saucers when his hand touched hers, she jerked her hand back as if, well...she'd been stung. She quickly wiped it on her even dirtier coat and retreated.

Rawlins frowned, cocking a brow at the girl's reaction.

She didn't know exactly what just happened, staring at her hand, but touching him, sent some kind of jolt up her arm, like... like when lightning hits a tree and makes the air crackle. That little motion of touching his hand had sent goose bumps all over her.

She quickly looked up to see if he had a reaction, too. *Nope,* he just stood there, studying her with a silly grin on his face.

"Half-pint...huh..." he said, pausing as if he was pondering looking at the dark sky then back at her again. "I think I'll just call you Carlie Anne, I like that much better than Half-pint, or I might just call you Carlie..."

She just stared at him, not sure what to make of his response.

"Mind if I join your fire?"

Coming back to earth with a thud. "Uh...sure..." Carlie answered. Going back to her saddle and bedroll, she plunked down on the ground. Draping an arm over Wolf's shoulders, she kept a tight grip on the animal. She kept stealing glances at Rawlins while she watched him hobble his horse next to her's, her eyes cutting away quickly when he felt her watching him and glanced her way.

Bringing his saddle and gear bag back to the camp and placing them nearby, he dug his cup out of the bag and walked over to the fire. Kneeling, Colt poured himself a cup of coffee and stared into the black brew before gesturing with the cup at her. "You make this?"

Carlie nodded.

"Is it as bad as last time?"

She rolled her eyes in response.

As soon as the ugly brew hit his tongue, he spit it out. He grabbed the pot and emptied it out on the ground. Gesturing with it, he ordered, "You take this down to the creek and scrub it out good with sand..." Standing and walking over to his gear, he rummaged around in his saddlebag and pulled out a towel and a sliver of soap. "And while you're there, scrub some of that dirt off. Start looking like a human being again."

Eyes round as saucers at his demands, Carlie continued to just sit and stare.

"Carlie Anne, did you hear me?"

She just blinked.

Colt moved to stand in front of the girl.

Wolf uttered a warning growl.

She tightened her grip on the animal as she almost busted her neck looking up at Colt Rawlins.

Eyeing the beast and resting his hand on the butt of his weapon, Colt testily asked, "You gonna move, or am I gonna have to drag you down to the creek and wash you myself?"

Her eyes flashed. "You're still mad at me because I bested you the first time, ain't cha, Mister?" Carlie taunted him.

Rawlins eyes narrowed at her reference to him. "You gonna move?"

"Alright, alright...you don't have to be such a bully about it..." she groused, rising. Plucking the pot from his hand, she headed for the creek.

"Wait..." Rawlins said.

Carlie stopped and turned around slowly.

"You forgot something..." shoving the towel and soap into her belly. "...And this..." he added picking up the pan with the burnt beans and laid that on top of the soap and towel.

Carlie's mouth sagged open.

"You do those three things and I might...just might fix something edible to eat," Rawlins said.

Her mouth snapped shut as her eyes fanned fire. "I'm not hungry..." she mumbled as she turned and headed back in the direction of the creek.

"Yep..." Colt muttered, pushing his hat back from his forehead while he stuffed a hand in the pocket of his bulky coat watching her walk away. Rolling his eyes to the star-studded sky as he sighed, "Yeah...Harley...it's gonna be a long winter..."

16

Hearing Wolf's call enter her subconscious sleep, Carlie flew up from under the wool blanket. Grabbing her rifle, she ran to Waldo releasing the hobbles and flung herself up on his back.

Long legs traveled the distance quickly as Colt's hand grabbed the bridle strap stopping her. "Where the hell do think you're going?"

Carlie uttered three words. "Wolf, danger, herd." Slapping his hand away from his hold on her horse, she banged heels into its ribs and took off.

He heard the cat's scream then, causing him to sprint back to his saddle and pull his rifle from the scabbard. He rushed after Carlie into the night.

Rawlins found the horse tied to some brush near a granite rock strewn bluff area, but no Carlie Anne. Slipping quietly off his bay, he quickly tied him securely next to her horse. As he edged deeper into the dense undergrowth, Colt would occasionally stop and listen. He heard nothing. Moving cautiously further into the undergrowth, a sixth sense made him stop again; his senses tuned to pick up the slightest sight, sound or scent that didn't belong.

Colt swiveled his head to the left as the hairs rose on the back of his neck, *There...something is there...* Easing to the left some more, he still couldn't see any movement, but he felt the presence of the cat.

*Damn...where in the hell is Carlie? She'd probably mistake me for the cat and shoot me instead...*he thought wryly.

The cat screamed again followed by a rifle shot. It came from below and to his left. Picking up speed, dodging the brush, he slid down the embankment and could just make out the form of a big cat in the starlight several yards away.

He looked around and still didn't see the girl as he moved toward the cat. Finding her rifle lying a few feet away, his eyes darted to the big cat. Seeing two legs sticking out from under the body, he reached for the scruff of its neck and hauled it off exposing Carlie underneath.

She rolled onto her knees then and began sucking in air and coughing as she heaved in huge breaths.

Grabbing an arm encased in the sleeve of that overgrown coat, Colt yanked her up. "What the hell did you think you were doing going after that big cat by yourself? It could've torn you to pieces!"

Sucking in more air, she glared back. "I wasn't afraid of him...Mister!"

"You would be, if you had enough brains to spit!"

Carlie's mouth gaped, then closed as her head swiveled when she heard Wolf's threatening growl. She watched his head sink between his shoulders, getting ready to attack.

She shouted, "No...Wolf! No!" Looking back over her shoulder she saw Rawlins taking a bead on Wolf with his rifle.

Her arms stretched out to stop Wolf from attacking and Rawlins from killing him. "No!" she yelled. Carlie whirled instead toward Rawlins, jumping and throwing her body into his.

The girl slammed into his chest, catching him off guard. His feet stumbled backwards over the cat's body as his finger pulled the trigger in surprise. The rifle went off as it sailed through the air and clattered against the rocks behind him. Her actions sent the both of them to the ground with Carlie ending up on top of him.

She whipped out her pistol and jammed it hard into his ribs. Her forearm pressed against his Adam's apple.

Damn! That's twice the girl laid me flat! his brain buzzed. He wheezed out something entirely different. "You're choking me."

Pressing harder on his Adam's apple, "I'll do mor'n that, you keep trying to kill my friends," she hissed, jamming the barrel harder into his ribs.

"Ow...that hurt..."

"It'll hurt worse Mister, if you make me pull this trigger..." Carlie replied tersely, giving him an evil eye for a few more seconds before pushing against his chest and rising as she continued to sit on him. "I cut my lead..." she explained, shaking a cartridge out of the cylinder and holding the tip close to his face, "...See, when it hits flesh it shreds everything in sight..."

Carlie Anne held that damn cartridge so close it made his eyes cross. Colt shoved her hand away.

Glancing and nodding over her shoulder towards the dead cat, she said to him, "...How do you think I killed that cat with one shot? I'll do it to you too, you keep trying to take out my friends..." she threatened.

"Friends? Hell..." he spluttered.

"I told you once before, he was just protecting me," Carlie said pushing hard on his chest as she rose.

Colt grunted.

Carlie continued to hold her pistol on him.

Rawlins remained flat on the ground, trying to wrap his mind around her craziness. It was maddening to think that this was the same girl from years ago. *The girl is loco, plumb loco.*

"Mind if I get up now?"

Carlie narrowed her eyes at him, saying, "If you promise not to shoot Wolf."

He shifted beginning to rise. "No..." he snapped, stopping when he heard the metallic click of a hammer being pulled back and a cylinder rolling. His eyes flicked up, Carlie had a two-handed bead on him.

"I mean it Mister, no more taking pot shots at my friends. You hear me, Mister?" the girl warned him again.

Colt knew the best way to deal with an insane person was to go along with them, until you could get the drop on them. "Alright," he agreed.

"You promise?"

Rawlins exhaled annoyingly, "I promise."

Carlie nodded, sliding the pistol back into the leather. She then turned and stepped over the dead cat, picking up her rifle and pointed with it. "If Harley was here, he'd want the pelt. You can have it, if you want. I'm too tired to mess with it right now. I'm going back to bed," Carlie said, then turned and faded into the darkness.

Brushing the dirt and leaves from his shirt, Colt bent and retrieved his hat, jamming it back on his head "Yep Harley, ya old coot, it's gonna be a long winter," he mumbled following the girl through the brush to pick up his horse and head back to the makeshift camp.

17

Sipping his coffee the next morning, Rawlins glanced over at the sleeping figure of Carlie Anne Russell. She was wrapped in her blanket like a little worm with only a smidgen of her head showing. Wolf had disappeared, but Colt knew he'd be back ready to protect his mistress if there was any threat to the girl.

And therein lay the problem, that damn wolf. Colt Rawlins didn't know exactly how he was going to deal with an insane rattlebrain eighteen-year old and a wolf that wanted to attack him at the drop of a hat.

He sure as hell wasn't going to walk on eggs around them, but that girl was going to have to do something about that grey monster. He'd just as soon kill the damn thing and get it out of his hair, but the girl would probably make good on her threat to shoot him if he did.

Colt didn't know how good a shot she was, she did okay with the cat, but that was at close range. Most women he knew couldn't hit the broad side of a barn. He had no way of knowing if Carlie was a good shot or not or whether she would carry out her threats.

Rawlins sighed heavily. He rose and strode over to the girl, "Time to get up, you're wasting daylight..."

Carlie rolled over, blinked and tried to sit up, but fell back. She was stiff and sore this morning from the weight of the cat landing on her.

"You're wasting daylight..." he said again as he walked away from her.

Carlie gingerly sat up and tried to stretch the stiffness out, but it wasn't working. Crawling from under the blanket, she squatted, *even that hurts.* She folded and rolled her bedroll up then wandered over to the fire. Picking up her cup, she held it out and waited for Rawlins to pour her some coffee.

Colt glanced at her cup, and then his gaze traveled up her hand to the dirty sleeve and followed that to the ragamuffin's face. Besides being filthy again, it was splattered with blood from the cat along with blotches of dried blood on her already dirty coat and her face. His eyes traveled back down to her hand. The girl obviously didn't give a hill of beans about her appearance as the dirty hand still patiently waited for him to fill her cup.

Refilling his cup, he saw hers wiggle in midair. Colt looked up.

Carlie wiggled the cup again.

"Naw-uh...you go wash up first. I don't care to set down to breakfast with someone as rank as you..."

Carlie blinked and gestured with the cup again.

"Nope...you go wash up first, then I'll give you some coffee," Rawlins repeated.

It dawned on Carlie then what he was talking about when she glanced down at the blood-spattered coat. Her filthy hand tried to brush off the dried blood.

"Go on, get washed up, we got lots to get done today..." Colt prodded her.

A half-hour later, Rawlins watched as Carlie trudged back up the hill. This time Wolf was at her side.

Carlie stopped in front of him, giving him that evil glare and spoke curtly, "Am I presentable enough for you now...Mister Rawlins?"

Carlie's face was shiny and flushed from scrubbing it so hard in the cold water. Taking a hand, he examined it as one would do a child before coming to the supper table.

She rolled her eyes.

"It'll do..." he said dropping the hand and filling her cup, handing it to her.

Colt handed Carlie a plate piled with food and observed how quickly she inhaled the grub, scraping the edge of the fork across the now empty plate getting every last scrap of food. "There's more," he grinned.

A deep rosy glow began rising from her neck, flushing her cheeks that continued up under her sun lightened bangs. Carlie realized she was acting like a starving animal. "I'm sorry," she said, as her dirty sleeve raked across her mouth. "I lost my manners there for a moment," rolling her eyes up and nodding at the lightening sky. "Mama and Grandma would have my hide if they saw me acting like this," she said. Eyes rolling back down, her hand gestured with the plate. "May I, please?"

Colt cocked an eyebrow for a second, then filled her plate once again, then sat back and watched her clean that one, too.

Carlie sighed; her tummy was finally full again. Her eyes skated over the air finally landing on Rawlins, then tapered, studying him.

"You one of them daffy drifters who ain't worth a plugged nickel? That why you've been following me, hoping for a handout?"

Handout? Daffy? Got moss growing on me, and now the damn girl is calling me a daffy drifter? Colt blinked, raising a dark brow. "Uh... not hardly," he replied.

"You said you was jus' passin' through?"

"Maybe," Rawlins said.

"I ain't hiring no two-bit saddle tramp..."

"So ya said..."

"Ya just passin' through?" Carlie asked again.

"Maybe, but that's my business."

"Meaning, maybe it's my business. You're the one following me..." she retorted.

Damn girl is gonna make things difficult. Harley, if I survive this, you owe me, you old coot." He was still having a hard time wrapping his mind around the difference between the girl in front of him with the memories of the one long ago.

"Maybe I'm passin' through, maybe not," Colt returned.

Carlie persisted. "What 'da mean, maybe, maybe not?"

Colt inhaled some coffee and answered lamely. "I've been asked to help someone."

"Help someone? Who?"

"You wouldn't know 'em," he lied.

"Shoot, there's not anyone I don't know around Kaskaskia. Who asked you to help? Who you supposed to be helping?"

"Never knew anyone who could fire off so many questions in such a short span of time."

Carlie wasn't satisfied with that. "Who?"

"Persistent little cuss, ain't cha?"

"Seriously, who are you s'posed to be helping? What's your story?" Carlie insisted.

"I'm helping out a friend and that's all you need to know for the moment..." Colt said. "...And as to my story...well...I've killed twenty-five men..."

Carlie Anne's face blanched as her mouth dropped open.

"...And been married four times...and might still be married to all four...but don't rightly know for sure..." enjoying her reaction to his lies.

Her mouth snapped shut.

"Now...which of those things scares you the most?"

Carlie Anne swallowed as she backed away from him, her eyes narrowing, not sure whether he was funning her or not.

Colt dropped his head hiding the faint smile that tried to bust through the three days' worth of stubble sprouting on his face. Lifting his head, he watched Carlie stride over to the edge of the little rise.

Sensing Rawlins moving towards her then coming alongside, standing close, Carlie began talking as her finger pointed. "See that dapple-grey mare? I call her Shoshone Princess, Princess for short. The cinnamon colored one with the blond tail and mane, that's Joy. The dark bay is Liberty. The chestnut, I call her Copper. She just had a foal. The three standing together are Winken, Blinken and Nod," Carlie told him. "The one standing by herself, that's Gypsy, she's about ready to drop her foal."

Finger pointing again, Carlie named off her three seed bulls. "The one over on the far side of the herd, he's Samson, he's kinda lazy, but gets the job done when he wants to."

Colt smiled faintly at her reference.

That finger continued to dance over the backs of the herd. "That darker red one, that's Dundee," her finger finally coming to a stop. "The one near the front, I call him McDuff, he's the one I use to lead the herd," she finished.

Rawlins raised both brows this time. *That did it, the girl is a bona fide crazy.* "You got a name for everything?"

Carlie nodded. "More often than not. It kind of makes...well... to me, it makes them not an object but..." she hesitated, then speaking softly. "...More like...uh...a friend..." she said as her eyes dove to the ground. *I know he thinks I've got bats in my belfry,* she thought.

Carlie Anne Russell must be lonely as hell... Colt's mind replied.

"The stallion, I call him Thor," Carlie said.

"Thor?" Rawlins queried as he took another sip of coffee.

"Uh-huh, when I was little..."

Rawlins watched her eyes develop a misty haze as she stared into the past.

"...I had read stories about Greek Gods and when he runs it sounds like thunder, so I named him Thor, the God of Thunder," Carlie said.

Now I know she really is loony, Colt thought again.

Turning to him, Carlie asked, "Do you read, Mister Rawlins?"

"Don't get much of a chance to do that."

"Do you like to read, Mister Rawlins?"

"Do you?" he asked, avoiding her question.

"Uh-huh...books can open up a whole new world. Did you know that, Mister Rawlins?"

"Hadn't thought much about it," he said.

"Well, they do," Carlie smiled as she closed her eyes. "It takes you places you'll never go..." opening her eyes, giving him a shy look. "I mean...go physically..." she paused then continued. "...I enjoy reading about the kind of lives other people lived and the land they took care of along with their customs..." she said.

The child-like demeanor continued as she inhaled and went on, "...Did you know there are all kinds of different names and customs other countries have for Santa Claus? For example, the Dutch children place their wooden shoes by the fireplace filled with hay and carrots for St. Nick's horses and then in the morning the shoes are filled with nuts and candies and other toys. And..." Carlie glanced at his face and saw Rawlins looking at her like she had just fallen out of a tree losing all her marbles in the process.

Sighing inwardly, she added softly, "I'm sorry, I didn't mean to bore you..."

Not only was the girl loco, lonely, and fired off questions faster than a repeater, she could talk you ears off, too. Colt mused to himself. Another memory surfaced; the child she had been long ago had done the same thing.

Taking another sip of coffee, he stuck his hand in his coat

pocket and continued to gaze at the mustangs and the mixed white-faced stock.

Carlie rolled her eyes. She'd embarrassed herself again, talking about stuff no one wanted to hear. From the look Rawlins just gave her, *"He probably thinks I'm a blithering idiot..."* she thought.

Digging a hole in the dirt with the toe of her boot, she then smoothed the dirt back over the little hole, sighing quietly. Glancing up and scanning her mares once again she saw that Gypsy had collapsed.

She gasped as she whispered, "Gypsy's down..." Carlie spun around too quickly, causing her to fall. She scrambled up and ran to Waldo, jerking the reins loose from the brush, she grabbed a handful of mane and flung herself aboard.

Surprised by the sudden departure, Colt yelled. "What's wrong?"

"Gypsy's down..." she shouted as she rammed her heels into the horse's ribs, taking off down the rise.

His eyes tracked her and that horse skedaddling down the slope into the draw and riding hard towards the downed mare before jumping on his own horse and riding after her.

Quickly sliding off Waldo, Carlie hurried to Gypsy's side and dropped to her knees, cradling the mare's head. "Gypsy...Gypsy, I'm here. It'll be all right...you can do this. I'm here for you, baby...I'm here..." Carlie crooned softly, gently stroking the mare's face and neck trying to soothe her.

The mare stiffened with a long spasm then tried to lift her head giving the girl a wild-eyed look. A desperate whinny rose up out of her throat as her head fell back into Carlie's arms.

"Oh...Gypsy..." she whispered as she gently laid the mare's head down. Carlie then moved to the rear of her and pushed the tail out of the way so she could peer into the entrance of the womb. Not glimpsing a tiny hoof or nose, she frantically removed her coat and rolled up her shirtsleeve to her shoulder. Speaking softly once again to the struggling mare, "I'm not going to hurt you Gypsy, just want to see where your baby is…" she proceeded to gently slide her arm into the birth canal.

Taking stock of the situation, Colt slid off his bay and walked over and knelt by the mare's head. He realized that she wasn't moving or breathing; the mare had died trying to give birth.

"Ugh…I can't reach the baby! My arms are too short," she cried out in exasperation. Glancing over at Rawlins, "You've got long arms, come here and see if you can pull that baby out!" she ordered him.

"Carlie…it won't do any good…" Rawlins replied.

"What do mean it won't do any good? You gotta help me… Mister Rawlins! You help me!"

The girl was frantic. Grabbing her arms with his two big palms, Rawlins squeezed her still. "Carlie! Carlie listen to me! She's gone…Gypsy's dead…" his deep voice calmly stated.

"Gone? No! She can't be," she cried out in fear. Turning her panicked gaze to the mare's eyes, Carlie knew then it was true. Half whirling, she yelled at the stallion stand thirty yards away, "Damn you Thor! Damn you! Throwing those dad gum big bullets, killing my mares!" Carlie cried out.

Colt blinked, he didn't know what the hell that meant.

Carlie whirled back on Rawlins, taking a big breath she held out her hand, "Give me your knife…"

Colt hesitated. "Why?"

"Damn it, give me your knife…there isn't much time! Give it to me…" she frantically cried out.

Handing Carlie his knife, asked. "What are you going to do?"

Taking it and sliding back down to the mare's swollen belly, she told him, "Cut the baby out…"

"What? You can't do that!"

She didn't bother to respond.

"Do you know what you're doing?"

"No…but I saw my Daddy do it many a time. I have to save this foal…" she explained.

Colt sighed as he slid down next to Carlie, his hand reaching for the knife. "I'll do it."

"No!" Carlie cried, jerking her hand away from his. "This is my problem, you're making me waste valuable seconds..." she said. Looking over at the mare's head, "...I'm sorry...so sorry... Gypsy..." Carlie breathed.

Damn horse is dead and the girl is talking to the animal like it was still alive. Lordy, Harley! What the hell did you get me into? Rawlins thought.

Taking a deep breath, Carlie drove the knife into the belly of the mare, slicing the skin down to between the mare's hind legs stopping just above the milk bag. Tossing the knife, she pulled opened the cut wider as fresh blood soaked her hands and arms.

A rich copper smell filled the air as other not so pleasant smells did also.

Stopping briefly to wipe her hands on her britches so that she might get a better grip, her hands dove into the back belly of the mare hoping to find the foal. She did. Her fingers slipped and slid trying to break the sack, causing her to groan in frustration several times.

Retrieving his knife, Colt slipped in next to her. Bending his head, he saw what Carlie was trying to do and slit the sack for her.

Water poured through the opening drenching her arms and shirt along with her pants and Colt's knees. Finding two tiny hooves, she reached in further grasping slippery legs and began pulling the rump of the foal through the opening.

Colt reached in, his arm wrapping around the back part of the body and pulled; the foal slipped out onto the dry grasses butt first.

Quickly they both removed the sack from around the mouth and nose along with the rest of its tiny body. Carlie reached behind her and grabbed her coat to begin vigorously rubbing and drying the newborn.

Colt took his bandana and cleared the mucus out of its nose and mouth.

The foal kicked.

"That's it baby...you can do it..." Carlie whispered.

The foal lay there heaving in air from its difficult birth while Carlie continued to rub its coat trying to dry it. She kept whispering softly to it, encouraging it on.

When the foal seemed to have gained some strength, it half sat up then flopped back down. After resting for a few moments, it tried again to stand. This time it got its front legs stretched out in front of him and tried to rise but fell. After the fourth time, the foal stood up on very wobbly legs, but it was finally standing.

Carlie and Colt helped support the unsteady foal by standing on either side of it.

Reaching down Carlie picked up and threw her coat over the foal. Her face glowing, she looked over at Rawlins. "We did it!" she whispered.

"I think so..."

She saw that he too was smiling; even his eyes beamed back at her.

It was then Carlie saw something white flutter down and settle on his black hat, followed by more. Looking up, she saw the air was filling with snowflakes.

Rawlins' eyes followed Carlie's.

"The first snowstorm of the season," she whispered.

Stepping forward she knelt and gently took the foal's face in her hands making eye contact with the colt's soft brown eyes, "Your name will be Storm and you will grow up to be big and strong and brave just like your Daddy. You too, will sire a many great foals," Carlie whispered, planting a kiss between its eyes. Standing after releasing the foal's face, her eyes found Rawlins grey ones again. "I'm gonna bring Copper closer, so he can nurse..." she stated moving off.

"That ain't gonna work, Carlie...that mare won't accept him."

Carlie turned smiling softly. "Oh…yes she will. Copper will do anything I ask of her…"

Frowning, Colt was flummoxed again at the magic the girl seemed to have over these wild horses. He watched her coerce the chestnut to accept the orphaned foal. Putting her coat on the colt wrapping him in her scent so that Copper would accept him was a smart move. He was surprised at her instinct of knowing exactly what to do.

After he was nursing contentedly, she walked back over to him grinning, "See…I told you…"

"That you did…" he agreed, nodding.

They continued to watch the new colt as he suckled from his foster mother, his little swatch of a tail flicking contentedly.

Her eyes rose. "Thank you, Lord," whispered Carlie.

Surprised, Colt glanced down quickly hearing Carlie's words. His body turning, he watched Carlie walk back over to the dead mare. Kneeling down and speaking softly to it, she rubbed Gypsy's neck for the last time. As she stood, she wiped away the single tear that had dropped onto her cheek.

Rawlins heard her sniffle as Carlie reached down to pick up her coat and put it on. He studied Carlie gazing at death one more time, then at the new life they had both brought into the world together.

Reaching for Waldo's reins, Carlie faced Rawlins. "Storm will be alright now, Copper's a good mama," she informed him. Turning and pulling her mount, she headed back towards the camp. Stopping abruptly, Carlie twisted back around. "I'm sorry, I'm forgetting my manners again. Thank you for helping…" she said, then looked back down at the dusting of snow covering the ground before she resumed her trek back to camp.

Picking up his own mount's reins, he continued to watch the girl followed by the mule trudge away through the light snowfall.

His glance once again touched on the newborn foal now trying out his new-fangled legs, tentatively taking a few steps in the first snowfall of the season.

Helping Carlie birth that foal, well...maybe she wasn't as crazy as he first thought. Maybe she was just...oh...what was the word he was looking for...*eccentric*. Yeah, that was it, eccentric, peculiar, a nonconformist. It was a lot of big words to describe someone who was maybe only fourteen, fifteen hands high.

Resettling his hat on his head, Colt Rawlins trudged after the girl.

18

Returning to the fire after washing off the blood and after birth the cold stream, Carlie was freezing. Kneeling as close to the fire as she dared, her hands stretched out to the welcomed warmth. Her shirt was soaked as well as the inside of her coat from rubbing down Storm, chilling her through to her bones. It had been warm so she hadn't dug out her long-handles to put on yet and now she was paying the price for that mistake.

Rawlins had finished tying off his bay and observed that the girl's teeth were chattering. Walking behind her, he stuck a big paw down the back of her neck and felt all the wet material she was still wearing.

"Hey! Cut that out!" her fist erupted slamming into his thigh. "Your hand is like ice," Carlie fussed at him.

Continuing to the girl's saddlebags Rawlins asked, "You got any dry clothes in these bags?"

Carlie shook her head. "No…all my spare clothes are at the winter cabin…I'll be alright, soon's I warm up."

"I don't plan on nursing you when you get sick…" he replied.

"I can take care of myself, Mister Rawlins," she replied crossly.

"Yeah, when you finally get enough brains to spit," he returned testily as he reached into his own bag, pulling out a spare shirt and coat and tossed them both at Carlie.

Carlie gasped when they landed on her head and shoulders. Pulling them off her face, she gave Rawlins another hard glare.

"Put 'em on," he ordered her.

Ignoring what he had told her earlier. "I don't need your help..."

"I said put them on," Rawlins ordered again.

"They won't fit."

"Yeah, well...if you had a thought far enough ahead..." he paused for a moment then plunged on, "...Didn't anyone ever teach you to be prepared? Kinda like never holster an empty gun?"

"Uh..."

"Thought so...if you did...you wouldn't have to be wearing my clothes. Now put them on or I'll strip you myself and put them on for you," he warned.

Carlie just stared into the fire, teeth chattering away, refusing to rise to his baiting her.

Colt stood watching her, refusing to help herself. His anger grew, "Dammit..."

Her head jerked up, staring at him and seeing his visible temper.

"...You have no business trying to run this ranch...you're too green...ain't got the sense God gave you..."

His words stabbed her deep in her heart. Tears sprang. She dropped her head so he wouldn't see how much his words stung.

"I mean it, get out of those wet clothes," he threatened again.

Blinking rapidly dissipating the tears, Carlie glared up at Rawlins. "You just got to be in charge, don't you? Bossing everyone around..."

"Someone's gotta be in charge with a rattlebrain like you..."

"I ain't no rattlebrain!"

"Well...you ain't proved me wrong yet..." Rawlins fired back.

Carlie squeezed her eyes shut, clamped her lips tight then expelled a noisy sigh. "Turn around," she finally agreed.

When he didn't move, she repeated, "I said, turn around."

Rawlins smiled and did as she requested.

"You can turn back around now."

When he did, he grabbed his blanket, walked over and draped it across Carlie's shoulders.

She pulled it tighter around her, huddling into the wool.

Rawlins handed her a cup of hot coffee.

"Thanks…"

"Welcome…"

After hanging the girl's wet shirt and coat on some nearby brush, Colt sat down next to her. Two sets of eyes stared into the fire, ignoring each other as only the crackling and popping of the wood broke the silence.

❧

RAWLINS PICKED up the dirty plates and forks and handed them to Carlie. "Take these down to the creek and wash 'em good."

Standing, Carlie asked, "Why do I always have to do the washing up?"

"You sure are a spoiled-rotten little brat…you know that?"

"I am not a spoiled-rotten little brat…" she retorted. "…I just want to know why I always have to…"

"…Because I do all the cooking…" he interrupted. "…Now go on, wash those plates…"

"I'm not your slave…Mister Rawlins…"

"Didn't say you were, but as long as I do the cooking, you'll do the washing up…" Rawlins replied simply.

She gave him a black glare. "Sheesh…you act like I ain't got no brains a-tall…" Her hands full, Carlie then turned and strode off to the creek below the rise.

"Yeah...or...grass growing betwixt them ears of yours..." he muttered when she was out of earshot.

Carlie kept mumbling to herself, "Men...always gotta be bossing you around, why even Harley has to..." Her feet flew out from under her on the muddy bank, plates going in one direction, the forks another as she slid on her backside into the icy creek.

"Ugh...Jeepers creepers...that water's cold..." Scrambling quickly up out of the creek, she tried to stand and fell on the slick bank, sliding back into the water. "Sheesh," she said as the icy water covered her limbs again.

Crawling on her knees this time, she carefully inched up the slippery bank and began a frantic search for the plates and the forks. She found the plates, but even with her hands digging in the mud, she couldn't for the life of her find the forks. Sitting on her knees, she heaved in a deep breath. "Rawlins is gonna kill me," she sighed heartily and whispered. "Now he'll really think I've got bats in my belfry..."

Carlie stood and inched her way up the rest of the bank. Standing at the top, she gazed at Colt Rawlins in the distant firelight, sitting there sipping his coffee. *He's gonna kill me, he's gonna kill me...* Carlie sang to herself.

Heaving in air, she walked into the firelight and came to stand in front of Rawlins, plates clutched tight against her chest. Carlie saw his eyes go round as he gazed at her over the brim of his cup.

Looking up at the dark sky, she heaved in another deep breath then refocused on him. "You're gonna kill me...I found the plates but couldn't find the forks in the dark..." Carlie said thrusting the plates at him.

Colt stared intently at the ragamuffin, her britches dripping water making a puddle right in front of him. "Guess you fell in the creek?"

"No. I slipped on the icy bank and the plates went that-a-way..." she began gesturing with the hand still holding the plates.

"...And the forks the other..." she said as the right arm flung out in another direction.

Colt's eyes followed each arm, then resettled on her face.

"...Then I slipped into the creek..." she replied seriously.

Rawlins tried to keep a straight face as he took another quick sip of coffee. He cleared his throat again trying to hold back the laughter threatening to bust out any second. "Trouble always follow you around like this?"

Heaving a deep sigh of relief, Carlie plopped down next to him.

Colt cut her a cock-eyed look.

"Like my Granddaddy always said..." Carlie began, pulling a boot off and pouring the water out, setting it next to the fire.

Rawlins had to button lips even tighter when he saw how much water she poured out of that boot.

"...Life's an adventure with Carlie around..." she said repeating the process with the second boot. "...Never knew what was gonna happen next with Carlie Anne... he'd say..." she added. Taking her socks off she twisted the water out of them and laid them next to her boots. Carlie heaved out yet another sigh, with arms between her knees and hands wrapped around her calves, her toes curling from the cold. Carlie Anne peeked at Rawlins, flapping those ridiculously long lashes framing impish eyes at him.

Harley, you were right, the girl was green, a real shave-tail, and still as pretty as four aces sitting in your hand during a high stakes game, Colt thought.

"Girl...don't know about you," he said, an eyebrow going up for emphasis. "First that cougar, then the foal, and now you falling into the creek," Rawlins said, handing Carlie a cup of hot coffee.

"I didn't do it on purpose," she fired back. "And I didn't fall in the creek, I slipped!" Carlie continued to glare at the man sitting next to her. "Oh...what's the use trying to explain anything to you! You wouldn't believe me anyhow..." she said bristling, rising quickly and moving to stand as close to the fire as she could,

86

trying to dry out those baggy britches as water continued to drip on her bare feet. She glared down at Rawlins. She saw his eyes twinkling in the firelight. "You think it's funny...don't you?"

Rawlins grinned. "You could say that..." he tipped the cup up to take another swallow.

"Pffftt!" Carle exhaled as she turned around to dry the front of her britches.

Rising, he strode to his bags for the second time that day and pulled out his extra pair of britches, walking back to the girl and thrusting them at her. "Here...put these on," he said.

Carlie glanced at the britches, then back up at his face. "I'll be fine," she said.

"You're wetter now than when we birthed that colt..."

"No...I'm not..."

"You got granite in your skull?"

She looked at him then, "Huh?"

"You don't listen worth a lick...I ain't gonna say it again."

Carlie's eyes narrowed. "You're just as bad as a gnat dogging a fly...you know that?" she fussed.

"I don't give a damn about any gnats chasing flies, just get out of those wet britches," he ordered her.

Carlie jammed hands in his borrowed coat's pockets and stood her ground.

Running a hand through dark hair, he sighed. "Alright...suit yourself, but if you get sick, I'm not taking care of you, you're on your own," he threatened.

Turning around to put his pants back in his saddlebag. Colt kneeled, rolling it up small enough to fit. Suddenly something sopping wet plastered itself across the back of his neck.

"Hey..." his hand reached behind and removed the wet object as he stood and swung around. She was standing in a defiant pose wearing ratty looking pantaloons encasing her thighs. *Girl's got some nice legs...* he thought. Giving himself a mental shake, *Don't even go there...* he told himself.

Carlie asked flippantly as she crossed her arms in a huff. "Happy now...Mister Rawlins?"

"Uh-huh," tossing Carlie his britches as he walked to hang the wet ones on scrub with the rest of her things. "Looks like someone has been doing laundry around this camp..."

Ignoring him, she held up the britches. When she realized that they would swallow her whole, she tossed them back to him. "I'll just wrap up in the blanket," she said, doing so, plunked down on the log, stared into the fire.

He could strangle the kid who acted like she didn't have the brains God gave her. No wonder Harley wanted to get rid of her. And he wasn't sure if he'd be able to help, anyhow, *if* he lasted with Carlie Anne bucking up against everything he tried to do to help. Colt sighed inwardly.

R eady to move out the next morning Colt stepped into the leather and asked, "Know how many head you got?"

"Nope..." Carlie replied.

"What about them harses, know how many you got?"

"Nope..." she said again.

Colt just stared at the girl. "When was the last time you counted them?"

Surprise crossed Carlie's face as she spluttered, "You mean I'm s'posed to count them?"

"How the hell else you supposed to keep track of them?"

Carlie shrugged.

Rawlins pushed his hat back and fixed a hard look on her.

*He's looking at me like I just ate locoweed...*she thought as her fingers fiddled with the reins.

"You got an iron?"

"A what?"

"A branding iron? You got one?"

"What for?"

Colt bent his head, gazed at his hands resting on the horn, pursed his lips and blew loudly.

"Why do you need a branding iron?" Carlie asked again.

Colt looking over, saw the kid's innocent expression. "Because, it looks like we'll be doing some branding here shortly, and that's when you count them cows," he said.

"Oh..." her eyes wide as she processed this. "But...I branded what I could this past spring..."

"You did?" forgetting that Harley had told him she had when he first came to town. "Well...there is also a fall branding time too. Branding the calves born late spring and summer," Colt explained.

"Oh..."

"Well...you got an iron or not?"

Her head nodded south. "At the cabin..."

"Fine. How much further?"

"Two...three days..." Carlie answered.

"Let's push this red river south," he said, picking up his reins.

Colt heard her give a sharp whistle after which he saw Wolf come running out of the brush. He watched as she gave him hand signals, then saw him take off for the other side of the herd. Carlie was riding toward the front, neatly circling and cracking her whip over those red backs, forcing the herd to begin moving.

Rawlins blinked at her use of hand signals for the wolf along with her skill at the whip and he realized she was pretty handy with it. He closed his eyes for a moment as he slowly shook his head. Dealing with Carlie Anne Russell was turning into more of a chore than he wanted. All he was hoping for was a nice easy job when Harley had approached him. But it didn't look like that was gonna happen with Carlie Anne around. *Aww...hell, I did promise Harley*, he thought. Opening his eyes, he sighed as he muttered, "Yep...a saddlebag just chock full of trouble..." and with that statement, Rawlins urged the bay into motion.

Several hours later, Colt heard a shrill whistle. He glanced to his right and saw Carlie Anne hopping up and down, arms flailing away signaling him. He reined his mount around and rode toward her. "What's up?" he asked as he dismounted.

Carlie dove behind the boulders and picked up two snowballs she had made and popped back up. "Over here…got a calf down, need your help getting him back up…" Carlie shouted.

"Damn critters worse than sheep…" he muttered when he began walking in her direction.

Splat!

"What the hell?" he exclaimed as he looked down at his coat and saw the remains of snow.

Carlie's aim took off his hat this time. The next one caught his shoulder.

Laughter tinkled through the air.

"Damn you…Carlie Anne! We ain't got time to be playing…we got a herd to move!" he yelled just as he saw another snowball sailing through the air at him making him duck quickly.

More laughter.

Colt dodged a few more.

"Aww…Mister Rawlins, haven't you ever been in a snowball fight before?" she cried gleefully.

"No!"

"It ain't gonna hurt you…" Carlie said as she popped up ready to hurl another. She suddenly she stopped. No Rawlins. *Where'd he go?*

A big paw grabbed her ankle.

Carlie yelped.

Rawlins yanked her feet out from under her, landing her flat on her back.

Carlie yelped again when she hit the frozen ground.

Rawlins quickly sat on Carlie with both hands holding her arms down by her side. He growled. "You gonna quit playing games now?" He watched as the merriment faded from her eyes.

Carlie looked into the granite face of Colt Rawlins. His eyes had gone to dark slate, a testament to his anger. "You don't play much, do you?"

"Not when there's work to be done…" Rawlins gritted.

Carlie said flippantly. "You sure are huffy. What's the matter… your boots pinching your toes or something?"

"We's got work to do…"

"…All work and no play…" Carlie teased in a sing-song cadence.

"Shut-up, we got cattle to move…"

Carlie resignedly blew air. "Pfffttt, you sure are a wet blanket…" she paused, waiting on Rawlins to get off her. "…Well…get off of me, you big moose…" she told him.

Moose? Harley where in the hell does she come up with this stuff! Rawlins mind buzzed.

He rose then and dusted the wet snow off his knees and picked up his hat slamming it back on his head. He briskly turned and strode back to the bay.

Scrambling up, she wiped the melted snow off her backside. Carlie trotted after him saying, "And it was perfect, too. Pretty soon the snow will be too dry to play with and you had to go and ruin my fun. You big walrus."

With one foot in the stirrup, Rawlins half turned back toward the ragamuffin. "Good," he said, mounting and moving back toward the herd.

"You know something else, Rawlins," she shouted giving a hippity-hop after him. "You're a…you're nothing but a…" thinking. "A snake on stilts…" she said, skipping after him. "And you got…" thinking again. "…You got bats in your belfry," she yelled after him.

"Yeah…maybe I do," he muttered to himself out of her earshot. "But not nearly as many as you have, not nearly as many…" he said as he rode away toward the herd.

Not getting a response as she watched the distance grow between them, finally muttering, "Pfffttt," she swung into the leather and rode out after Rawlins.

20

Keeping his distance from the girl to give him some kind of peace, Rawlins remained on the other side of the herd chasing down some young strays and heading them back into the main body of cattle. His eyes skimming over the stock, he searched for brands keeping a mental tally on how many did or did not have the Russell mark.

His eyes grew wide with anger at what he was seeing. Brands were marking the hides on necks, backs and ribs of the cattle. They were everywhere except where they should be.

Colt whirled his big bay around and raced the horse to the other side of the herd. His hand snaked out grabbing Waldo's bridle strap, hauling him up short and surprising the sorrel and Carlie.

Rawlins bellowed at the girl. "What the hell did you think you were doing when you branded those beeves?" Eyes the color of a couple of .45 slugs zeroed in on Carlie Anne.

She blinked in surprise as confusion crossed her face. "Whatever on earth are you talking about?"

"I'm talking about you marking up good hides," he yelled. "Instead of placing the brands where they should be."

Carlie looked down at her hands. "Ooh...that."

Colt rolled his eyes and spoke to the clouds above. "Ooh that... she sez..." He returned dark steel to the ragamuffin's dirty face. "What the hell did you do, brand 'em from horseback?"

The angry reaction from her eyes seemed to make them dance, "Well...just bust my bustle Mister Rawlins, that's exactly what I did..." She gave him a shrewd glance, "I didn't think you were smart enough to figure that one out..." Carlie taunted him.

"Hell-fire...Carlie Anne! You lost fifty cents to a dollar on those hides, marking them up like that."

"So?"

"So? So...she sez?" Rolling his eyes again, "Dammit...Carlie Anne, if you had enough brains to spit, you would've hired some men to do this work for you by now."

Quick as a flash Carlie's hand grabbed Rawlins' coat and yanked on it, expecting him to move. He didn't. Instead the movement brought Carlie's face to within inches of his. Eyes flashed with anger. "I've got more brains then you or that hammerhead you're riding put together..." she gritted through clenched teeth.

Rawlins kept quiet.

Carlie's breath stopped when she realized she could feel heat waves pulsing off his body into the air between them. Her hand shoved at Rawlins' chest trying to push him away. He didn't budge, *again.*

Sitting up straighter in the saddle, Carlie breathed air into her starved lungs, then settled a black look on him.

Rawlins observed a deep flush creep up under that dirty face as her eyes smoldered with anger. *Got mor'n a temper than I figured and still as pretty as four aces sittin' in my hand.* He waited to see what else she would say; you just never knew with Carlie Anne...

"So...I got a little creative, Mister Rawlins," she finally puffed out.

He exploded. "Creative? You call marking up hides creative?"

Silence stretched between them from two saddles.

Carlie's next words surprised even herself. "You're a handsome man, Mister Rawlins..." she began softly then quickly darted her eyes down, staring at her hands loosely holding the reins and swallowed hard.

Looking back up, she narrowed her eyes trying to cover up her embarrassment of what she had just revealed. "...But I'm not some girly girl batting my eyelashes at you or swooning at your feet just because you happen to be good looking." Carlie pulled her gaze from him looking instead out across her cattle.

Rawlins watched the rosy hue slowly climb from Carlie Anne's neck all the way into the roots of her hair.

"This is a big spread, Mister Rawlins..." she said, cutting a glance in his direction again, then her eyes darted away before speaking. "...And yes...sometimes more than I can handle..." she admitted, looking down at her hands again. She continued, "...So...sometimes I have to be a little creative..."

Carlie sat straighter in the saddle and squared her shoulders. "But I'm not going to cry trying to weasel pity out of you. I cried enough when my folks died and sat on my pity-pot then..."

Colt had to admit the kid had spunk.

"...I really don't care if you think of me as a blithering idiot..."

*Well...that's true...*he thought.

"...Or that I have peculiar ways of accomplishing chores."

True again...

"But I still have a ranch to run, Mister Rawlins, with you or without you...and that's that," she finished quietly.

She gave him one last hard look before jerking Waldo's head around and heading him back toward the herd.

He pushed his hat back on his head and rested forearms on the saddle's horn as he watched her ride the horse into the brush. The kid had surprised him with her little sermon. In a roundabout way she had told him she didn't want his pity. Reading between the lines though, Carlie Anne wasn't that opposed to him helping her either, Colt reckoned.

21

C arlie reined in her sorrel and cut a glance at Rawlins, then nodded down the hill. "Home," she said, tapping her heels into Waldo's ribs taking off.

Dismounting by the corral fence, he took a slow look-see around, observing that these structures were as well built as the main house and barn. Unsaddling the bay and carrying his gear, he followed Carlie into the lean-to barn.

Stepping into the doorway after Carlie, they ended up in a walk-thru between the cabin and the barn. His eyes roamed around the main room of the cabin. Peeking around the corner to his left, he saw a sleeping alcove that held one big bed and two sets of bunk beds. Walking over he threw his gear down on the big bed. Turning and taking a few steps his gaze traveled again noticing the big rock fireplace and to the left of that, a wall of built-in bookshelves filled to overflowing. To the right, a nice sized kitchen was tucked into a space of ten feet with a big cook stove, its pipe stuck into the stone of the fireplace chimney. It also contained a sink counter and water pump. Shelves all around were well stocked. Next to him was a table with a coal oil lamp sitting on it under a big window.

His gazed at Carlie as she was trying to get a fire started. He walked over and knelt down. "Here…let me…" he offered.

Eyes flicked up.

Their hands touched.

His eyes and hers held each other along with his hand touching hers for just a second too long. Clearing his throat, he finally took the pine straw and matches from her, "Seems your folks were good at building solid structures," he said for something to say, stuffing the straw between the wood and lighting it. He focused hard on the fire instead of the girl, watching it begin to flare up and lick the wood.

Carlie slowly stood and retreated, wiping her hands down her britches as she backed up some more. *When our hands touched there was something familiar with…naw…we've never met before he came into my camp…or have we…?* Her thoughts became even more puzzling. She wrinkled her brow in confusion.

Rawlins felt the girl silently withdrawing and knew she felt the way he had when their hands had touched and their eyes had locked. *That's the last thing I need, is to get attached… our worlds are too far apart…I can help her but that's all…*his mind reflected. Shoving the thoughts away, he concentrated on feeding the fire.

Carlie couldn't take her eyes off Colt's lean features, watching his hands deftly and surely build and feed the fire. This was the second time, *it* had happened, when he had touched her hand. *Falling for someone like Colt Rawlins would just be trouble, a saddle bag full of trouble,* she thought, *If his name really was Colt Rawlins.* Then a niggling thought appeared. "Who are you really?" Carlie asked abruptly. "What are you doing here?"

Half turning, he replied, "I already told you, Colt Rawlins."

"Yeah…but why are you really here?"

Throwing a log on the fire, he answered, "I already told you that, too…"

"No, you didn't. You ran around my questions before…" she

hesitated then plunged on, "...Don't you think it's time you gave me a straight answer?"

Standing, he replied, "I did."

Crossing her arms, Carlie gave him a dirty look. "Hell's bells... you're lying to me...and you know it...I want to know why?"

Resting his elbow on the mantel and clasping both hands together, Colt returned her stare, remaining quiet. *Well, I ain't exactly lying, just not telling her everything either,* he reasoned with himself.

Carlie heaved in air than expelled it quickly, the breath lifting the hair off her forehead.

Colt watched her spin and walk away. He bent down and threw two more logs on the fire. When he heard footsteps coming back toward him, he turned again and there she stood.

"Um...I figured you'd like a bath," she said thrusting clothes at him. "My Granddaddy was a big man like you and I think these may fit and this is Gramma's special soap..." she added.

Colt took the items, "We callin' a truce?"

Stuffing hands in her britches' front pockets, Carlie shrugged.

Sniffing the soap, "Lavender? Why...that's a woman's soap!"

"Well, I can give you a bar of lye soap if you prefer, then watch you shrivel up into nothing in this dry air."

Colt tentatively smelled the soap again, "What's in it?"

Carlie shrugged. "I don't know exactly, but Gramma put something in it so our skin wouldn't get so dry."

Pulling her hands out of her pockets, Carlie edged toward the door. "Well...you want a bath or not?"

Looking around, "Where? I don't see a wash tub."

She stepped off the porch and motioned with her hand. "C'mon, I'll show you..."

HEARING THE DOOR OPEN, she turned, speechless for a moment at the difference in his appearance. "Uh...you feel better now?"

Colt smiled. "Yeah...that was a nice surprise."

She nodded. "My turn," Carlie said, relieving him of the soap. "I made up the big bed for you and put some potatoes in the fire. When I get back, I'll get a rabbit for supper..." she said closing the door softly in her wake.

Well, now...Carlie Anne is being right hospitable... Colt mused.

Laying his things on the bed, Colt allowed his eyes to travel over the contents of the cabin once again. Drawn to the over-stuffed bookshelves, he strode beyond the sleeping alcove to them, surveying the overflowing shelves. The only time he'd seen this many books had been in a lawyer's office. And that was some time back.

Tilting his head, he read some of the titles. A Tale of Two Cities, the Iliad, *however you pronounced that one,* he thought. Don Quixote, Charles Dickens; there were several by him. Encyclopedias, a dictionary, Washington Irving, William Shakespeare, Gunn's Domestic Medicine, and a ton of other titles as he read the names silently. Well, at least he'd have something to do this winter, but reading that much would probably cross his eyes.

Spotting a long thin box, he pulled it towards him and opened it. *Chess and checker pieces, Alright...something else to do.* Replacing the box, a pad of paper fell, its individual sheets scattering across the floor. Squatting, he noticed the drawings. Gathering them together, he began flipping through the pages. The paper contained beautiful intricate drawings of butterflies, needle-flies, flowers, and mule deer, along with different poses of Wolf. There were several drawings of the horses, especially that stallion. She had captured his muscular lines and stature and the way the light caught his dark coat.

Colt glanced quickly at the door, then back at the drawings. *Carlie Anne Russell is a very talented young lady, well...I wouldn't exactly call her a lady, but she sure as hell is talented.* Replacing the pad, he edged back to the hearth and threw on another log. Straightening, his eyes were once again drawn to the shelves holding the beautiful drawings. He didn't remember Carlie drawing all those years ago. *Must've been something she picked up over time. Seems that crazy rattlebrain girl is talented in several ways...*he thought as his mind tried to wrap around this new revelation of his long-lost friend.

22

As Carlie swam around in the hot spring, she thought, *This sure beats washing up in an icy stream.* Ducking under the water again, she broke through the surface, the warm water cascading through her hair and down her back. She flipped over on her back and hand paddled around, staring at the geese honking overhead, heading south, *They're late...*she realized.

Her mind wandered back to Colt Rawlins. She felt it in her gut that he was lying to her, well...maybe not lying, just not telling her everything. He said he was just passing through *maybe*, but for a *maybe*, he sure was hanging around a lot longer than a *maybe*.

Sighing, she turned another back flip underwater then broke the surface again as her hands smoothed back her hair.

It had been kind of nice having company the last week. He reminded her of daddy and granddaddy the way he handled the cows, except when he got mad at her.

Turning a front flip underwater, she came up again.

*Problem is I have no money to pay him and once he finds that out, well...he'll be gone in a flash...*she thought as she made another front flip then resurfaced again. Glancing at the bank she saw Wolf waiting on her. "You ready for me to get out...big boy?" she asked softly, swimming over to him. Stretching her hand out, Wolf came closer to sniff then lick her wet palm. Carlie reached up and rubbed his ears, then her hand trailed down to scratch the black tipped furry chest.

Climbing out of the water, she dried and dressed quickly in the frigid air.

Pulling her boots on, Carlie spoke to her four-legged companion. "What are we going to do about Mister Rawlins, huh...Wolf?" she asked rubbing his head. "I'll bet you'd like to chew another hole in his arm, wouldn't you?" she grinned, ruffling fur.

A shot rang out, making Wolf spring to attention.

What the dickens did he do now? she wondered. Picking up her belongings, she headed back to the cabin with Wolf right on her heels.

A deer hung from the porch beams, already gutted with a hindquarter missing. She stepped on the porch and looked over the deer noting it's nice size. A big dishpan full of scraps for Wolf sat by the door. "Hey look...Wolf, he left you supper," she said, taking a foot and sliding the pan closer to him. "Eat up big boy." Smiling when he dove into the raw meat.

Opening the door, she saw Rawlins squatting in front of the fire, turning the spit. The rush of warmed air felt good on her skin as did the scent of roasting meat tickling her nose. The sizzling splatter of juices on the coals was music to her ears making her realize how much she missed her folks. Sighing internally, she shook off the memories and put her dirty clothes in a pile to wash later. Then she grabbed her brush and strode over to stand next to Rawlins. "We've got the big cook stove, you know," she said, beginning to comb out the snarls in her hair.

Colt smiled as he glanced up. "Guess I'm more used..." his voice trailed off. Cleaned up, Carlie Anne Russell had turned into a beautiful girl...uh...young woman. That thick sun-drenched honey-brown hair flowed free reaching almost to her waist took his breath away. Her eyes were wide and with an innocence he hadn't seen in a long time in a female. *Damn, she's beautiful!* And would become even more so when she finally grew up.

Ducking his head, *Don't even go there...* he reminded himself. He was just here at Harley's request, it didn't matter that he had once known her long ago.

Clearing his throat, his eyes refocused on the spit. He began turning it again. "Uh...I guess I'm just more comfortable cooking over an open fire."

Carlie chewed her bottom lip with her teeth and just nodded in response. She had witnessed those unusual eyes turning into a darker grey. Scooting the footstool closer to the fire, Carlie plopped down and continued to comb the snarls out of her hair.

Silence reigned except for the juices sizzling on the coals.

Carlie spoke quietly. "Um...thank you for feeding Wolf," she said.

Colt nodded. "You're welcome..."

THE CABIN CONTINUED with its deep silence except for the fire crackling and popping as Carlie finished up the dishes. She poured them both more coffee before coming back to the table and sitting down across from Colt.

There hadn't been much conversation during supper. Carlie hadn't talked a blue streak like she normally did, Rawlins noted. He had noticed her eyes skittering away from his every time he glanced at her.

He finally broke the silence. "What do you do during these long winter months up here by yourself?"

She hesitated, smoothing crumbs into a little pile.

Colt raised a brow at her silence.

Finally, she replied, "I stay busy."

"Doing what?" he asked, nodding at the bookshelves. "Reading a lot?"

Carlie shrugged, "That and other things."

Forearms resting comfortably on the big wooden table, Colt observed the girl still being shy with him after all that bluff and bluster on the trail.

"Where'd you learn to cut your lead like that?"

"Harley taught me. You don't know him...but I mentioned him before..."

*Yeah...the lying ol' skinflint...I don't know him...*he thought.

"...He said if I was gonna take out someone, make sure my mark counted, instead of just winging them," she explained.

Colt frowned. "When did this happen?"

Carlie shrugged. "Couple of months back..." she informed him.

Rawlins saw her hesitate again and decided to wait.

Carlie sighed. "...Ever since Mama and Daddy died, Tom Riley has been playing games with me. At first it was just him, wanting to buy me out. Offering me only diddly-squat sums for this place, I kept turning him down. Then he started sending out his hired hands to threaten me and to...well...do other things. I winged the last two who ransacked the main house while I was hiding in the barn."

"You tell the Sheriff?"

"Who'd believe me? It's Riley's word against mine. They all think I've got bats in my belfry anyway, what with Wolf. Only Harley believed me..." she finished quietly picking at her ragged fingernails.

Colt sat back in his chair studying the girl. Harley was right, *Carlie had a wagonload of lemons dumped on her, and she was trying so hard to make lemonade.*

Rawlins sat up wrapping both hands around his cup. "Is that why you attacked me by the corral?"

She nodded. "I thought you were one of Riley's hired hands," she said.

"Maybe I am," he deadpanned.

Carlie looked up. "What?"

"One of his hired hands."

Carlie folded her arms on the table and rested her chin on them. A smile crossed her face as she studied him.

Rawlins witnessed how that smile seemed to light up her features like mountain sunshine. Her unusual eyes were shimmering like the sun on a fast-flowing creek. It dredged up memories when she used to smile like that when they were kids.

"Naw...you're too nice, except when you get your britches all in a twist at me. You're not like the others..."

"Maybe Riley hired me to try some other type of tactic with you," Colt stated.

Her head rose, but the smile remained. "Naw...you're too honest, you wouldn't play Riley's type of underhanded line of attack. You'd figure him out too quick and then walk away," Carlie said seriously as she resettled her chin back on her arms.

"Besides knocking big men like me to the ground and pitching snowballs, what else do you do in the winter?"

Raising her head, she asked seriously, "You really wanna know?"

"I saw your drawings..." he said nodding toward the books.

Carlie's head swiveled around toward the bookshelf. "You did?"

Colt nodded, "They're very good, you know that?"

Carlie shrugged, pushing herself up from the table and walked over to her bunk. She dug out an old wooden ammo box from underneath and brought it back to the table. Taking off the lid, she pushed the box toward him, then stepped back, tucking fingers in her hip pockets as she did so waiting on his reaction.

Colt peeked in. Vibrant colors seemed to splash his eyes. Dipping a hand in, he picked up a small branch. Tiny intricate trout flies dotted the wood. Delight crossed his features. "You make these?"

Chewing on a bottom lip, Carlie nodded as she moved to her chair, then sat on one leg resting her arms on the table as she leaned over the box. One hand reached in and removed more of the box's contents. She spread them out in front of Rawlins.

Her hair still loose fell across her shoulder and down one arm gracing the table with its thick strands. The lamp picked out the contrast between the light and dark, making it shimmer.

He became mesmerized, his fingers just itching to run through those thick strands to see if they felt as silky as they looked.

Oblivious to him staring, Carlie Anne continued spreading the lures on the table.

Colt swallowed forcing himself to come back to earth. "Do they work?" he asked lamely. "I mean do they actually catch trout? Not just pretty things to stick in your hat?"

Carlie frowned. "Of course they catch trout! My Granddaddy taught me..."

Rawlins removed one from the wood and held it closer to the coal oil lamp. Turning it, he saw how the light picked up the iridescent colors of the feathers gracing the hook's back. "Where did you find the materials?" he wanted to know picking up another.

Carlie still sitting on one leg leaned in closer and lightly touched one, "All over. Have you ever really looked at a bird's feathers?"

"No...can't say that I have, it was just supper to me," Colt replied.

Carlie nodded. "Well...underneath the outer feathers there's all kinds of different colors, I just saved them..." she said sitting back.

Colt reached into the box and removed a few folded papers. Opening them he saw drawings of the lures that were now hooked into the wood. Gesturing with them, he asked, "And these?"

"Those are my models...I guess that's what you would call them," Carlie said, leaning forward, her finger traced the pencil and charcoal drawings. She shrugged again. "So now you know what I do to pass the winter up here," she replied, getting up and pouring more coffee for them both.

Colt tipped his chair back on two legs and folded his arms. *The girl might be a little off in the head, but she was talented as hell.*

Rawlins allowed his chair to come back down, resting his arms back on the table. "Ever thought of selling the lures? Make yourself a little extra cash? I'm sure there's a market for them back east."

Carlie packed up the box, then walked over to her bunk and slid it back underneath before answering him.

His eyes followed the child-like body and continued watching as she turned around and walked back to him.

"I did once," she said, tucking fingers in her hip pockets again. "At Sam's, but then, well...things got kinda topsy-turvy, what with Mama and Daddy dying. The fever hitting the town like it did and Riley pulling his stunts and well...trying to run this ranch and..." she hesitated as her eyes found his. "...Guess I'm not doing a very good job, am I?"

"You could with the right kind of help," he said.

Shaking her head, "I don't want to discuss it right now. It's late...I'm going to bed," ending the conversation right then and there. She didn't want it to accidentally slip out that she had only eighty-three cents in the Ranch's account.

WASHING THE TWO CUPS, Colt contemplated what he'd learned about Carlie Anne Russell that evening. The girl, despite being a real shave-tail, had grit and determination besides being talented as hell in some areas.

Walking over to the fire, he threw on two more logs and eased his long lanky body into the rocker. Placing an elbow on one of the arms, his finger rubbed his chin as he sat there thinking. The kid had somehow started to grow on him. She didn't know yet that Harley had sent him to help her. He'd have to tell her soon, not yet, but soon. When the time was right, he would also have to let her know that he was actually Lone Wolf, her friend from long ago. But for now, it needed to remain his secret.

It pained him to see Carlie struggling under the weight of all that responsibility that had been dumped on her. He could hear it in her voice earlier that night. She'd been hanging in there, barely.

The anguish he saw in her eyes when she mentioned the death of her folks still hit Carlie pretty hard, even now, over a year later. *Must've been hell on her, spending that first winter up here alone,* he thought.

Colt had learned to steel himself from looks like that from other women a long time ago, that and their sob stories. But Carlie's was genuine, she wasn't play-acting with him, hers was real.

"Well, old man...now I know why you're so attached to the girl, 'cause I'm falling under the little witch's spell, too." Rawlins whispered into the quiet air surrounding him.

23

"Half-pint..."

Carlie turned, "Thought you weren't gonna call me that?"

"Changed my mind..."

"Only women are allowed to change their minds..."

He grinned at that. "Where's your branding iron?"

With a soapy hand she pointed, "Hanging on the wall in the walk-thru."

Colt found it and walked back over to Carlie. "That's an interesting brand," he commented as he turned it over in his hand gazing at it. It was composed of three flat rods, one about an inch and a half, another two inches and the last one three inches long. Smaller bits of metal were attached to resemble limbs of a pine or fir tree, making it look like a grouping of three trees.

"After they had decided on *Three Pines* for the name, Mama designed it and Daddy and Granddaddy made it," she replied

"It's not a standard brand. Be kinda hard to take a running iron and alter this brand with that design."

"I know...that's what Daddy said too," Carlie agreed.

"We're gonna be up there for a week or more. Pack all the gear you think we might need," Rawlins stated heading for the door while he pulled on his coat. "I'll get the buckboard ready," he added settling his hat on his head.

"Why can't I get the buckboard ready and you put the gear together, you know more about that stuff than I do," Carlie insisted.

Colt Rawlins turned toward the girl. "Because you're gonna learn," he answered back.

"Your boots must still be pinching your toes," she retorted.

Colt rolled his eyes as he closed the door in his wake.

"Pfftt! Harley, he's worse than you bossing people around..." Carlie whispered.

COLT CHEWED a hole in his cheek that afternoon, trying to keep from laughing out loud as he watched Carlie's facial expressions every time he gave her an order. Despite all the huge sighing and eye rolling she did, Carlie Anne hadn't argued with him. He didn't know if that was a good sign or not.

"Better hit the sack, we'll be up before daylight," he told her.

"Before daylight? You can't brand in the dark, even I know that," Carlie retorted.

"No, but it'll give us time to eat and build the branding fire. Now hit the sack," he ordered her.

Carlie just rolled her eyes as she wandered over to her bed and flopped down. Hands under her head she lay thinking. *I'd like to get on Colt Rawlins like ugly on a gorilla,* but knew she couldn't, she needed his help too much right now.

Of course, when he wanted his pay, she'd have to tell him she was broke. She could just envision those eyes of his going from that nice light grey to dark 45 slugs. When they did that, she'd be in trouble again, *with a capital T.*

Rolling on her side, Carlie Anne studied Rawlins. He was right pleasant to look at with the firelight highlighting his features; he was one long drink of water. The only time he didn't tower over her was when she was sitting on Waldo. The rest of the time she would almost bust her neck looking up at him. In town there were a few good-looking boys, but none of them had piqued her interest, besides they were just boys. But Colt Rawlins wasn't a boy, he was a man, all man even with that stony face he put on sometimes. At least it seemed like with her he did. Carlie had never run into a *real* man before, not all by herself. Her daddy and granddaddy had always been around to keep the young bucks at arms-length. But there was something familiar about him, too. What? She hadn't figured that out, yet.

Sighing, she rolled on her back again, sticking her hands beneath her head as she gazed up at a star-studded sky. "I miss you all so much," she whispered.

Wolf lay down beside her, heaving a huge sigh that made Carlie's hand instinctively reach out to rest on his back. Her hand rhythmically rubbed his fur, falling asleep as she did so.

RAWLINS PUT Carlie on first shift bringing the calves in for branding. He wanted to see if she could manage them without falling out of the saddle, being trampled, strangling herself or cutting off her fingers with the rope.

The first few she brought in were small heifers. He told her, "I want you to bring me all sizes, not just the ones easy to handle. You got that?"

Carlie rode back to the herd, muttering under her breath, "All right, Mister Rawlins, if that's what you want, then that's what you'll get."

Picking out a larger bull calf, she nudged Waldo forward. Walking quietly amongst the herd, Carlie guided him alongside the bull calf. She quickly sent her rope around his horns and snubbed it hard around the saddle horn.

Carlie reined the sorrel around and dragged the bellowing fighting calf behind.

Colt had seen Carlie snag the young bull. He quickly mounted as they weren't going be able to topple this one. They would have to stretch him out, brand him, and then hog-tie him to cut him.

Colt came charging up behind the bull on his bay. Watching his hind feet, he threw the lasso catching those two, then jerked hard, pulling his legs out from under him, quickly slapping half-hitches around his horn.

Colt yelled at Carlie, "Stretch 'em! Hold 'em there!" Hopping off, he ran the few yards and grabbed the iron. Trotting back, he laid it against the hide. The calf bellowed.

The stench of burning hair and flesh filling the air caused Carlie to wrinkle her nose.

Gesturing with his gloved fingers, "Come here...you know how to hogtie?" he asked when she was alongside of him.

Carlie nodded.

"Do it, then. I'll get the disinfectant," he said ordering her. When he returned, he frowned looking at the hog-tie, but it would do.

Kneeling alongside the bull, he looked up at Carlie. "Do you know how to cut him?" Colt asked.

Carlie stared blankly at him. She was already tired and it wasn't even noon yet. "Huh?"

"Do you know how to take a bull calf and turn him into a steer?"

"Of course I do," she said grabbing his knife. She knelt beside him and quickly made the cutting swipe to the bawling complaint of the calf. Swabbing on the disinfectant, her eyes seemed to spit at him. "Satisfied now?"

"Good enough," he said. "Go get another one," handing her the rope. *If looks could kill...I'd be dead right about now...*he thought seeing the last glare Carlie had sent sailing through the air before she mounted. She jerked Waldo back around toward the herd.

Colt just grinned.

Besides being so tired she could barely throw a rope, much less stay in the saddle, she was spitting mad at Rawlins. All he was doing was touching iron to rumps, except when she brought in a bigger calf and then he'd help some, but she was having to do all the cutting too. *Men, what a sorry lot they are....*

Dragging a small heifer to the branding fire, she slipped off Waldo hanging on to the fender for a few moments to gain her strength. Heaving in a big breath, she was going to have to topple this one all by herself, *again,* as tired as she was. Carlie threw a dirty glance in Rawlins' direction.

His face remained deadpan watching her.

Leaning over the body, she latched onto a front and hind leg and tried to toss it. That didn't work. Carlie had no strength left to topple the calf. Besides its stiff little legs were too splayed out in resistance along with bawling her head off for her mama.

Her patience gone, she twisted its face to look at her and threatened it, "Now you listen here...you little four-legged milk guzzlin'...grass burner. The sooner we get this over with, the sooner you can go back to your Mama. You hear me?"

With those words, she quickly kicked out her foot, knocking the legs out from under it, making the calf topple to the ground.

Colt doubled over in silent laughter as he heated the iron.

Throwing her body across the calf, she tried to hold the squirming heifer down.

Carlie yelled, "I ain't got all day...Rawlins! Ya nit-wit! Move!"

Still chuckling, he finally touched the brand to the calf while she bawled loud and long. Glancing up he shouted a warning. "Carlie! Look out! Here comes Mama!" He quickly jumped out of the way himself just as the mother charged in his direction.

Ducking her head as she tried to get the rope off the squirming calf, she rolled out of the way and stood quickly ready to run. The calf took off back to its mother's side.

Heaving in the missing air from her lungs, she whirled on Colt, "Damn you...Mister Rawlins!" she yelled. "Damn you! Ya work my ass off then almost get me killed...you jackass!"

Trying not to burst out laughing as he gave his answer, "I was mesmerized by the way you toppled that calf...never saw anyone do it quite like that before."

Carlie threw her arms in the air, exhaling, "Aauugh!" She whirled around and stomped back to Waldo. Sticking a foot in the stirrup, she was abruptly halted by Rawlins' voice.

"I'll take over from here."

Carlie tossed him a glance of gratitude as she slipped her foot out of the stirrup. "Bout time..."

"Your sorrel needs a break, go take his gear off him so his back won't get sore. Water him good, then you can brand for a while."

"You mean I don't get a break?"

"You've got a few more hours left in you. Go on...hurry up," he returned.

Carlie gave him another black look as she pulled Waldo along. "You sure are bossy," she mumbled.

"How's that?"

Carlie stopped and turned around, then said a little louder, "I said...you sure are bossy!"

"Really?"

"Really..." she remarked.

Mounting his bay, he watched Carlie trudge tiredly toward the camp. He grinned as he reined his pony back toward the herd.

TOWARD DUSK, Colt held down a young heifer while Carlie held the iron to the calf's rump.

Colt looked up then knocked the iron out of her hand.

Carlie's eyes followed the iron sailing through the air, then came back to rest on his face.

"What the hell you trying to do? Burn all the way through and brand both hips?"

Carlie stared tiredly at Rawlins.

Colt knew then that Carlie Anne was done. She was beyond comprehension.

"Alright young'n," releasing the calf and slapping its rump. "Go find your Mama..." Colt said.

Staring at Carlie's tired face. "I guess we'll call it a day. Let's go wash up and get something to eat. We got calf fries for supper..." he grinned.

Pulling the bay, he draped an arm across Carlie's shoulders.

Carlie tottered under the weight of his arm then shoved it off her body, stumbling away.

Colt caught her. "You alright...?"

Carlie just nodded and waked away.

His dark brows rose, then he grinned.

STRETCHED OUT ON HER BEDROLL, Carlie felt that every square inch of her body hurt. Taking the hot coffee Rawlins handed her, she rested the cup on her tummy. Too tired to even take a sip, she thought she would just close her eyes for a moment.

Rawlins dished out a plate of the fries, then he held it out to Carlie. When she didn't take it, he chuckled and gently removed the cup from her hands to pour it back in the pot. He took a sip from his cup as he looked over at the girl and smiled. He wouldn't be hearing a peep out of her tonight because Carlie Anne Russell was dead to the world.

Finishing his supper, he continued to stare into the flames, his ears picking up the distant lowing of the cattle and his bay and the three mules blowing behind him. Colt thought back to the last two weeks. Carlie wanted to march down her own trail, oblivious to the amount of work it took to run a spread this size. She had to have a thousand to twelve hundred head, judging by the size of the herd. No telling how many of those weren't branded or how many were still in the brush unaccounted for. *Her herd was ripe for someone to come in and clean her out,* he sighed inwardly at that thought.

Rawlins had seen that Carlie knew how to ride while working a calf out, even knew how to rope without losing any fingers. But it was still going to be a long winter.

Trying to show her how hard it would be to ramrod this spread by herself, he had worked her little fanny off today, not that she had much of one. She hadn't even filled out with any real womanly curves yet. But those innocent eyes had a way of mesmerizing him.

Never in his born days had he seen any cowpoke knock the legs out from under a calf like she did today and it took everything he had not to burst out laughing at her.

Carlie Anne had hung in there though, not arguing with him, going back time after time bringing calf after calf, until both her and Petey were done in.

Maybe it won't be such a long winter after all, he thought, finally settling down for the night.

2 4

For some reason Colt woke up dreading the day. *One of Harley's premonitions,* he figured as he observed the sky lighten in the east. Something was niggling at his stomach and it wasn't because of all the fries he'd eaten last night either, but he just couldn't shake the feeling.

He glanced over at the sleeping girl. Even if he taught her everything he knew about cattle, Carlie Anne Russell still wasn't going to be able to handle it all on her own, she was just too tiny. She looked more like a twelve-year old than a girl of eighteen. But he had to admit, she had spirit, guts and gumption, but that would only carry her so far.

Throwing another chunk of wood on the fire, he watched as it caught. His mind turned to what he knew about her history. Her folks had planned toward the future, buying that good red stock to mix breed with their other scrappy beeves. Carlie Anne had a lot of money standing out there eating grass. Those white-faced cows were bred for meat and would likely bring a better price then the scrawny cows he was used to doggin'.

Rawlins sighed heavily again. There was a hell of a lot of work to do here as he looked around and that girl could do only so much. Meaning, he had to take up the slack.

"Damn you, Harley," he whispered. "I don't mind working hard, but right now I can't see the forest through the trees. No wonder you passed that damn kid off on me! You're probably sitting in your rocker in front of a warm fire, laughing your fool head off, ya little sidewinder," he muttered. Rawlins stared at the dirt between his boots, fingers slowly turning the cup in his hands. But something remained niggling at his stomach. He'd learned a long time ago to listen to his gut.

He already knew Carlie Anne Russell was just a saddlebag full of trouble waiting to happen. The problem was, *When...*

25

Squatting and shaking Carlie's shoulder he said, "Time to get a move on...we're wasting daylight..."

"Go away..." a muffled voice said.

"Can't...we still got a lot of cows to brand. Coffee's hot, let's go," he ordered her.

"No, I'm tired," her muffled voice returned.

"Too bad, you got a ranch to run. The boss always goes to bed after his men and gets up before they do, lining up the day's work. Roll out, you got work to do," he said.

Carlie rolled over, half sitting up and squinted at Rawlins through tired, swollen eyes asking, "Why were you so hard on me yesterday?"

"Because you have a ranch you need to learn how to run, you don't...you'll lose everything your folks worked so hard to get," he answered back.

"Yeah, but did you have to be so hard on me making me do every little thing? You wore me out," she admitted.

Squatting again alongside her, "Because you needed to learn. Most cowpokes ride twelve to sixteen hours in the saddle at certain times of the year. You barely put in ten yesterday," he explained.

Letting her head flop back on her shoulders, Carlie groaned.

Rawlins stood. His normally pleasant baritone took on a sharp edge. "I'm showing you how hard it will be if you keep holding onto this damn fool idea of yours...that you can run this spread by yourself..."

Carlie sat up, crossing her legs under the blanket as her fingers began playing with the frayed strings on the edges.

Rawlins rubbed his tired eyes as he gave Carlie Anne another hard look. "I'm trying to show you what you have to look forward to: sixteen to eighteen hours in the saddle, days so cold your britches freeze to the leather, days so hot you break a sweat standing still. Drought, disease, wind storms. Beef prices bottoming out, maybe rustling," he warned her.

Carlie's head popped up at that.

Colt's eyes softened as he offered, "If you don't trust your own judgment of picking out good men, I could help you with that if you'd like."

Carlie shook her head. "I can't."

"Why?" he asked, folding his arms and staring down at her, "Because of your stubbornness and pride?"

Carlie shook her head again then whispered, "No...it's not that."

"What then?"

Carlie's eyes rolled up and then away from Rawlins' scrutiny. "It's because well..." her finger scratched an eyelid, "Well... because I'm broke," she said. Frustration showed itself when she hopped up and folded her arms in defiance glaring at him. "There I said it! You happy now, Mister Rawlins?" Angry color flushed her cheeks as Carlie shouted. "You can pack your bags now and git, okay! Go on! Start packing since you know now I can't pay you!"

Rawlins cut her a sideways look, his gaze becoming shrewd. "Harley know about this?"

Eyes went round with surprise. "Harley? What's Harley got to do with this?" Then she tapered her eyes at the big man. "How'd you know about Harley? Does Harley have anything to do with this?"

Folding his arms once again, "Because it was Harley who sent for me to help you out," he said.

"I don't need your help," she said her eyes beginning to spit fire. "Harley and I can do this..."

"No, he can't, honey..." Colt interrupted softly. "...Harley's not well..."

Butting in, "...Hell's bells..." she said. "...Why, he's fit as a fiddle..."

"No, he's not," Colt returned quickly.

"Dammit, you're lying to me again, Rawlins!"

"Carlie Anne...I've known Harley a long time and..."

She interrupted him again, "...How long?"

"Long enough to know when he's spinning a yarn and when he's telling the truth," Colt answered.

Carlie bowed her head and began picking at her fingernails, chewing on one. Her head came back up with her eyes in slits. "I still say you're lying to me, Mister Rawlins, but only you know the lie from the truth. Pack your gear, get off my land," she said quietly.

"What the hell is wrong with you, Carlie Anne? I'm trying to help you. I owed Harley a favor, he asked me to come help you, and then you call me a liar when I tell you why I showed up and not him! What the hell you trying to prove, Carlie Anne? You trying to prove to four people buried six feet under that you can run this ranch all by yourself? Hell! They're gone! Dead! They wouldn't notice the difference anyway."

Her head spun. "You take that back, Rawlins! You take that back!" she shouted.

"No! It's high time you got a dose of reality!"

Tongue running across her lips, Carlie reached down and released the whip from the side of her saddle. She whirled toward him, snapping it out as she did so.

His face turned hard, his eyes becoming cold as 45 slugs. "Put that thing down," Colt said quietly.

Carlie snapped it around his ribs, his coat softening the blow. "Not till you get off my land, Mister Rawlins," she threatened him.

"I'm warning you Carlie Anne, you'll be sorry if you hit me with that again."

"That so, Mister Rawlins?" Carlie taunted him, the whip catching him alongside his neck and cheek before he could duck. "Now git off my land! I'll not say it again," she said, readying the whip once again.

Colt's fingers touched his cheek, lowering them he saw the blood she'd drawn. His eyes the color of gunmetal, he watched that whip flying through the air once again toward him. Catching it, he yanked the girl off her feet.

Stumbling, Carlie landed flat on her belly.

Rawlins quickly grabbed a handful of that overgrown coat. Picking up the little hellion and taking hold of the arm that was threatening to hit him in his most private of parts.

He marched over to a log and sat then laid her across his knees. With one arm holding down the squirming she-devil, Colt began pounding that fanny hard. When he was through, he shoved her off his knees.

Carlie rolled away from him getting up, tears burning the backs of her lids. She rubbed her stinging fanny. "That was the wrong thing to do Mister Rawlins, the wrong thing to do…" she whispered hoarsely.

"Maybe that will teach you not to hit a human or beast with that whip ever again," he gritted out.

Stepping closer Carlie repeated, "That was the wrong thing to do, Mister Rawlins," she stepped closer still. "The wrong thing to do," she hissed, small hands clenched into fists by her sides.

Colt warily watched, realizing that he could overpower her again if needed. As insane as the kid was, no telling what the hell she'd do next.

Her fist slammed hard into Colt's jaw, sending him sailing ass backwards off the log. The momentum of her follow-through sent Carlie to her knees. Rising quickly, she held her hand shaking it. The pain went all the way up to her elbow. She doubled over from how bad her hand hurt. Sucking in a ragged breath, she aimed eyes that seemed to be on fire at Rawlins, still lying on his back, legs resting on the log.

"Get off my land, Mister Rawlins and don't ever come back. You hear me? Never come back," Carlie whispered. Picking up the whip, she turned and hauled up her saddle with her good hand and moved toward her sorrel.

Colt just laid there, blinking and moving his jaw around. *Damn, where the hell did that come from?* Expecting words or maybe the whip again, but not a fist. He stood, trying to shake the ringing out of his ears as he caught sight of Carlie Anne riding off down the hill.

Anger renewed itself as he gathered up his gear. "Harley, I don't know where in the hell you got the idea that me or anyone else could help help, she's beyond help," he said and without a backward glance rode north toward Harley's.

CARLIE SQUATTED NEXT TO A STREAM, holding her hand in the icy water, bawling her eyes out. Lifting her face to the sun, tears glinting in its rays, she whispered, "What have I gone and done now?"

Pulling her hand out of the freezing water, she saw that her hand was puffing up and becoming discolored. She stuck it back in the water and blubbered some more.

Later sitting on the bank, chin resting on her arms, she looked at her hand again. She was able to wiggle a few fingers, but it was going to be sore and bruised. She just hoped she hadn't broken it pulling that stupid stunt.

Regret at what she had done to someone who was only trying to help made her realize how stubborn and hardheaded she really had become since the death of her folks. Rawlins was right, she *had* been trying to prove she could run this ranch all by herself. "You stupid fool..." she whispered aloud as she laid her head down on her arms once again.

Eyes rose to the clouds scudding across the sky. "Lord, why do I always have to be so stupid? Why, Lord, why? I just ran off a good man, why did I do something that dumb, why? Mama and Daddy, I miss you so, please tell me what to do, please?" Carlie whispered the prayer then buried her face in her arms again.

Wolf nudged Carlie. Her arms went around his neck as she buried her face in the silky fur. Her voice mumbled, "It's just you and me Wolf, just like it was in the beginning," she said raising her face. She gazed at her only companion in the whole world. "Think you and me could do this together? It would be awfully hard work, really long days and no more playing games," Wolf licked her cheek. "I guess that's a yes, huh, big boy?" she said as she ruffled the fur between his ears.

Drying her tears on her filthy coat, she stood to her full five feet, Carlie told Wolf. "Let's go see if Rawlins left us any coffee," she said.

She stood by the cold remains of the branding fire, cradling her throbbing hand. She unconsciously began chewing on a fingernail, thinking. Teeth ripped off the nail she had been gnawing on. Realizing what she had done, Carlie watched the blood ooze from the torn skin. She quickly stuck it in her mouth to stem the bleeding.

Picking up the iron with her left hand, she walked back to camp, pouring the last drops of coffee from the pot. She was going to have to ride into town and have Doc take a look at her hand. Until then everything else was just going to have to wait. She exhaled heavily, muttering, "Nothing is going right…"

Loading everything in the buckboard, Carlie struggled with tying the tarp down. She could only use her good hand and her teeth. Letting the other two mules free to roam, she'd leave everything here at the campsite. Mounting Waldo, Carlie Anne headed for town.

26

Sheriff Page saw Carlie Anne Russell riding in on her sorrel and strode out to meet her. "Howdy Carlie Anne, hain't seen you in awhile. How ya been?" he asked.

Carlie stuffed her hand in a coat pocket so Ed wouldn't see it. "Been doing a little fall branding," she replied.

"How's that new hand working out?"

Now what am I going to tell him, that I ran Rawlins off after slicing him with my whip? "You seen Doc?" she asked instead.

The sheriff noticed her eyes had sparked when he had asked her about the new hand. "He's over in his office," Ed replied, nodding up the street.

"Thanks," nudging her mule forward.

Ed narrowed his gaze as he watched her ride toward Doc's. *Something's up.*

❧

THE THROBBING from her hand had not eased, making dismounting difficult. Throwing the reins around the hitch rail, she stepped up on the walk. Taking a breath then wincing from the on-going pain, she opened the door and strode into Doctor Ben Caldwell's office.

The office was small, but neatly kept with his living quarters in the back. Doctor Benjamin Caldwell had given up on striking it rich in the goldfields. Traveling back east he had stopped in Kaskaskia and liked what he saw and knew this small town needed a doctor so he had hung out his shingle. And that was some fifteen-odd years ago. He eked out a living doctoring, but he still enjoyed prospecting the area always dreaming of that one big strike he might find some day.

Turning around, Doc asked. "Well, Miss Carlie Anne, what brings you here?"

Taking her hand out of the pocket, she showed it to him. "I think I broke it."

"Humm...well now, let's take a look..." as he gently handled the injured limb, pressing on a few spots.

Air whistled through her teeth when the Doc did that making her sag against the table from the extreme pain he had caused.

Her reaction left no doubt in Doc's mind. "How'd you manage to do this, young lady?"

Now what am I going to say? Closing her eyes, Carlie whispered, "Uh...fell off my mule...landed wrong," she lied.

Eyebrows jerked up. "You fell off your mule? Thought you could ride like the wind?"

"Yeah...well...accidents happen..." Carlie answered lamely.

"Yes...yes, they do," Doc Caldwell replied.

After he finished wrapping her hand in the splint, he smiled saying, "That should make it feel a lot better." Walking over to the medicine cabinet and opening one side, he read the labels before finally selecting a bottle. Reaching for a small envelope on the next shelf, Doc poured a few tablets into it and handed it to Carlie. "Take one or two of these when the pain gets a little feisty. It'll ease off in a week or so," he instructed.

A week or two? she thought. *Ugh...* Instead of voicing them, Carlie nodded her thanks and left without another word.

Standing in the open doorway, his gaze followed the girl watching her mount with some difficulty. Doc thought, *Carlie Anne had looked like hell. Something's up...*

LEADING WALDO INTO THE BARN, Carlie had to unsaddle, grain and hay the sorrel with one hand and it took her longer than normal. Walking out of the barn she stopped and stared at the big log structure, *Home*, she thought.

Tiredly, she trudged up the three steps, opened the door and stepped over the threshold. She stopped, listening to the house's deep silence. Carlie squeezed her eyes shut as tears stung the backs of them, there used to be so much laughter, fun, and noise in this house. Now only silence greeted her every time she walked in, making her feel even sadder and twice as lonely.

Boots heavily trounced up the stairs, her footfalls echoing loudly in the silent house. *Maybe things will look brighter after I get some sleep.* Carlie sank down on her soft bed, laid back and was gone in seconds.

27

C olt Rawlins reined up in front of Harley's place calling out, "Harley, Harley, you here?" Not receiving an answer, he dismounted and opened the door. Harley was sound asleep in the old rocker.

Shock registered across his face as Colt softly closed the door. In just the short time he'd been gone, Harley's dark grey hair had turned snow white, his skin as grey as his hair used to be. Clothes that had once fit him were limp hanging off the small frame as if they were strung on a clothesline. Blue colored veins stood out across the tight thin-skinned gnarled hands resting on the rocker's arms like crooked little rivers snaking across land.

Kneeling next to the old man, Colt noticed he was still breathing, but barely. Harley was taking in shallow breaths, then they rattled as he exhaled. Colt puffed out the breath he had been holding. Closing his eyes, he pinched the bridge of his nose, then reopened them. Colt lightly touched Harley's arm.

"Hey, you old bandy rooster, wake up!" Rawlins spoke softly. "Loafing time is over. We got traps to set out."

A familiar voice entered Harley's subconscious. Raising his

head, turned it toward the voice before opening his eyes, "Son? That you?" A raspy voice asked.

"Yeah Harley, it's me."

Harley reached over and patted Colt's arm. "Where's Half-pint?" he wheezed, then a coughing fit racked his body. Gasping for air after the spell, Harley panted the words out, "Son...pour some hot water in that cup on the table and fetch me a fresh bottle out of that cupboard..." his finger pointing while hauling in a short breath. "...And grab that honey while yore at it..." he wheezed.

"That what you been doing since I left Harley? Tying on a twister every day?"

Harley smiled weakly, "Not hardly...boy. It helps with the pain and the coughing spells..." he said as his watery eyes watched Colt pour hot water, add the honey then the whisky.

Before raising the cup, the old man asked, "What happened to yer face?"

His fingers went to the cut, gingerly touching it. "Uh...tell ya later..." Colt replied.

Harley gave him a slit-eye glance, "Uh-huh..." He gave another weak smile. "Through the lips and over the gums, look out belly here she comes," he said drinking it all down.

"Harley, this ain't the time to be funning," Rawlins said disgustedly. Throwing more wood on the fire, he turned toward Harley, speaking quietly, "What's going on with you, you old coot?"

"Well, I hain't been doing so well lately...son..." Harley wheezed out again.

"I can see that! You grizzled old buzzard!"

"Here..." he gestured with the cup. "Fill me up again," Harley said as another fit of coughing racked his body.

Deep concern for the old man swept over Colt as he listened to the intense spasms that seemed to come from within the bowels of Harley's living skeleton. He handed the cup back to Harley when the spasm had ceased.

The old man gasped the words out, "Thankee son."

Pushing Harley back in the rocker, "You rest some, I'll take care of the mules and horses and when I get back, I'll fix you something to eat." Colt said as he gazed somberly at the skeleton that was his friend. Without another word, Colt turned and left the cabin.

28

Glass tinkled then a whoosh as flames ignited the coal oil in the dark house. More glass shattered as another soft explosive sound filled the air igniting more flames in a different room. Dark figures quickly mounted, digging heels into their horses' ribs, bolting away from the burning structure.

CARLIE WOKE UP COUGHING. Opening her eyes, she gazed at her foggy room. Choking some more as she sat up, she smelled the smoke. She didn't remember lighting a fire, scrambling off the bed, *I didn't! The house is on fire!*

Racing out of her room, she slid around the corner and stopped before she tumbled down the stairs. Flames were everywhere, creeping across the floors, climbing the walls. Her eyes found the two shattered windows. "Damn...you, Tom Riley," she whispered, "Damn you!"

As she hurried down the steps her feet tangled with each other, and Carlie stumbled head over heels to land at the bottom, the breath knocked out of her. Blinking against the smoke, she pulled the end of her coat up over her nose and mouth. Crawling over to the couch, she reached for the coverlet across the back, wrapping her body and covering her face with it against the smoke and flames. Using the back of the couch she pulled herself up and saw a path through the fire. She ran into the kitchen, whirling, as she gazed over her shoulder one last time, realizing that the house had become a blazing inferno. The heat and smoke rose, becoming unbearable. Her eyes burned as if wind-blown sand was scratching them. She began coughing again trying to gasp for air in the thick haze. It was suffocating her. *I have to get out of here.*

Flying out the back door, her fingers entwined in the coverlet in a death grip, she stumbled toward the four graves fifty feet away. She collapsed in a heap when she finally reached them. Rolling on her back, she gulped in big doses of fresh air, coughing as she tried to clear her lungs of the smoke.

Above the din of her home going up in flames, she heard Waldo nickering frantically. "The barn..." Tossing off the coverlet she stood and raced around the heat and flames to the barn entrance in panic. She frowned, it wasn't on fire. Rescuing a wild-eyed jumpy sorrel, she gripped the lead rope firmly in her one good hand and led him to safety, towards the back of the ferocious burning structure to a small watershed seventy-five yards away and tied him securely to a tree. Running back, she grabbed the bridle and her saddle in case the barn did catch flying embers and burn, too. Catching her breath, she ran and picked up the coverlet, then stumbled back to where Waldo was, collapsing on the dew damp grass. She watched the blue and yellow flames crawl up the wall like fingers continuing to lick and grow consuming the only home she had ever known. Flames were reflected in the tears that coursed down her face flowing like a river.

29

K neeling before the fire, Colt stirred the rabbit stew, then ladled a small amount onto a plate and set it in front of Harley. "You gonna tell me what's going on now, Harley?"

Harley picked up a biscuit, crumbling it into the broth, watching as it soaked up the juices. "Half-pint been eating better since you been cooking for her?" he asked spooning a small bite in his mouth.

Colt stared at the skeleton in annoyance, then straddled a chair and sat down. "This ain't about Carlie Anne, old man," he said picking up a spoon.

"You always was a better cook then the rest of them girls," Harley offered up, making reference to some trapper friends he and Colt had, taking another bite.

"Cut it out, Harley! Quit side-winding around my questions."

Harley leaned back in the chair gasping for air, his hand limply holding the spoon. "Think I got some kinda canker eating at my insides," he said, nodding at the whisky. "That's 'bout the only thing that works for the pain," his anguished eyes fixed on Rawlins. "I'm glad you came...son...." Harley whispered.

JULIETTE DOUGLAS

Looking at his old friend, Colt spoke quietly, "So am I, Harley. So am I."

Scooping up another spoonful, Harley looked up as he asked, "How's my girl doing?"

Taking a bite of biscuit, Rawlins spoke around the food chewing out the words, "She ain't."

Bleary eyes widened. "What 'da mean, she ain't?" Harley spluttered.

"I mean..." Colt said, rising and going for more coffee. "...I mean, she's an insane, rattlebrain eighteen-year old kid who ain't got the brains God gave her..." he said, setting the pot back on the fire.

"Sounds to me you kinda like her," Harley chuckled, then lapsed into another coughing spell.

"What?" Colt said, whirling around. "Like her? Hell, Harley, she's nuthin' but a blithering idiot," he told the old man.

Straddling his chair again, Colt begin ticking items off on his fingers; "For starters, she asks if I got moss growing on me like some damn tree! Calls me a daffy drifter, accuses me of trying to kill that wolf, talks to dead animals." Finger ticking items off the other hand, "Cuts a foal out of a dead mare's belly, plays tag with that stallion, oh...and we don't want to forget all the names she has for her *friends*," Colt added sarcastically. "Winkin, Blinkin and Nod. Thor and his harem. Samson, Dundee, and McDuff. Hell Harley, the girl's a bona fide crazy..." Fingers continued to tick off the items, "...Throws snowballs when there's work to be done. Then calls me a snake on stilts, got bats in my belfry, and let's see what else?" His eyes stared up at the rafters. "Oh yeah, falls in the creek, lashes me with her whip, punches me in the jaw, and..."

Harley wheezed. "Ahh...that's how ya got thet scratch on yer cheek...she slapped you with her whip...huh?"

Colt threw a dirty look at him.

Slurping some broth from the spoon, he added, "Sounds like you've been busy, son."

136

"Hell, yeah, I've been busy, so damn busy I can't see the forest through the trees," Colt fired back then took in a huge breath. "Harley, you got me belly deep in quicksand, ain't nobody gonna be able to help that girl," Colt finally finished, turning back to his food.

As sick as he was, Harley managed a slight twinkle in his eyes as he mused. *I think the boy might actually like Half-pint.*

Rawlins eyes became shrewd. Thinking out loud, he asked, "You knew all of this when you wrote me, didn't you, you slick old fox?"

"I figured if I tol' you everything, you never would have hepped out," Harley admitted.

"You're damn right about that! You sucker punched me good, Harley! Next time you ask me for a favor, the answer will be no!"

Harley nodded. "Yeah, I figured as much. Half-pint got yure dander flaked up a bit, didn't she?"

"My dander? Hell, ya little strip of dried buffalo hide! She did mor'n that! She marches down her own little trail. Try to teach her anything and she's got to argue with you about every dad-gum thing. Why I bet if you were to blow in one ear it'd come whistling clear through...out the other side..."

Harley's chuckle turned into a raging coughing fit.

"...There ain't nothing in there to stop it." Colt continued, "Harley, there's no rhyme or reason for the way she does things..." Colt stopped, inhaling more air. "...She gives me a headache just thinking about her, not to mention wearing me out," he finished.

Reaching for the bottle, Harley poured his cup full. After taking a sip, he replied, "I tried ta give ya a heads up on her...now ya know how I felt."

Tilting back his chair on two legs, Colt folded his arms. His eyes stared off at the wall behind the old man. "But you know something, Harley? For being a real odd duck, she's talented as all get-out," Colt said.

The older man nodded.

Lowering the chair back down, Colt added, "But ya know... watching Carlie Anne ride that stallion, well it was really something to see, and I'd never seen trout flies like the ones she put together, and she draws like...like she's gone to school for it," shaking his head as he stared back into his coffee.

Taking another sip of the golden liquid, he knew he had made the right decision bringing Colt Rawlins here. No matter how aggravating Carlie Anne could be, no matter how many times she tried Colt's patience, the boy would look out after her, Harley knew. A little reluctantly maybe, but he would still look out for her. Suddenly, he felt at peace, ready now to be reunited with his Katydid and their baby boy.

"Son, fetch me my Bible, it's on top of that cupboard ober thar..." the older man pointed.

Walking over and stretching out his arm, he grasped the book on top of the cupboard, giving it a long glance then looking at his frail friend while he strode back to the table and slid the Bible over to Harley.

Gnarled hands lovingly fingered the well-worn and frayed edges of the book. "I know'd Half-pint is a handful and she can raise yure dander like no other..." his rusty voice whispered softly. Seeing Colt about to interrupt, he held up his hand stopping the young man from speaking. "...Let me finish. I really don't know how her Mama and Gramma put up with her all those years, but all that aside, I love that kid like she was my own. In fact, since her folks passed away, she has been my girl," Harley finished quietly.

Harley leaned across the table toward Colt. "Son, I need one and only one promise from you. I want you to promise me that you'll keep a watch on Half-pint. I don't mean you have to marry her, just keep a lookout fer her, make sure she don't get herself into too much trouble. Would you grant me that one promise?" he asked solemnly.

"Harley..." Colt began, then stopped. He rose and wandered

over to the fire. Picking up the pot, he refilled his cup giving him some time to digest Harley's wish. His gaze traveled back over toward the skeleton of a man who through the years had become his best friend. Friends were hard to come by out here and even harder to hold on to. It was just a simple request from a dying man. One last wish asking that he take care of Carlie Anne Russell.

He noted Colt's hesitation. "Yure not gonna refuse a dying man's last request, are you?"

"Harley, she ain't gonna believe me."

"Well, jus' tell her I sent ya," he replied.

"Sheesh, old man! That's what I did the last time! She nicked me with that whip, then punched me in the face. Naw, if…I said if…I keep an eye on her, it'll be from a distance, far enough away from her where it's safe, Harley."

Leaning back in his chair, Harley sipped his whisky. He knew the boy wouldn't be able stay away. He had won the battle. "If that's the best you can do…son…"

Adding too quickly, Colt said, "…That's the best I can do, Harley."

"Much obliged," Harley said, ignoring Colt's fast reply as he opened the Bible and pulled out some papers, handing them to Colt. "That there is my will, hit's on record at that lawyer's office in town, and this here…"

"Will?" Colt interrupted. "When did you have time to make out a will?"

"That day I came to see you in the saloon," Harley answered. "Now you and Carlie Anne is in that thang and here's the paperwork on the six hundred and forty acres, and I want you to…"

"Harley…" Colt held up a hand stopping the old man. "…Harley, will you just slow down a minute, I'm not…"

"…Son…" the old man butted in. "…Now you listen to me," his weakened voice becoming sharper. "I made myself stay alive, hoping and praying you'd show up to give you these things. I'm at peace now. I'm ready to go be with my Katydid and baby boy, you hear me, son?"

Colt rested an elbow on the table, forefinger lightly tracking back and forth across his lips, his eyes still focused on his friend.

"My time is come and knowing you'll be keeping an eye out for Half-pint, well, that jus' makes me a whole lot more peaceable," Harley confided.

Sometimes the Great Spirit or God put people in situations, for whatever reasons the Man above had, taking control. Colt thought, *And, I'm in one of those situations right now. I can tell Harley no, or promise to do whatever I can to help Carlie Anne giving him the peace he wants. Heavens knows she can't run that place by herself.* Taking a sip of now cold coffee, Colt said, "Alright Harley, you can rest easy. I'll do whatever I can for Carlie."

"Thankee, son," Harley said as he drained the liquid, the empty cup hitting the wooden table with a light tap. "Mind helping me to my bunk, I'm kinda tired."

Easing Harley down on his bed, Colt noted the old coot was nothing but skin and bones, whatever he had was eating away on him mighty quick.

Harley lightly touched Colt's arm as he covered him up. "Thanks again for coming, son," he whispered.

Tucking the blanket in, Colt looked over and saw cloudy brown eyes that had become bright with moisture. "I'm here old man, and I'm staying till you get better," he said reassuringly.

"Ain't gonna get better."

"Carlie needs you, old man," Colt replied.

"Naw...she's got you now."

"Get some rest, old man," Colt said, patting Harley's shoulder. "I'm going to check on the horses," picking up his coat. "See ya in the morning," he added as he walked out the door.

Colt Rawlins leaned against a porch post, heaving in the crisp night air, watching the fog as he exhaled. His life had been getting

awfully complicated lately, *And I don't want that, I don't need that.*
All I wanted was a nice, simple easy job, he thought, sighing heavily.

He didn't like dealing with Carlie Anne. Not only did she
continue to complicate his life, but he found himself getting
attached to the little bugger as well. Something he didn't want to
happen, but happen it did, thanks to Harley. And now, it looked as
if he just might lose a good friend, too.

Studying the situation in his mind, about all he could do for
Harley was to make him as comfortable as he could, and wait, just
wait. Something Colt Rawlins wasn't going to take pleasure in,
watching his friend die.

Bowing his head, staring at his boots, he looked up at the lean-
to barn. "Damn it, the horses can wait," he mumbled. He fiercely
needed a drink so he turned and went back into the quiet cabin.

A rancid smell assaulted Carlie's nose forcing her to open her eyes. Reality smacked her senses as she gazed at the still smoldering ruins of what used to hold so many happy memories. Sitting up, she stared in shock at her former home. She wanted to cry, but no tears would come. She pulled the only thing she had saved from the fire closer up around her ears warding off the morning chill. Carlie knew she would treasure that blanket for the rest of her life. Drawing it in tighter, she willed its presence to comfort her.

"Tom Riley, you bastard," she blurted into the smoke-filled stillness. Her mind became cluttered with revenge. *Tom Riley has played with fire, now I'm going to return that fire. Riley is gonna wish he'd never heard of Carlie Anne Russell. If that's the last thing I ever do, I'll get you Tom Riley! I'll get you, even if it kills me!* Her mind nailed in the final words as if nailing the lid shut on a coffin.

Standing she looked over the four graves. "I'm so sorry, Mama and Daddy. I'll make sure Riley pays for this," she said as her voice took on an even harder edge. "I swear to you with the last breath in my body, he'll pay for this..."

After a difficult forty-five minutes trying to saddle Waldo with only one good hand and fingers of the other, Carlie stood and feathered the reins across her fingertips and stared at the still smoking remains of her beloved home. She couldn't cry anymore. *No sense in reporting this to Ed, I don't have any proof that Riley was behind this, just my own gut feeling. Most of the town would probably just say I let a fire get out of hand and burned down the place myself.*

She determinedly grabbed a handful of mane and mounted the sorrel, riding out of the yard towards Tom Riley's place. She planned on confronting the weasel and giving him a piece of her mind.

31

W aldo kept up his mile-eating trot as they neared the outskirts of the Riley Ranch. Carlie's eyes were constantly on the move, flicking and darting this way and that, looking for any of Riley's hands that might be in the area. She saw nothing but his herd off in the distance.

Dull thuds traversed the bridge before entering the two-track lane that led to the main house of the Riley empire. Carlie reined the sorrel over to a hitch rail. Before stepping down off the leather, she stared at the log home with its wide expanse of covered porch and the ornate heavy door. She heaved in air to calm her sloshing insides. Licking dry lips, she dismounted, wrapping the reins around the post and marched determinedly to the front door. Pounding on it with her good fist, she then stepped back a foot and waited.

Hearing footsteps, Carlie braced herself, ready to do battle.

Opening the door, Ruth Riley stared at the figure on her doorstep a few seconds before recognizing the waif. "Why...Carlie Anne what brings..." Her voice trailed off then exclaimed in surprise. "...Lordy...young lady...what happened to you?"

"Never mind that..." pushing her way past the matronly

woman and spinning around, Carlie asked with a sharpness in her voice. "Where's your husband, Miz Ruth?" She folded her arms taking a stance that meant business, hazel eyes glaring at the woman.

Surprised at the amount of hostility emanating from Carlie, Ruth replied, "Why…he's at the logging camp…"

Leaning forward with venom in her eyes, "That…so…"

"Well…yes. This country is growing…and the need for lumber is huge…"

"More like butchering…" Carlie mouthed, dropping her arms and striding past the older woman as if she was dirt on the floor.

Ruth's mouth dropped open at the girl's response.

Flinging the door open hard enough it bounced against a side-board behind it and swung back, she marched out, heading towards her horse.

Stopping the door before it closed, Ruth ran after her calling out, "Carlie? Carlie Anne…what's the matter…what's going on?"

Jerking the reins off the post so hard it made Waldo fling his head up in surprise, Carlie turned towards Ruth studying her and decided not to mince words. "Your husband tried to kill me last night…"

Gasping, Ruth's hand flew to her mouth. "No…"

"…By burning down my house…With…Me…In…It!" she shouted.

Reaching for Carlie, "No…no…"

Slapping at the hands trying to grasp her and backing up, "Git away from me…you're no better than your lowdown weasel of a husband!"

"Carlie…I knew nothing…"

"Yes…yes, you do…ever since my parents died, you and your husband have been conspiring to run me off my land because you want it so bad your mouth is watering…you hired backwater drifters…gunslingers to scare me off and try to force me into selling...so you can butcher it like you've done your land...but I ain't sellin'!"

"Carlie...I'm so sorry...I had no idea...that Tom would..." her voice trailed off.

Sticking one boot in the stirrup, Carlie looked over her shoulder at the woman. "...That your husband would do something so horrific?"

"Yes...he's not like that..."

"Liar..." Settling in the saddle, she nudged the sorrel up a few steps to come alongside Ruth. She leaned into the woman making her take a step back, disbelief still etched across her features. "You don't believe it...ride out to what once was my home and see for yourself...it's still smoldering..." With that she kicked Waldo hard in the ribs, he grunted and bolted. Hooves clattered against the hard-packed earth then echoed loudly when they hit the bridge.

"Carlie...Carlie...?" Ruth called out, but her words fell on deaf ears as she watched the girl fade into the distance.

ABRUPTLY REINING THE SORREL UP, Carlie gasped seeing the stark barren hills and the carnage that remained from stripping the beautiful forest and turning it into a wasteland. When the spring and summer rains came all the soil would wash into the valleys and streams polluting them. Tears rose in her eyes making tracks through her sooty face. A dirty hand angrily swiped them away smearing it further. The words came out guttural and soft, "And you think you can do this to my land? Like hell...Tom Riley...like hell..."

She nudged Waldo forward riding into the camp.

rusty voice broke into Colt's sleep. Coming fully awake, he walked the few paces between the bunks and knelt down by Harley, gently resting his big palm on the old man's wrinkled forehead and brushed the unruly hair back. "I'm here, Harley..."

The old coot smiled faintly, then opened timeworn bleary eyes. "Thankee, son..."

"Do you want a shot of whiskey?"

Colt could barely hear Harley's reply his voice was so weak. "That'd be good..."

Returning to the old man's side, Colt slid his arm under Harley's bony shoulders and gently lifted him, noticing again how light he felt. Resting the rim of the tin cup on his bluish thin lips, he tilted it so Harley could sip the whisky.

When it was all gone, Colt laid his friend back down and pulled the blanket up higher. "Anything else?"

Barely shaking his head no, Harley whispered, "Think I'll jus' close my eyes and rest a spell...but I'll be back..." and with those words, Harley Trimble died.

❧

THE PICK-AX RANG hollow digging into the frozen upper crust of ground. Colt Rawlins didn't want to think of the body waiting on its grave, pounding that pick deeper into the ground with each blow. He'd buried many a man in his time, but not with the fondness he had felt for Harley Trimble. He slung that pick even deeper still, loosening more earth. *No, they didn't make many men like Harley.*

Colt's mind retrieved the memories of the old bandy rooster. Raising the pick over his shoulder, he slammed the point into the ground. *Nope, they sure didn't make many men like Harley,* his mind repeated.

The pick hit cold ground.

That old man could argue with the best of 'em, over any kind of nonsense, just because he liked to argue. Colt remembered. *Then laugh his fool head off about it.*

The pick struck another blow to the cold earth.

He said Carlie Anne had a wicked sense of humor, hell, that old geezer could run circles around her with his crazy nonsense.

Throwing the pick aside, he retrieved the shovel and began digging at the loosened dirt.

And the tales he could spin, he could get you so engrossed in a tale, you'd be hanging onto every word, thinking it was the truth. Then wham, he'd start cackling like an old hen, he'd suckered you again. You did that to me many a time, old man. Rawlins thought fondly.

His boot jammed the shovel into the softened soil.

Harley, you was one of the few men I'd trust my life with and I think you felt the same.

He tossed a shovel full of dirt to the side.

Yeah Harley, the world ain't gonna be the same without you, you old coot.

Colt stepped into the grave, continuing to toss out more soil making the earthly casket.

Yeah Harley, it's gonna be tough breaking this news to Carlie Anne. It's likely going to hit her pretty hard, and so soon after losing her folks, too. I'm kinda dreading telling her, but it's got to be said. Can't never tell what that little shave-tail will do, especially with news like this. Colt sighed, heaving another shovel of dirt.

Standing next to the fresh mound, Colt pounded in the simple marker; all it said was Harley Trimble.

"Never knew when you were born or even how old you are. But you're with your Katydid and baby boy now. Take care of yourself old man, I'm gonna miss you," he said quietly.

Resettling his hat, Colt mounted the bay. Pulling Harley's sorrel and his two mules, he set a course for running smack dab into saddlebag just full of trouble, Carlie Anne Russell.

33

Hazel eyes scanned the roughshod muddy camp. Grungy tents to house the loggers in were scattered and shoddily thrown up in no particular order with fire rings in front of them still smoking from the night before. A mess tent with a wooden lean-to attached to the side of the tarp had a stovepipe sticking through the roof with smoke curling lazily from it into the windless air. The ground around the camp was trampled so bad it was hock deep in mud.

Carlie lifted her eyes to the hills beyond the camp where she heard the shouts and yelling coming from. At the top of the ridge, she could see teams pulling logs and the men guiding them to roll into a large pile waiting for transport. Her gaze shifted to her right where another huge stack was waiting. It was going to take some doing to load and ship those logs and then traveling to the nearest railroad that was in Missoula, some one hundred miles away, unless they took them to Flathead lake and floated them down river to Missoula. "But that would take experience and knowing how cheap Tom Riley is, he jus' picked up wandering cowpokes..." she muttered to herself.

It pained her to see the land butchered for greed. Most of the trees in this section had to be hundreds of years old. Stately sentinels guarding the land for centuries now reduced to bare stumps. No thought had been given to caring for the land after scalping it. Carlie sighed. She had to stop Tom Riley in his land grab, but how? She didn't know but confronting him was a start, letting him know that she was no pushover.

Nudging the sorrel with her heels, Carlie neck reined him to her left, his hooves sinking and making sucking noises when he pulled them from the mire.

Stepping off Waldo, her boots sank ankle deep in the muck. "Ugh..." as she slowly made her way to the cook tent. She saw slabs of wood had been laid for a makeshift floor underneath the canvas. The flaps were closed but she heard voices from inside. She eased closer to try and make out what they were saying.

"You boys sure that girl was in the house when ya lit it?" her eyes narrowed as anger sent a rosy flush climbing her face. "Damn you, Tom Riley," she whispered. She reached for her pistol with her right hand, then realized the splint hindered her. But she could still pluck it out of its boot with her fingers and transfer it to her left which she did.

"Her harse wuz in tha barn..."

"Hum...you boys go back out there and see if ya can find a body...I need proof she's dead."

Abruptly, the flap to the entrance was whipped back and a gun exploded. Three bodies hit the floor as a bullet embedded itself into the boards at the men's boots under the table. Automatically drawing their guns in response, their eyes focused on the small figure standing there.

Carlie stepped further inside, "You need proof I'm dead?" Flicking her glance over each man, two she had never seen before, she settled her eyes on Riley.

Surprised and flustered at her abrupt arrival out of nowhere, Tom's mouth hung wide open as he stared at the girl. He slowly rose, keeping his palms up in the air and away from his gun.

She spit the words like bile, "Sorry to disappoint you...you damn scalawag..." Catching movement out of her left eye, she pointed her gun and fired. Splinters flew into one of the two men's face. "Drop 'em, boys...or you'll not see a 'nother sun..."

"Toss 'em...men." Riley ordered. They did. He refocused on the girl, "Now...Carlie Anne...there's no cause..."

Butting in, "...You jus' shad-up, Tom Riley! I've had enough of you trying to scare me, run me off my land and...Kill...ME, you bastard!"

"Me? Why now...child...you must be plum loco...to think that!"

Hazel eyes narrowed into slits. "Yeah...I'm plum loco for not killing you where you stand, Tom Riley! Burning down my family home last night...with Me In It! Yeah...I'm loco..."

"You'd hang..."

A head tilted, "No...I think you would...the ring leader behind an attempted murder plot..."

"You can't trace nothing to me..."

"Oh...but I can..." Carlie lied as she began backing away. "I can prove it without one shred of doubt..." With those words, she spun and raced towards Waldo, mounting and riding hard out of there.

Rising, the two men stood looking at Riley. "Damn...now what?"

"Kill her..."

W hen she was out of sight of the camp, Carlie rode the horse behind a stand of fir and pine and dismounted. She quickly loosened the cinch on the saddle so the he could have a breather. She stumbled a few feet away and collapsed weakly against a boulder. She slid to the ground, trying to catch her breath and stop her stomach from feeling like it was full of rocks tumbling downhill in a barrel. She gasped more air into her starving lungs, thinking, *I just put the last nail in my own coffin...shutting the lid for good.* She breathed deeply again. *Now I'm gonna half to play a cat 'n mouse game jus' to stay alive...* Carlie exhaled noisily. Standing up, her good hand brushed the needles off her britches. She walked over to the horse, tightened the cinch, mounted and said, "C'mon, Waldo...we's got work to do..."

CARLIE HAD BEEN WHISTLING for Wolf for more than hour and still no Wolf. She knew he would disappear for days on end when he had caught the scent of a bitch in season, but Carlie couldn't remember if it was time for that now. Her brain and body were still numb from what had happened last night.

Standing in her stirrups, Carlie whistled again as her squinted eyes traveled over the rugged terrain. Then she spotted the buzzards, circling in the sky. *Not a good sign, something is hurt or dead,* she thought. It looked like they were about a mile away. She nudged Petey forward to investigate.

Reining the horse up so short he half reared when she saw Wolf's grey body, the buzzards pecking away at it. With her fingers she pulled her pistol and quickly switched hands and began firing into the congregating crowd of birds.

"Get away from him," she screamed, firing again. Slipping off the mule, she kept firing as she ran to Wolf's side. "Stay away from him," Carlie screeched, firing again at the birds.

Dropping the pistol, she fell to her knees as her hands begin roving lovingly over that silky pelt. Then she found it, a little bullet hole. "Ooh...Wolf, no wonder you didn't come..." she breathed softly as more tears began coursing down her sooty face.

Carlie whirled as she stood, shaking a fist at the sky. "Why Lord, why? She shouted at the clouds. "What have I done so wrong for you to punish me like this? Why, Lord? Why?" Carlie heaved in air and screamed again at the clouds. "You took my grandparents, then my parents, my house burned down around my ears! Now Wolf! What have I done to make you so mad at me? Why?" Tears were streaking in rivulets, clearing a track through dirty cheeks, "Well, answer me, damn it, answer me!" Carlie shouted then waited, angrily swiping away at the moisture coursing down her face.

She yelled at the sky again. "Alright if you won't talk to me, then I won't talk to you either, ever again. See how you like that, Lord!"

Carlie heaved in a breath trying to calm herself. Her insides were sloshing around like churning milk going sour.

Turning back to Wolf, she knelt, fingers lightly tracing the soft black-tipped ears, swiping at her runny nose. Sitting down cross-legged now, one hand remained on her companion as an elbow propped itself on her knee. She rested her forehead in her hand, trying to think.

Lifting her head, Carlie looked at the sky again and spoke sarcastically, "Things get too quiet for you up there, Lord? So, you decided to create some mischief down here for me? Is that it Lord, so you could have a good laugh at my expense? That it?"

"I hate you, Lord. You took everything that I loved away from me. I hate you…" Carlie whispered.

Brows knitted together as her mouth firmed into a hard line. She willed her tired brain to work. "I need proof that Riley was behind this too, but what?" Carlie whispered as her hand absent-mindedly rubbed Wolf's soft pelt. As her hand reach the dried blood, it made her sit up straighter. Her hands began digging through the matted fur. Finally, she found the little hole again.

Rising, she got her pocketknife out of the saddlebag and came back to Wolf. She sliced away at the matted fur until she had a clear view of the bullet hole. She began digging in the pelt. Soon a piece of lead popped out into her hand. Holding it, Carlie stared, she didn't know what caliber it was since she wasn't that knowledgeable about weapons. Tucking the bullet in her pocket, she wiped the knife on her already filthy coat and slid that into another pocket. She began gathering rocks placing them around and on Wolf's body, shedding a few more tears as she did so.

Rising, Carlie gazed at the mound of rocks. "Happy hunting, big boy. I swear to you I'll make sure I get the bastard who did this to you," she whispered. Without another word, she mounted the sorrel and headed back in the direction of the herd.

35

Carlie sat in the dark at the edge of her herd, giving Waldo a break. She had ridden him and the others hard the last ten days or maybe it was only a week. She didn't know for sure, she'd lost track of time, but it was showing on him. Sliding out of the saddle, she stood next to him, loosening the girth then gently rubbing between his eyes. Lightly moving her hands to his neck and withers, she allowed her tender touch to ease the exhaustion out of him.

Carlie spoke softly, "Hang in there, Wallie, I need you."

Carlie caught the flicker of light out of her peripheral vision as soon as she mounted. Standing in her stirrups, she saw the campfire had been stoked and was blazing since she had left the campsite early that morning. It looked like a lone figure was reflected in the light. *Tom Riley...* was her first thought. She urged Waldo toward it.

Dismounting in the shadows, she quietly eased the whip out of the leather strap, and then ambled into the firelight ready to do battle with Riley. She gasped at who sat on the log staring into the fire.

Colt heard the quick intake of breath and looked up to see the small figure walking into his sight, taking him by surprise.

Carlie shook the whip out. "Thought I told you to stay off my land, Mister Rawlins," she said as the whip neatly flicked the cup out of his hands.

Colt pulled and fired his weapon as fast as he rose.

Carlie yelped, dropping the whip, her eyes going big as wheel hubs as she cut a glance at her stinging hand. Seeing the blood, she jammed the wounded part of her hand in her mouth.

A deep baritone spoke with deadly quiet. "I told you once before not to use that black snake on me. Maybe that'll teach you a lesson," he finished, tucking his pistol back into its leather.

Continuing to suck on her hand, *Damn, he's quick and good...*her brain realized. Carlie stared venomously back at Rawlins. Taking the hand out of her mouth, she demanded, "What are you doing back here?"

Resuming his seat after picking up and refilling his cup, he answered, "I came back to help."

Her eyes became shrewd. "Ha. Ha. Ha. Mister Rawlins. That is So...Not Funny..." Carlie replied flatly. "...You just came to bring me more trouble..." She took a spread-eagled stance, folding her arms across the front of that filthy coat.

Colt hid his smile at Carlie's physical display of defiance. As the sleeves of that oversized coat pulled back, he saw the splint on her right hand and wondered what had happened. His brow inclined up, "Like I said. I came back to help," he repeated, ignoring Carlie's last comment.

"Well...ain't that jus' real noble of you, Mister Rawlins...to gallantly come riding to my rescue! I told you once before, I don't need your help," Carlie declared, as she resumed sucking on her hand.

"Knock it off, Carlie Anne. I ain't in the mood for your sarcasm."

Taking the hand out of her mouth again, she mustered up what she hoped sounded like authority and gritted the words out, "Pack your gear, Mister Rawlins and get off my land!"

Colt watched the firelight flickering along Carlie's gaunt features. The dark circles accented her eyes like hollow bruises. The girl looked worse than when he had found her on the trail the first time. "You look like hell, Carlie Anne," he said.

"My appearance is no concern of yours, Mister Rawlins."

"When was the last time you ate?"

Surprised at the shift in conversation, "I eat..."

"What? Nuts and berries you find along the trail?"

Taking that spread-eagled stance once again, she threw a dirty look in his direction. "You needn't concern yourself with my health either, Mister Rawlins," she answered.

He continued to gaze at the ragamuffin. It was time to change his strategy with the girl. "I've got hot coffee and plenty to eat, come..." he said, patting the log next to him. "Come get something to eat, Half-pint," he added softly.

"No! Get off my land, Mister Rawlins, now!"

Tapering his eyes, Colt said. "Not till I say what I've come to say."

Silence.

"Well..." she finally intoned. "...Say what you've come to say, then git off my land."

Carlie needs to be sitting down when I tell her about Harley. The way the she looks right now she'd probably collapse on me.

Patting the log once again, "Come sit, have some coffee and something to eat..." he repeated.

"No."

Damn kid ain't gonna budge. Colt silently whistled in air between his teeth. "Alright have it your way, you damn stubborn woman," he said as the muscles contracted in his jaw. "...Harley's dead, Honey...." Rawlins paused waiting on a reaction from

Carlie; only puzzlement crossed her tired face. He continued, "After I left you, I went back up to his place...he went peacefully in his sleep. I came back because there are things I needed to give you. Harley wanted you to have them..." he added quietly.

It finally dawned on her what he was telling her. Shock then disbelief tracked across her face. "No! No, no!" Her voice becoming shrill, escalating in pitch with each word. "Lies, lies, all lies! You're lying to me again, Rawlins!" she screamed. Her words bounced against the mountains.

Colt winced, Carlie's voice sounded like two limbs screeching against each other during a storm.

Taking a few steps toward him, she pointed crying out, "You take that back Rawlins, you hear me? Harley is not dead! Why do you want to lie to me? Why? Is it because you want to get back at me?" Giving him one more angry look, she finished in a whisper. "Why are you playing such cruel games with me?"

Rawlins witnessed the agony on Carlie's face and her unusual eyes filling with anguish. "Honey, I'm not playing games with you nor would I lie to you about something like this," he ended softly.

Carlie whirled away from him.

Colt stared at the small back encased inside that overgrown coat, then at his boots. "Honey...Harley was my friend, too. I'm going to miss him..." his gaze rose staring again at the back of that dirty oversized coat. "...We both are..." he stated quietly.

Carlie spun back around. "Why? Why is God not smiling down on me anymore? Why?" Tears began to flow freely. "Why? I don't understand?" Her emotional anguish again filled the night. "Why is He doing this to me?" Carlie cried.

Colt looked up in surprise at her words. Her eyes were bright with renewed moisture, overflowing and running a course through Carlie's dirty cheeks, her torment shining through the tears.

"I don't have the answers to those questions, Honey."

"But, why?" she asked. "I don't understand, why is God punishing me? I tried to take care of His land like I thought He'd want me to," she said, searching Colt's face for answers. "He took my grandparents, then my parents, Wolf…"

That beast is dead?

"…And now Harley…why? What have I done so wrong that He wanted to take everything I loved away? What have I done so wrong for Him to punish me so hard?"

"I don't have the answers for the reasons why God does some things, and not others," he said. His chest felt like it was being squeezed in a vice, witnessing Carlie trying to come to grips with Harley's death.

"What did you do?" Carlie accused Rawlins, taking a dirty sleeve and wiping her runny nose with it. "You talk to God, tell Him I needed to grow up, quit being such a spoiled rotten brat? You tell Him that? Is that why He's punishing me?" Heels of her hands swiped angrily at her wet cheeks, smearing them further.

Colt had to smile at her words. "No…God and I ain't exactly on speaking terms."

"That just figures…"

The girl is exhausted. Ignoring her barb, he patted the log again. "Come, sit," he said again. Pouring her a cup of fresh coffee, he gestured with it. "Come sit and have some coffee, at least…" he said.

Carlie sniffled as she finally nodded, plunking down beside him. She took the cup he offered, but just stared into the brew. Carlie finally spoke in a voice husky with emotion. "My Gramma used to say bad things always came in threes," Carlie heaved in air. "I've had more than a few threes lately. Had a few wagonloads of lemons dumped on me, too. I can't make lemonade anymore, ran out of sugar a long time ago…" she said, trailing off.

Rawlins smiled sadly at the kid's attempt at humor. Glancing at her profile, he watched her try and swallow down the tears threatening to erupt again.

Angrily, she threw her cup across the fire.

Colt's eyes followed the cup sailing into the darkness.

"Guess God's trying to tell me something. Maybe I should sell out to Tom Riley, but…" big round eyes searched his face for more answers. "…I didn't want this beautiful piece of land to go to ruin like he's done to his land. Is that so wrong, Mister Rawlins?"

Colt remained silent.

Carlie slid off the log, wrapping her arms around her knees, pulling them in close, resting her chin on them. Speaking softly once again, "That's why he wants my land, so he can butcher it like he did his. Clear cutting the timber, shipping it east just to make a few dollars. Now all the dirt washes down the hillsides during the rains, ruining his grazing. I couldn't allow him to do that here. Lone Wolf told me a long time ago to take care of the land so it will take care of you," she sighed.

Startled when he heard his old name, Colt tried to remember that particular conversation, but couldn't dredge it up out of his memory bank. He looked at her thinking, *She's just trying to save something that means the world to her.*

"Maybe…" Carlie choked. "…Maybe that's what God is trying to tell me, to let Tom Riley have it. Let him ruin this beautiful land…" she said as she buried her face in her arms hiding the tears trickling once again.

Colt tilted his head and gently took a stringy strand of hair and tucked it behind one ear. He was on the verge of revealing he was Lone Wolf but bit his tongue so the words would not come.

"Maybe God is trying to give you another message," he said instead.

Her head shook briskly. "No…God has made it way too plain on what I'm supposed to do…" Carlie mumbled through her knees.

Hand resting on that tangled mess of hair, his fingers gently tucked the flyaway strands back into her braid, "It will get better Half-pint, I promise you that, it will get better," Colt said quietly.

"No, it'll never get better, it's over and done with," came the muffled reply as silent sobs began shaking the thin shoulders inside that overgrown coat.

Hold her, son...

Startled at the voice coming out of nowhere, "What the hell..." he whispered, swinging his head around trying to figure out where the voice had come from.

Tol' ya...I'd be back...

Harley...? His mind asked.

Yep...

Where are you?

Up...here...

Looking through the darkness scanning the tops of the trees, *Up...where?*

Well...it's kinda hard ta figure, but I got me a birds-eye view...guess ya could say I'm kinda hangin' in the rafters of the sky...

Harley...you're dead...

Peers so...but I kin see you jus' like I was a standing right next ta ya.

*This is crazy...it's plum loco...*Colt thought, shaking his head.

Yeah...it does right spook ya a tad...but well...got some last minute details ta take care of fer I go see my Katydid...

Huh...what?

...Makin' sure you stick wit Half-pint...She'll fill ya in when hits daylight, 'bout what's been going on...Now...you jus' hold her, cause that's what she needs the most right now...I'm kinda outta reach...things 'll begin ta straighten out...now's that youse be there...

Harley...

Don't go getting obernoxious wit me boy, jus' do as I tell ya!

Sheesh...Harley! Even dead...you're gonna ride herd on me?

Colt heard Harley's rusty laugh coming from the darkness making him roll his eyes in response.

Sliding off the log, he pulled the girl onto his lap, wrapping his large arms around the child-like body of Carlie Anne Russell.

Carlie felt those big arms pull her into his embrace. The gentle gesture just made her cry all that much harder. She buried her face in his coat sleeve and sobbed.

36

Rawlins woke with a jerk, realizing he'd fallen asleep still holding Carlie. Gently placing her on his bedroll, he covered her. Sleep would be the best thing for her right now, he knew.

He ambled over to the sorrel and began stripping the gear off him. Pulling the saddle off, he saw the horse was almost in as bad of shape as Carlie was. He quickly glanced at her other stock. Even from this short distance he could see the weariness shrouding them. She'd almost run all of her riding stock into the ground. *That's not good,* Colt thought. Out here, your ride could mean the difference between life or death. You get stranded on foot...well...things could turn nasty pretty quick. Having Harley's stock now would help spare the small remuda they had.

Hauling her saddle to the fire, he set about making up his bed with her blankets. Untying the coverlet, he became aware of the thick putrid odor of lingering smoke within its folds. He smelled Carlie's blanket. *No, it didn't smell like the coverlet,* his eyes glanced over at the sleeping girl. *I know I've seen that coverlet before, but where?* Then it hit him, *In the house...when Carlie first brought me inside, it was draped over the couch.* Puzzling him further, *Wonder when she went back? And why?* He'd ask her when she woke up.

Digging in his bag, he found a clean bandana and some of Harley's all-medicinal salve. Rawlins picked up the canteen and squatted next to Carlie to begin cleaning his bullet graze on her hand. Looking over her hand Colt gave a double take. The girl had chewed her nails down to raw skin. For all the mud-slinging and shooting off her mouth did, Carlie Anne was nervous as a cat, chewing those nails off to the quick.

Carlie Anne Russell had a lot of questions she was going to have to answer for when she finally woke up.

ROLLING OVER, Carlie opened her eyes. The day was cloudy, dismal and cold. Snuggling deeper into the blankets she thought, *I don't want to get up.* Then she finally remembered finding Wolf dead and the horror of her house burning down. But she had made Wolf and her folks a promise, *I'll get the bastards who did that to you.*

Flinging back the covers, Carlie rose to her feet. She spied her grandmother's coverlet lying on the log. Glancing around, she noticed that Rawlins was nowhere in sight.

She poured herself a cup of coffee and after sipping it, decided, *That sure tastes a lot better than that mud I used to make.* She guzzled the brew, liking the way it warmed her insides all the way down.

Refilling her cup, Carlie wandered over to the buckboard and leaned against its side as she stared off into the distance, forcing herself to think through the fog of exhaustion.

Rawlins had seen Carlie by the buckboard as he rode back into camp. Studying her for a few moments before dismounting, he realized she looked as if she hadn't a friend in the world.

Loosing the cinch on his mount, he walked over to the fire, knelt and poured his own cup of brew. Sipping as he observed the lonely figure, he finally walked over to stand alongside her, allowing their silence to blend with the quiet cold.

Carlie spoke softly. "I'm sorry I unloaded on you last night," she said.

"Last night? That was three nights ago," he said as his eyes traveled over the still fatigued features of the little ragamuffin. "You were exhausted, you needed the rest," Colt quietly added.

Carlie cut him a sideways glance as she chewed on her bottom lip, deciding that she could trust him. Inhaling Carlie whispered, "Tom Riley burned down my house and killed Wolf," she confided.

His eyes deepened to dark slate. "When?"

Carlie shrugged thin shoulders. "I don't know, a week, ten days, maybe a month. I don't know," she said.

"You tell the Sheriff?"

"The Sheriff? Whatever on earth for? He can't do anything without proof, and I don't have any proof, just my gut feeling. Ed ain't gonna do nuthin' without evidence of the crime," she said disgustedly.

Pushing his hat back from his forehead, Colt said. "Alright, I want you to start from the beginning and tell me every fact you can remember. You got that? Every little detail," he insisted.

"Why? You can't do anything without proof?"

"Well, let's just see if we can dig up some proof, shall we?"

Carlie threw Rawlins a cock-eyed look. "Why?" she asked again. "You can't dig up proof where there ain't none."

"Oh, you'd be surprised at what you can dig up when you ask the right questions," Rawlins grinned.

Brows knitted together, her eyes thinking, she asked, "You some kind of lawman?"

Colt smiled. "Have been..." he said and watched as Carlie's nose scrunched up thinking of the likelihood of that idea.

Colt asked softly. "Now...how'd you know the house burned?"

Her head swiveled, "Because I was in it! You ninny!"

Colt's heart dropped to the soles of his boots when he heard that. He softly sucked the air back into his lungs.

"Um...when I slugged you, I broke my hand..." embarrassed, she showed him the splint.

Ahhh...that's where that came from... Colt remembered she did wallop him pretty good.

"...I...uh...went into Doc's in town and he put this splint on it...it was hurting pretty bad and I didn't feel like riding back to the winter cabin, so I went home and fell asleep. Later, my coughing woke me up and that's when I started downstairs...well, it was all engulfed in flames..." she trailed off going silent.

He waited.

"...I saw the two busted windows..."

Colt stopped her with his hand. "The two busted windows? That means the fire was set on purpose."

"Well...bust my bustle...Mister Rawlins! I think that's just what Tom Riley had in mind. Besides when I went to his logging camp I ..."

"...You went to his camp?"

"Yes...to let him know that no matter what he did, I wasn't gonna be run off my property...But I overheard him tell someone to go diggin' around in the ashes for my body..." she sucked in more air and continued, "That's when I surprised him and the two saddle bums discussing my death...When I confronted him, he said that I had no proof he was connected to burning my house down or anything else...I lied and told him I did...then I skedaddled outta there...

"Well...Hell...Carlie Anne, he sure fire now is gonna try harder to kill you..."

Looking down at her cup, she tossed the contents heaving a huge sigh, "I know...now it will be like playing a cat 'n mouse game with him...trying to stay one step ahead...trying to stay alive..."

"Need to find some proof that would convict Riley in a court of law...not just your gut feeling, Carlie..."

"But any proof would have been burned up, so you still don't have any proof, Mister Rawlins," she threw back at him.

"Oh...I don't know about that. Sometimes proof can show up in the damn 'dst places," he assured her.

Carlie shook her head. "No. You stay out of this, Mister Rawlins. This is my problem, not yours. Riley played with fire and now it's my turn. I'll kill him if it's the last thing I ever do," she gritted out.

"This is something the law needs to handle," he said.

"Law? What the hell is the law gonna do without proof? No, I'll just take care of Riley and whoever else is in involved myself," Carlie stated vehemently.

"And maybe get yourself killed in the process? It's different when the target can shoot back, Carlie," Colt said quietly. His hand rested lightly on her arm again.

Her head spun around. "So? I don't care anymore," she said. "My family is gone, my home burned down around my ears," her voice rising into a shriller pitch. "Wolf killed. Just what exactly do I have to live for, Mister Rawlins?"

Her arm swung toward the herd. "A bunch of damn red cows, fuzzy tailed nags? Harley's gone now, too," she said as eyes angrily flashed at him, giving way to moisture making them glisten. "Tell me...Mister Rawlins, what do I have to look forward to?" she asked, breathing heavily. "Nothing...Mister Rawlins, nothing! That's what!" Carlie finished. Spinning on her toes, she headed back toward camp.

Colt followed, taking hold of her arm stopping and spinning Carlie around. "You've got me, I told you I came back to help," he said.

Carlie's eyes dripped with disgust, her voice loaded with bitterness. "You? Well, just bust my bustle, Mister Rawlins," she said. "Why don't you just go roll over in clover, you think so highly of yourself," she said insulting him.

Colt reached out and jerked Carlie toward him. "Listen here, Miss High and Mighty, you're out of your league dealing with Riley, you let the law handle this!" His big palms squeezed her thin arms. "You hear me Carlie Anne? You let the law handle this!"

"Your brain is all clouded up, Mister Rawlins, and let go of me, quit dogging my tail. I'll handle this my way," Carlie argued with him as she tried to jerk out of his grasp.

Two sets of eyes quietly challenged each other.

Abruptly, he wanted to kiss this stubborn firebrand, but he but held himself back, after all she was just a kid. Finally, he released her.

Colt rested his forearms on top of the buckboard's wooden side and watched Carlie march back to the camp, stumbling a few times in her hurry. *She's nothing but a bundle of nerves.* It wasn't going to do any good talking or arguing with her anymore. Carlie Anne was just going to march down her own little trail no matter what anyone said to her, digging herself an early grave. And it was up to him to make sure she didn't wear a permanent dirt blanket whether she wanted his interference or not.

37

Colt Rawlins' nose whiffed the unpleasant odor as he pulled up in front of the Russell homestead. He sat astride the bay gazing at the ruins. A light snowfall overnight had made an interesting study in contrast, turning the scene into a black, gray and white tintype, the white layer attempting to hide the black charred remains.

Dismounting at the corral, he tied the bay's reins to the rails. He went looking for a shovel or hayfork, anything to dig with. Finding both, he walked back to the ruins.

Stepping over the stone foundation into the rubble, he gazed at the charred remains, his breath adding to the emotional fog hanging over the site. He tried to jog his memory. *Carlie Anne said two windows were busted.*

He turned back around toward what had been the front of the house, estimated about where he remembered those windows had once been. Slowly he turned facing back into the burned-out rubble, brows knitted together thinking.

Climbing over half burnt beams, he crunched through thick ash and cinders. Colt scuffed and kicked through the powder gray-black silt. When he had estimated he was about eight feet within the original structure, he took the hay rake and began lightly pulling it through the debris.

What he was looking for he wasn't rightly sure; he'd know when he found it.

🙢

SHERIFF PAGE WALKED across the street thumbing through what little mail he had. Mail wasn't real regular out here. Once a month mostly, lucky if it was twice a month, then pretty soon there would be no mail till spring. Hearing hooves squishing along the muddy street, Ed glanced up. Walking over, he stopped by the bay. "Well, what brings you back to our little mountain hamlet?" Page asked, gazing at Colt Rawlins' smudged face and hands.

"You got some place where I can wash up and we can talk?" Rawlins asked.

He stepped on the walk. "Sure, come to the office," Ed said, opening the door, leading the way.

Pouring a cup of coffee, the sheriff handed it to Rawlins then asked, "Now...what's on your mind?"

Taking a sip, Rawlins inquired, "You been out to the Russell place lately?"

"Not lately, why?"

"When was the last time you were out there?"

"Ooh...maybe three-four weeks ago. I check on it now and then for Carlie when she goes to winter grazing," he replied. "Why?"

"Somebody burned down the main house," Colt said.

"What? Why?"

"That's what I'd like to know, too..." He proceeded to open his saddlebag, dumping the contents on the desk. "Found this digging through the rubble," he revealed, pointing to a melted whiskey bottle. "It was set, coal oil. Carlie was sleeping inside when these were thrown, jury might call it attempted murder," Rawlins said.

171

Page's gaze became shrewd. "Attempted murder? That's a heavy charge, Rawlins...based on just speculation..." the sheriff commented.

"That's what it would look like to me."

Ed pulled on his ear, then picked up the bottle and smelled the inside. "You're right. Coal oil. It must've just happened, but why? The Russells were good folks..."

Colt nodded. "Carlie broke her hand then came in to see the Doc? Did you see her then?"

"Yeah...I talked to her. She wasn't none too friendly neither, especially when I asked how you was making out," Ed said.

Colt's jaw muscles contracted, hardening his features hearing the sheriff's words. "No, we don't get along. Now answer my question, Sheriff. When did you last see her?"

"I guess it was about ten days ago, why?"

"Thanks."

"Why is that so important?"

"I'm trying to narrow down the time frame since Carlie couldn't remember," Colt said. Pouring himself more coffee, he turned around and faced the sheriff again. "Did you know Tom Riley has been hassling, threatening and scaring Carlie to sell out to him?"

"Threatening Carlie? No, she never said a word to me..." he replied.

Rawlins offered a thin smile. "She said you wouldn't believe her, because you all think she's got bats in her belfry," he said.

Page grinned sheepishly as he scratched his head. "Well...I wouldn't go so far as to say that. But...Carlie is, well...you know, just different..." He warmed up his coffee, then turned again, "... So you think Riley is behind the burning?"

Colt shrugged. "And a few other things, won't know till I see the man face to face," setting down his cup. "You say his place is south of here?"

"Yep," Page said as he saw Colt opening the door. "You planning on paying him a visit?" following Rawlins out the door.

Sticking a boot in the stirrup. "Figured I would," Rawlins replied, slipping easily into the leather.

"Mind if I tag along? I'm none too happy about someone burning down a defenseless little girl's home," Ed said.

Looking down from his saddle. "I wouldn't go underestimating Carlie, Sheriff. She ain't as defenseless as she appears..."

Ed grinned, "...I know. But any which way you look at it, it ain't right burning down her home."

38

K nocking on the door, the two men waited.

Opening it, Ruth Riley's eyes went wide. "Why, Sheriff what brings you out here?"

Removing his hat. "Afternoon Ruth, mind if we come in? We need to talk to Tom."

Stepping aside, she allowed the two men inside. "Tom's out on the west slope with the logging crew, if you need to see him…" her eyes continued to send questioning glances at the two men.

After whisking off his hat, his fingers held it in front of him while he asked, "I'll get right to the point, Ruth. Someone burned down the Russell house, and I won…"

Ruth interrupted. "…I know…Carlie stopped by and told me. She was accusing Tom of being behind it…but Tom wouldn't…"

"I'm not accusing anyone, Ruth. I'm just asking questions."

She nodded, "I understand."

Ed nodded at the tall man next to him.

Her eyes flicked to him then back to Ed.

"This here is Colt Rawlins, he's been helping Carlie some, and brought me evidence the fire was set. Tom hire on any new hands the last couple of months?" he asked.

"I...yes. He's logging a new section, needed some more men," she answered.

"Alright, Ruth. Thanks for your time," the sheriff said, heading to the door.

"Wait. Mister Rawlins? Is Carlie Anne alright? She looked frightful when she was here last." Ruth asked.

Colt turned and looked at her. "In a way, Miz Riley, she's dealing with a lot of grief right now. But she's strong, she'll make it," he said, then followed Page out the door.

It closed softly in their wake. Ruth leaned against it and closed her eyes. "Tom...Tom...I hope you're not behind this...the Russells were good neighbors..."

The sheriff handed Rawlins his reins. "Well, that wasn't real enlightening."

Sticking his boot in the stirrup, Colt mounted. "Either she doesn't know or knows more than she's telling," he said. Reining the bay around he headed toward the west slope where the mining camp lay.

❦

GAZING AROUND IN DISGUST, Colt realized Carlie Anne had been right. Riley had clear-cut the mountainsides. He sat staring at the stumps dotting the now bare hills, not even leaving saplings to start new growth timber. Leaving the land bare and open for disaster, turning Rawlins' stomach.

"Hey Page, hold up," Rawlins said pulling in next to the sheriff as he rested an arm on the saddle horn.

"You know much about Riley's holdings?" Colt asked, flicking a couple of fingers toward the bare hills.

Ed Page tapered his eyes at the man next to him. "What are you thinking?"

"I'm thinking he may be on Government lands. Do you believe he got any Government contracts for this?"

"I see what you mean, trespassing, scalping the land in the process, without no one the wiser back east," the sheriff offered up.

"Uh-huh," Colt replied. "Where's the nearest telegraph?"

"Missoula," the sheriff said tilting his head. "You planning on taking a visit to Missoula, see the sights?" Ross grinned.

Colt smiled right back. "Maybe, hadn't been to a big city in a while, might do me some good," he said urging the bay forward.

TOM RILEY WAS OVERSEEING the new section and they were making good progress. Since the snows were late this year, keeping the ground partially frozen enough to allow the skids to work without much opposition hauling the logs down the mountain was a good thing.

Now if only he could get his hands on the Russell ranch, but that fool girl was standing in his way. Progress; it was what separated the men from the boys. The country was changing and that damn girl didn't want to change with the times. She was standing in the way of progress, his progress, his money.

So far, that little upstart had turned down every offer he'd made, and they had been good offers. A lot of people would have been glad to have one third of what he'd offered her. But, oh no, that wasn't good enough for her, Miss High and Mighty.

Moving the chomped end of the cheroot from one side of his mouth to the other, Riley squinted up the slope. Pretty soon when the snows finally came this year, they were going to have to halt the operation. Too bad burning the house down didn't kill her, then he could have started the process of filing for her land over the winter. There were no heirs to impede his desire of claiming the best land in this section if she were dead.

Frowning, Riley turned sticking hands in his trouser pockets. He walked back to the cook tent as his eye caught the two men riding up. Sheriff Page and someone he didn't recognize. Wondering what they were doing here he walked over to them to find out for himself.

"Howdy, Sheriff," Riley called out the greeting as his gaze drifted over toward the stranger, sizing him up. Riley's eyes narrowed when he realized the man might be trouble. His focus resettled back on Page as he asked, "Long way from town ain't cha, Ed?"

"Just came out for a visit, Tom," Ed replied.

Riley's eyes kept skittering back to the big man quietly setting his bay.

Rawlins noticed Riley's unease. He continued his relaxed non-threatening pose, while his peripheral vision continued to scan the camp. When he found two unlikely candidates for loggers, he stared openly at them for a few moments, studying the two men. He gave them a slight nod, then returned his attention back to Page and Riley.

"You say someone set fire to the Russell place? Now why would anyone want to go and do something like that?" Riley queried. "The girl, is she all right?"

"Yeah, she was lucky," Ed answered, eyes traveling across the makeshift camp. "How many new hands you hired on in the last three weeks?"

Riley looked around. "Oh...about a dozen or so...why?"

"They local boys, or from out of town?" the sheriff inquired.

Scratching his head then resetting his hat, Riley answered. "I guess it's about half and half, why? You don't think it was some of my boys playing games, do you?"

"Boys playing games under orders..." Colt answered quietly. "...Trying to scare a kid half to death into selling her family's land. Or maybe murder was on your mind, enabling you to lay claim to her property, just so you could butcher more terrain. That about size it up, Riley?"

Yanking the cold cheroot out of his mouth, Riley angrily

gestured with it. "Now...you jus' hold on a minute...Mister! The Russells were good neighbors...what cause would I have to do something like that?"

Colt observed the two men stand and move slowly toward Riley's back. "Not man enough to tackle your own nasty doings?" Colt nodded at the two men behind Riley. "Had to hire someone to do your dirty work for you, so your lily-white hands wouldn't be soiled, eh Riley?"

Swiveling his head, Riley saw the two moving up behind him. He gave a nonverbal *No* toward the duo. They stopped in their tracks. He jerked his head back around. "Don't know whatever gave you that idea, Mister..." Riley answered smoothly.

"Rawlins, Colt Rawlins, and I'm sure we'll be meeting again," reining the bay around, he headed back the way they had come.

Riley heaved in air. "Ed, let me know when you want to get everyone together for a house raising," he said, hoping to throw suspicion off in another direction.

"Will do, Tom," Page said, turning the sorrel and following Rawlins.

Riley waited until the two riders were out of earshot, then whirled on the men behind him. Grabbing the shirts of both men, jerked them closer. "You damn idiots," he growled. "Apparently you two didn't cover your tracks well enough."

"Boss...we did what ya told us to do...even killed that wolf of hers...

Shoving the two away from him. "Let me think," Riley said walking away from the two men. When the idea flicked through his brain he walked back toward the duo stopping a few feet in front of them. "Alright this is what you're gonna do. I want you to go find that bitch and make her disappear, kill her for good this time then dump the body in an old mine not far from that place. You two jackasses got that?" he snarled.

"Where we gonna find her?" Luke asked.

"She winters in a cabin, two days north of here." Riley said. "I paid you two blokes a lot of money, and so far you haven't earned one penny of it. You keep screwing up, but you get caught, I don't know you. You were two drifters just passing through, you got that?" His voice took on a gravely edge. "You finish that job, you two assholes clear out, I don't want to see either of you ever again," Riley threatened. "You understand me?"

Both men looked at each other, then back at their boss. "Alright Riley, we'll do your dirty work for you, but get one thing straight. You get caught..." one finger jabbed into Riley's chest. "... And you squeal like a hog, you'll be the one we come gunning for. You understand *that*, Riley?" Luke threatened back.

"C'mon Stu, let's go, the air around here is getting mighty rank," Luke said.

❞

RAWLINS HAD PULLED up his bay waiting on the sheriff to catch up. When Page came alongside, Colt stated calmly. "Something's rotten in the manure pile, Ed. Riley is getting mighty greedy if he's hiring guns. He must want Carlie's land pretty bad. *And*, for that matter, how did he know Carlie Anne was in the house? Makes you wonder, don't it? For him to ask if she was alright," Colt finished.

"Say...that's right...and I didn't mention she was in the house neither," Ed agreed.

"You notice the two behind him?"

"Yeah. They're not loggers for sure, and not drifters neither, more like hired guns," the sheriff said.

"Yep. Stu Phillips and Luke Evans, up from Colorado way, hired guns," Colt added.

Ed cut Rawlins a cock-eyed look. "And you know these two how?" leaving the question hanging in the air.

Sitting up straighter in the saddle, Colt smiled as he answered.

"I was Sheriff at Leadville for a little while, until Baker could resume his duties after getting hisself shot."

Ed nodded. "I figured you was some kind of lawman, the way you found that evidence and talking about attempted murder charges," he said.

Colt squinted off into the distance. "Carlie Anne is in a peck of trouble with those two hanging around, and I can't keep my eye on her. I've got other things I need to check on first," he announced.

"You want me to go get her, lock her up until we settle this?" Ed offered.

Colt tilted his head at Ed. "Might not be a bad idea, but she'd never stand for it. Besides she's like an Indian out there in those woods. You don't find her, she finds you," he revealed. Closing tired eyes, he pinched the bridge of his nose with two fingers. "Naw…just try and keep an eye on her. It sure won't be easy, but I'd be much obliged," he said, thanking the sheriff in advance.

"Will do. You heading out now?"

"I've got to get some supplies first, and do you have someone who handles land acquisitions, deeds, government contracts in town?"

"We've got that lawyer in town, he came from back east, but been here for about five years. He might be able to answer your questions," Ed offered.

RAWLINS STEPPED BACK into the sheriff's office and was promptly greeted by a little black and silver fur ball dancing on its hind legs, front paws raking the air in a *Howdy*.

"Well, hello there, pup," Colt said, bending down rubbing its ears. "This your new deputy, Sheriff?"

Ed handed Rawlins a cup of coffee. "I guess," he said. "My wife doesn't want her around, so I bring her here with me. She's a good pup, smart. Know anyone who might want her?" he asked.

An idea flickered through Colt's mind, looking around. "What's today's date?" he inquired.

Ed looked at the calendar. "November 11, why?"

"Just wondered. Whoever burned down the house, also killed Wolf and Carlie's taking all of this pretty hard. That and the fact Harley passed away on top of everything else she's already struggling with," Colt said, taking another swallow of coffee.

The sheriff spewed his brew, his hand wiping at the dribbles. "What! When? What happened to Harley?"

"Said he had some kind of canker eating away at his insides..." Colt hesitated, then added, "...He went peacefully..." he said quietly.

"Damn..." Ed said shaking his head, "He was a good man..."

"Yep...one of the best..."

Changing tactics, Ed asked. "So, did you go see Josh Stokes? What did he have to say?"

Rawlins thought back to his conversation with the young lawyer.

"Umm...found out why Riley wants Carlie Anne's piece of land so bad. Most of it is government lease rangelands and her folks filed for all mineral rights on all the lands that come under the Russell name. Carlie Anne Russell is a very rich young lady, even though she says she's broke. I wouldn't doubt that Carlie Anne hasn't got a clue as to what her folks left her..." Colt surmised.

The sheriff nodded. "Find out if Riley is trespassing?"

"Stokes didn't have access to those records, said I'd have to go to Missoula for that," rising, Colt added. "Sam should have my supplies ready, I'll stop by when I get back," he said opening the door.

"Wait..."

Colt turned.

Ed went to his desk. The drawer gave a raspy sound when he opened it. Digging around, he finally pulled out an object and handed it to Colt saying, "This might give you some leverage if you was acting on my behalf…"

A brow cocked up as he took the badge, "Thanks. Oh, and save that pup for me, I want to give her to Carlie for Christmas. She won't replace Wolf, but it might heal Carlie's grief a little," and with that Colt Rawlins was on his way to Missoula.

39

Carlie was going stir crazy. She tried to stay busy, but it wasn't working. Her gut was churning all the time, keeping her on edge. She was skittish as a new foal, and Wolf wasn't around to warn her anymore. Every little noise made Carlie jump, her heart sticking in her throat each time.

She constantly checked her pistol and rifle, making sure the lead in each casing had an X or cross marking on them like Harley had taught her.

Heaving in air; she seemed to be doing that a lot here lately, trying to settle her quivering insides. Carlie sighed once again. *I'm just a sitting duck here, hanging around the cabin would just make me easy prey. I need to leave...but go where?* Gazing out the window by the table, it had begun to snow in earnest now. *Well, this will slow Riley down some,* but her gut still wouldn't let her relax. *I could go to Harley's place, but then there would be no one to keep an eye on the herd. Riley will never give up, not until I'm dead and he has my land...*she thought resignedly.

Carlie thought of Harley being gone forever and it made tears well up in her eyes. Blinking rapidly, she got out her drawing pad and sat at the table and began sketching.

The room had gone cold and dark, Carlie suddenly realized. Time always seemed to fly by when she was drawing. She lit the lamp and threw more wood on the fire and came back to her drawing. Her eyes went wide at what she had drawn or who for that matter: *Colt Rawlins.* He was leaning forward in the saddle, his rope gracefully arcing out in front of him, his bay stretched out, mane and tail flowing, a man and his horse working as one.

Carlie eased herself into the chair and quietly inhaled as she rested her forehead in her hand continuing to stare at the drawing. Her finger lightly traced the edges of the figures, *Maybe I miss him more than I realized.* Suddenly she was tired, so very tired. She got up and retrieved her pistol, making sure a cartridge was in the chamber under the firing pin. Lying down, she covered up with two blankets, one of which was her grandmother's coverlet. The pistol was tucked in next to her thigh. Carlie sunk into an exhausted sleep.

"You sure this is the right place, Luke?" Stu whispered loudly.

"Has to be, the horse's in the corral," nodding his head toward the sorrel. "We hain't seen nobody for three days now," Luke said pausing, thinking. "This is gonna be perfect, that bitch made it easy for us. Living way out here all by herself, the big snows coming now, hain't nobody ever gonna find that girl till her bones is bleached white by the sun," Luke said giving a soft laugh. "Yeah, she just made it perfect for us. Leave the horses here, we'll walk the rest of the way in," Luke said.

Two figures skirted the edge of the shadows, heading to the side of the cabin. They stopped, listening to the silence. Glancing at each other, both nodded. Tip-toeing across the boards of the porch, the men stopped suddenly when one cracked with the cold, stilling them. Only their breath pierced the cold with fog-like puffs.

Two sets of ears were greeted with more silence. Their boots began a slow advance on the door. Luke took off his glove, and gently lifted the door latch, pushing it open.

Squeak.

Both men stopped suddenly, listening hard. Again, they heard nothing. The duo moved inside and looked around, the low fire their only light. Stu tapped Luke's shoulder and pointed.

Squinting into the semi-dark, Luke saw what Stu had pointed out. Easing his pistol out of the leather, Luke tiptoed to the side of the sleeping figure.

Stu followed, stopping about six feet behind.

The muzzle of Luke's pistol zeroed in on Carlie's ear. "Wake up, bitch," he said in a harsh whisper cocking the hammer back. "Wake up bitch, we're going for a ride."

The metallic click of a pistol being cocked woke Carlie up. Cutting her eyes to the right she saw firelight reflecting off the steel-blue barrel stuck within an inch of her face. Her eyes rolled up the hand, then arm to rest on the face of the man holding the pistol. Her glance then traveled over his shoulder to his partner. His face was encased in shadow too, firelight highlighting his back.

Carlie couldn't breathe, her insides felt as cold and heavy as a huge block of ice. She swallowed, her left hand slowly reaching around the grip of her weapon, thumb on the hammer. Her finger slid quietly into the guard, resting on the half-moon trigger.

"I ain't gonna tell you again, get up, bitch, we're going for ride," the man growled.

Carlie slowly did as the man requested, sliding the pistol around under the blankets, allowing it to come to rest between her legs. The barrel was pointed up at the man's gut underneath the blanket's folds.

"C'mon, get a move on, bitch..." he said backing away as he spoke gesturing with his gun.

Placing stocking feet on the floor, Carlie half rose. The pistol slammed into her hand with its recoil from firing it.

The look of surprise and his scream would haunt Carlie for a long time. She watched him fall back landing hard, lying in his own blood pooling underneath him.

The whites of the second man's eyes turned yellow in the firelight as he fled through the open doorway.

Carlie fired wildly through the blankets at the second figure, missing him. The bullet slammed into the mantle instead. Her legs became tangled in the covers as she tried to give chase. She angrily kicked them aside, running after the second figure. Carlie stopped at the edge of the porch, leaned against the post, took a bead on the running figure, held her breath and pulled the trigger.

The man flipped, then after a few moments, he scrambled up running for the cover of the trees.

Carlie lost him then in the dark. Sinking down to the porch floor, she heaved in air, choking on it as she did so.

Later as her head rested back against the post, Carlie gradually opened her eyes and stared at the underside of the porch roof. Her eyes then flicked to the heavy snow coming down realizing it was covering her. She didn't know how long she had been sitting there, dreading going back into the cabin. She cut her glance to the right, gazing through the open doorway. From where she sat, she wasn't able to see the body, but her mind's eye sure did. Her ears could still recall his screams, echoing, bouncing off the inside walls of her skull.

Pushing herself up against the post, its solid presence steadying her weak knees, she brushed the dry snow off herself. She took tentative steps toward the door, and as her gait became more steady and sure, she walked through the open doorway.

Carlie laid the pistol on the table, lit the lamp and turned down the wick. The glass rattled against the brass when she replaced the chimney. Reaching behind her, she closed the door. Taking in a calming breath, she walked over to the man she had killed and stood staring at him, then closed her eyes against the scene. Opening them again she sucked in more air for her starved lungs, then knelt next to him. Glancing at his face she remembered him as one of the men that had been sitting with Riley in the cook tent that day she surprised them. Dragging her eyes away from his face, she concentrated on the entrance wound that appeared small. When she turned the man over, the rich copper smell of fresh blood made her gag. But it was the exit wound that made her cover her mouth. She rushed to the door, barely getting it open in time and just making it to the edge of the porch before emptying the contents of her stomach. That then turned into dry heaves, her body unable to control the retching.

When the spasms finally ceased, Carlie washed her face with the cold snow. She put a handful in her mouth, waited until it had melted, then spit it back out. Rolling over on her back she just laid there with her eyes closed. But her mind's eye kept replaying the scene over and over again, forcing Carlie to keep her eyes open.

"I've got to get him out of the house," she whispered to herself. Pushing up from the porch floor, she wobbled when she stood, her knees so weak she felt as if she would collapse any second. She barely made it over to the doorjamb, willing the wood to hold her up. Carlie walked over to her boots and pulled them on. She kept her eyes averted from the body on the floor by her bunk. Walking back to the pegs by the door she slipped on her coat. Turning, she staggered back and stared once again at the man she had killed. Breathing deeply to give her strength, hoping her legs wouldn't fail her, she grabbed the man's legs, swung him around and dragged him to the door. Finally, Carlie had him out of the house and on the ground. She heaved in more air as she continued to haul him toward the old wood sled.

Turning her back on the body she stopped to rest with her hands braced upon her knees, her mouth pulling in air. "I'll load him tomorrow, take the bastard to Ed," she mumbled to the snow-filled night air. Without another glance at the dead man, Carlie staggered back toward the cabin.

IT WAS FINALLY DAYLIGHT she noticed, blowing out the lamp. Carlie had scrubbed through the night's darkness trying to remove the bloody remains of the eerie incident. Even though she knew she had removed the red stains, they still haunted her thoughts.

Carlie began shaking uncontrollably. Taking her grand-mothers blanket, she wrapped herself in it. She scooted the rocker as close to the fire as she dared, then sat trying to get warm. Her insides still felt like a block of ice. The flames seemed to mesmerize her; finally, her eyes closed and her chin dropped onto her slender chest.

40

Leaving the bay with the hostler in the local stable, Colt tucked his bedroll under his arm and draped his saddle-bags over a shoulder. He pulled his Henry from the scabbard and began walking down Main Street in bustling Missoula, Montana toward the Rodgers Hotel. Stopping in the street, he let his eyes roam over the two-story white clapboard building. It didn't look to be very old. Dropping his gaze, he glanced around, his eyes flicking from one object to another gathering his bearings in the growing town. First, he'd get a room, then begin his inquiries.

STEPPING off the bottom step of the stairs, he approached the clerk. "Say...where can a man get a rib-stickin' good meal in this town?"

The clerk looked up at the tall stranger, "The Missoula Restaurant is the only eatin' place in town..."

"Alrighty...then, which direction?"

Pointing, "Out those doors, turn left, just a few buildings down..."

"Thanks."

❧

STEPPING INSIDE, Colt closed the door behind him. Glancing around he found an empty table against the wall. Making a beeline for it, he shed his coat draping it on one of the four chairs at the table. Taking a seat with his back to the wall, he waited for a waitress. Grey eyes scanned the few patrons, settling on a table of two men across the room, leaning towards each other talking earnestly. Both had beards and dark brown hair and dressed in business suits that said 'money'. His brow cocked up.

"You're new..." a plump brunette interrupted his thoughts as she approached the table. She pulled a pad from her apron pocket and pulling a pencil from over her ear, she poised it above the pad and waited to take his order.

Looking up he answered, "Uh...yessum...coffee and your special..."

"Beef stew suit ya..."

"Yessum..."

"Be right back..."

He watched as she sashayed through a swinging door, disappearing quickly. His eyes roamed back to the men in the business suits. Feeling eyes on him, one of the men glanced Colt's way, studied him for a few seconds, then nodded. He returned the gesture.

Returning with a mug of coffee, bowl of stew and a basket with bread, the waitress set them down in front of Colt. Pulling a spoon and a knife from the pocket of her apron, she asked, "Anything else..."

"Um...not right off that I can think of..."

She turned to walk away.

"Uh…Miss…there is one thing…"

"Yes?"

"I'm logging some of my property above Kaskaskia… wondered if there was anyone around here who buys lumber?"

Looking over her shoulder at the two men in suits still at their table, she returned her gaze to Colt. Thumbing in their direction, "They do…"

He flicked his eyes that way then back to her. "Much obliged…"

"That all?"

"Yessum…" He picked up a piece of bread and broke off small bites and dropped them into the stew. Picking up the spoon, he stirred the bread to soak up more of the gravy. He watched as his waitress walked over to the table across the room, bent over and said a few quiet words. He noted the one who had glanced his way earlier did so again. She left that table to check on another one in the back.

When Colt was halfway through the stew, the one who had nodded at him approached his table. He looked, sizing up the man with a full beard and well-cut suit.

"Hear you're looking to market your lumber?"

"Maybe."

Sticking out his hand, he said, "Andrew Hammond, I'm a partner in the Montana Improvement Company."

Rising, and taking the hand offered, "Rawlins…Colt Rawlins… have a seat…" resettling in his chair once again as Hammond sat down in the chair opposite his.

Glancing at Colt's half-filled cup, "May I offer you something besides coffee?"

"Coffee is fine…"

Looking for the waitress, he called out, "Maybelle…bring this man another cup of coffee and me, my usual…"

The girl nodded. A few moments later she returned and set the items on the table and remained standing there like she was waiting on something.

Colt asked, "Got any pie?"

"Apple..."

"Sounds good..."

She took his empty bowl and again sashayed through the swinging door. Returning once more, she placed the plate with a good-sized wedge of apple pie on it in front of Colt.

Leaning forward he smelled it, then smiled at her. Reaching into his pocket he inquired, "What do I owe you?"

Before she could answer, Hammond butted in saying, "Put it on my account, Maybelle..."

Colt's eyes questioned the man's generosity, but he remained silent.

"All right...Mister Hammond..." she answered, turning towards the swinging door.

"Much obliged..."

"No problem, especially if you become a supplier..."

A brow cocked up as he slipped a bite of pie into his mouth that set it watering. It had been a long time since he had apple pie. He reached for the coffee and took a sip and returned the cup to the table.

Hammond watched every move with curiosity.

Colt pushed the plate with the remaining pie aside, folded his arms and rested them on the table. He gave the man an inquiring stare. "What are you offering?"

"Thirty-seven cents on ten thousand board feet..."

"What about raw timber?"

"Twenty-five cents on ten thousand board feet..."

Colt feigned surprise. "Tom Riley told me you were good to work with..." he lied.

"Ahh...he supplies us pretty well from up that a way..."

Colt's jaw tightened remembering the butchered land he'd witnessed.

"...We've got orders to fill. Three thousand ties per mile on the railroad's contract..."

Leaning forward, Colt pulled the plate back in front of him and took another bite of pie, listening to Hammond.

"...Bridges and trestles to build, lumber to shore up inside the tunnels, mines when we get them operating. Wood to the steamboats, wood to fire the smelters for the copper...wood for building new homes across this land and Montana's forests are ripe for the pickin'...There is an unfathomable amount of timber in this territory...we will likely never see the end to the rich resources Montana has to offer...all free for the taking..."

His eyes narrowed at Hammond's last remark. "...And your company is just the sort to take advantage of it..."

Hammond smiled as he leaned back in his chair, picking up his glass and swirled the rye in it before taking a sip. He looked at Rawlins, "I...we as the company prefer to call it...opportunity..."

"I see..."

"Well...what do you say, Rawlins...ready to make a deal?"

Colt took another bit of pie and slowly chewed it, thinking. Swallowing he looked at the ceiling and replied, "Not sure...it's good timber...at least a good two feet thick and some three feet... not counting the height..." he brought his eyes back down to focus on Hammond. "That's a lot of board feet in one tree..."

Staring at the last bit of rye in his glass, Hammond swirled it around again before answering. "Thirty-eights cents a board foot for raw timber...that's my final offer..."

"Much obliged...I'll think about..." Colt replied.

Downing the rest of rye in his glass, Hammond set it on the table and rose. "You can just stop by our offices here on Main with your reply."

Colt nodded for his answer.

Hammond spun on his toes and headed towards the door, opened it and walked out.

41

Carlie was oblivious to the attention she kept drawing as she was standing up and driving the wood sled pulled by Harley's old mule, Jackass. A blanketed form lay in the bed of the sled as she drove through town, finally pulling up in front of the sheriff's office.

Ed came out of the sheriff's office as soon as he saw her pull up.

Her knees buckled as she climbed out of the sled. Ed barely caught her as she collapsed. He gazed into the haggard face of Carlie Anne Russell. "Girl...what the hell happened?" his eyes searched for answers within her gaunt face.

Carlie recovered, leaning back against the sled in exhaustion, "Got a body for you, Ed," she said as she began sliding down the side of the sled again.

Ed reached out to help steady the girl. "Come inside, you can tell me about it," he said wrapping a supporting arm around her waist helping her step into his office. He pulled out a chair and sat the girl down. "Now what is this all about, Carlie?" Pulling a bottle out of a drawer and taking down a glass off the shelf behind him, Ed sloshed two fingers of whiskey into it and handed it to her.

Carlie held up her hand shaking her head no.

"Drink it, Carlie. Looks to me like you need it, you look like hell," Ed ordered, thrusting the glass at her again.

Taking a sip, Carlie gagged. After all that upchucking she did, her stomach wasn't ready to tackle the hard liquor. She tried to pass it back to Ed.

Pushing her hand back. "All of it. Drink all of it," he commanded.

Glancing up at the sheriff, Carlie tried again. This time she coughed and spluttered, but it stayed down. She sucked wind first after draining the glass trying to cool the burning sensation in her mouth, then wiped her mouth with a dirty sleeve.

Ed watched all this, noticing how Carlie's eyes had a dull cast to them. Cheekbones seemed to protrude over hollow cheeks, lending a pinched drawn look to her pretty features. The girl looked like death warmed over, her face as white as the snow outside. Her only color was the dash of freckles sprinkled across her nose and under her eyes.

"You want to tell me what the hell happened out there?"

Carlie nodded.

Sitting down on the edge of his desk, Ed waited patiently.

"Two men..." she began softly. "...Came to the cabin the other night, they were going to..." Carlie swallowed. "...To take me some place and kill me," she said as her eyes drifted over to the window.

Ed observed Carlie's big hollow eyes recede into themselves.

She spoke so softly Ed could barely hear her. "They came to kill me, so Riley could take my land," she said.

"You sure about this?"

Her head bounced *Yes*. "I overheard Riley in the cook tent the day I surprised him..." She gulped in more air. "...Talking about finding my burnt body in the rubble of my home to make sure I was dead."

Ed stood. "You stay put, I'll be back in a minute..." he said, returning to the sled.

Pulling back the blanket, Ed gazed into the grotesquely frozen face of one of the two men he and Rawlins had fingered for hired guns at Riley's camp.

Rolling the blanket down further, he found the entrance wound. Rolling the frozen body up on its side, he gazed at the huge exit wound. He had to swallow the bile that suddenly found its way into his throat. He let the body drop back down with a thud.

His eyes glanced over to his closed office door, then swiveled back at the crowd gathering. "Here now, you folks go on about your business, nuthin' here for you to see." Pointing at a few men. "Take him down to Doc's office and tell him I'll be over in a little while." Ed said, as he stepped back into his office.

Carlie hadn't been able to remain still. She kept pacing the small space back and forth. Startled suddenly as the door opened, she resumed her pacing when she saw Ed come through the door.

The sheriff puckered the skin between his brows, his mouth drew into a tight thin line, *Nervous as a long-tailed cat in a room full of rocking chairs...* he thought.

Finally, Carlie stopped in front of the sheriff, and pulled a gun out of her britches, laying it on his desk. Digging in her pocket, her fingers grasped a piece of lead and pulled it out. "That's his gun, Ed," she said, as she placed it in his hand.

Ed studied it carefully, rolling it around on his fingers.

"And that's the lead I took out of Wolf, I don't know if they match up or not. I'm sure I wounded the second one pretty bad. I've got to get back, saddle up and trail him." Her hand rested on the doorknob. "He'll not get a second chance at me," Carlie said, going out the door just as the sled was returned minus the body. She climbed in and slapped the mule's rump with the reins. Turning around in the street, she headed back the way she had come.

Ed bounced the piece of lead in his hand as he watched her drive back towards her winter cabin. *Carlie's exhausted,* he thought. She had no business being out there in those mountains by herself. But as everyone knew, Carlie Anne Russell had a mind of her own, marching down her own little trail. You couldn't talk any sense into her once her mind was made up, and Carlie Anne could be one stubborn female. Closing the door, he headed to Doc's office, still bouncing the piece of lead in his hand.

4 2

C olt Rawlins lay back on his bed, the springs squeaking with his weight and laced his hands together under his head thinking. Tom Riley had private contracts to ship timber for the developing railroad and also east to the treeless prairies for the growing populations. Most folks in town were reluctant to give out any information as most worked for the Montana Improvement Company. The whole issue was beginning to smell worse then fresh skunk oil.

He was finally able to pry some information out of one lawyer not held hostage by money from the Company. But that just threw more kinks in the lasso. He had mentioned to Colt that the legal right to cut lumber in the territory besides on the property owned by the Northern Pacific railroad Company was very limited. Adding that the Timber and Stone act of 1878 was the only law which provides for timber to be harvested from public land. It allowed a one-time filing for one hundred and sixty acres of land not suitable for agriculture. So... Colt began thinking, *he could get his wife to file and bribe a few others to get them to file...*

Exhaling a loud "Damn it" as he sat up, Colt strode over to the window. Pulling the curtains aside, he stared out at the Bitterroot Range from his room on the second floor of the Rodgers Hotel.

Tom Riley didn't have an honest bone in his body. His face had revealed that the first time Rawlins had laid eyes on the man. Bringing in hired guns to scare Carlie into selling out to him or worse yet, trying to kill her to lay claim to her land; that was low, lower than a snake's belly.

Tomorrow he would begin his trek back to Carlie. He smiled. He was actually missing her.

43

After she had shot the two gunslingers and the one escaped, most of the storm had passed leaving just a mere dusting across the land. But as tired as she was, she had one urgent mission she had to complete: find the second one.

Leaning over Wallie's shoulder, she stared at the bloodstain barely covered with light snowfall. Sometimes it was heavy like now, other places the stain-blemished snow was lighter. The footprints became a beacon that allowed her to find the trail. Sitting up, Carlie's eyes intently followed the footprint blood marked sign heading south. Carlie sat very still holding her breath, listening to the sounds of the forest, *No wind,* she thought, nudging the mule forward again. *The bastard won't be much farther ahead either, bleeding like that,* as she continued to follow the red trail.

Gunshots made Carlie pull the sorrel up short. The sound reverberated against the granite hills. She sat there in confusion trying to decide which direction the sound had come from. Listening intently, she finally could pick out faint sounds coming from deep within the trees.

Carlie removed her rifle from its scabbard, dismounted and securely tied off the horse. Crouching low she began to make her way toward the faint noise, stopping every twelve to fifteen feet or so, listening. Different pitches of growling reached her ears, prompting her to move toward the sound. Another blast from a gun echoed against the walls of the mountains. Carlie moved quicker. Finding a break in the rocks, she climbed through them and doing a belly crawl to the edge, looked down.

There she found her wounded prey, trying to fend off a gathering circle of timber wolves.

His pistol fired again, taking one down. It yelped, then lay still.

Carlie waited until he had emptied his gun and had no more spare cartridges in his belt before making her move.

She fired the rifle in the air. That scattered the wolves into a short retreat. Turning, yellow eyes focused on her above them watching her warily. They'd close in eventually and she would let them have the remains, *after* she was through with her prey.

The man's head flopped to the ground when he saw her. "Thank Gawd you showed up, I thought I was a goner," he whispered hoarsely.

Taking a firm stance, Carlie rested the rifle in her arms keeping one eye on the pack. "You are…" she stated calmly.

Fear replaced relief in the man's face.

"…Or had you forgotten what you tried to do to me last night, or were going to do?" Carlie said quietly. "I outta let the wolves finish you off…"

The man tried to sit up but fell back in pain. "T'weren't my idea, that was Luke's and Riley's" he gritted out.

"Uh-huh…and burning down my house around my ears with me in it, killing my wolf, whose idea was that?" Carlie asked.

Spittle was forming around his mouth as he gasped for air. "Riley wanted you scared enough so you'd sell out to him…" he said flakes of spit flying with his words.

"He order you to do those things?"

His mouth tried to form the words. "Sort of…Evans…he got a mean streak…" he sucked in more air then continued, "He…he… wanted to do more than Riley tol' him…to…"

Hearing his words sent Carlie's insides to churning and sloshing again. She swallowed the bile that was rising in her throat. Silently she sipped more air, trying to ease the flip-flopping that was going on in her stomach.

Carlie sent the man a black look. "How much did Riley pay you to get rid of me?"

"Five hundred…" he whispered.

Carlie's eyes popped. "That's all? Mister, you got shanghaied! I'm worth way more than that! Where's the money?" When he didn't answer she knelt next to his shoulder and grabbed a lock of his greasy hair and shook his head hard. "Where's the money, you scum!"

The man didn't respond.

Carlie rose and looked around. She had forgotten about the wolves, they were closing back in. She fired the rifle into the air, and watched as they withdrew some distance, but not as far as before. She needed to get out of there. She quickly retreated back into the trees.

A voice stopped her.

"Help me, don't leave me here…"

She turned, staring at the man. Finally, against her better judgment, Carlie walked back. Keeping an eye out for the wolves, she asked, "Where's your horse?"

44

Colt Rawlins stopped at the rise before descending into the little mountain hamlet of Kaskaskia, Montana, still five hundred miles north of nowhere.

Pulling his collar closer up around his ears, he thought back to who had first brought him to this God forsaken piece of high lonesome ground. *Harley.*

So much had happened in the short time he'd been in this quiet peaceful little valley. At least it used to be a quiet peaceful little valley.

Things had gotten so whopper-jawed since he had come at Harley's request. So much so, that it was making his head spin. Harley sure knew how to tangle up a man's life, complicating it to the point where he had no choice but to help Carlie keep her land.

Looking up at the dirty gray skies, his mind asked, *You knew all of this, didn't you Harley? You knew Riley was behind this. You knew Carlie Anne was out of her league when you brought me up here, didn't you? And you knew I couldn't turn down a challenge either, didn't you, you skinny old coot?*

Yeah son, I knew.

Dammit, Harley, you made my life so complicated I can't think.

Shor ya can, son. You'll find the answers soon, I promise you.

Like hell...Harley...

Use them lawman instincts ya got...

Damn you, Harley, quit making my life so complicated, Colt's mind fired back. Rawlins would have sworn he heard Harley's rusty laugh coming from the heavens.

"Hup son, let's go find Ed," he said as he began moving toward the little hamlet that was still five hundred miles north of nowhere.

ROTATING the pencil through his fingers, Ed had been trying to get his mind wrapped around the incidents ever since Carlie Anne had brought Evans' body to him, then the next day, a wounded Phillips. He shook his head in disbelief at the turn of events.

Since Harley had brought Colt Rawlins to town, this place had gone to hell in a hand basket with murder and mayhem. And who was smack dab in the middle of it all? Carlie Anne Russell! It was enough to make a sane man go stir crazy. Ed looked up quickly when the door opened, disturbing his thoughts.

Colt Rawlins stepped through and made a beeline toward the stove, taking off his gloves warming his hands over the heat. He looked over at the cells and saw a body with a familiar face lying on the cot. "Well...I'll be damned...where'd he come from?"

"Well...howdy do to you too..." Ed answered crankily.

Colt grinned, turning to warm his backside.

"Ever since Harley brought you to town, there's been nothing but trouble!" Ed tossed out.

One brow shot up at the sheriff's response. Pouring himself a cup of coffee, Colt asked. "See you caught Phillips...Where's Evans? Lose him?"

"Nope...Carlie Anne did...caught 'em both...ya might say..."

Spurting coffee at the news, Colt wiped his chin, "What?"

"Those two blokes tried to kidnap and murder her…while'st you was gone…"

Rawlins moved toward the desk. "What? When did this happen?"

"Ta' other day for Evans…" nodding at the cell, "Caught him yesterday, she said…Doc patched him up…she took a hunk out of his arm when she shot him."

Glancing at the cell, "He talkin'?"

"Yup…like a stuck pig… 'n all pointing square at Riley."

"Well…that sure changes things…"

"Yep. What'd ya find out in Missoula?"

"Riley has contracts to cut timber for the railroad, on their property, but he's way far from that…"

"That…so…"

"Uh-huh…And he can file once to cut timber on one hundred and sixty acres, but what he's cutting is way more than that unless he got his wife to file and maybe some of his hands…"

"Hum…getting tangled bout as bad as barb wire…ain't it?"

"Yep…"

On that remark, the sheriff stood and retrieved his hat and coat. Putting them on, he said, "C'mon, got something else I want to show you," going out his door and leaving it open for Colt to follow.

Setting the cup down, "Where are we going?" Rawlins inquired, shutting the door in his wake.

"To the stable," Ed replied, as two sets of boot heels rang hollow on the swept boardwalk. "We got a room in there for those that die during the winter. We can't bury 'em till spring, the ground is too frozen," Ed explained.

Kicking at the snowdrifts blocking a side stable door, Ed pulled it open enough to slide in and waited on Rawlins to follow. "I don't know what the hell that kid used to kill this fella, looks like a damn cannonball went through his gut," Ed said leading the way into a small room.

Colt slipped past the sheriff, removing the shroud. "Evans..." he said. Rolling the dead man on his side, he examined the exit wound, then laid him flat again, replacing the shroud as he turned facing the sheriff. "Harley taught Carlie Anne to cut her lead. You cut lead like that, it rips your insides to shreds. He couldn't have been no more than three, four feet from her, from the size of the exit wound," Colt surmised.

The sheriff exhaled. "Damn kid, she keeps messing around like that, one of these days it'll catch up with her," he groused.

Colt offered a thin smile. "Do' no about that sheriff, I got a sneaking suspicion that girl has several guardian angels watching over her," he said, clapping a hand on Ed's shoulder. "Let's go back to your office, I'm not warmed up enough yet."

TURNING BACK TO THE WINDOW. Colt said, "I need to get a move on."

Ed swiveled his chair around. "Back to Carlie?"

"Not right away...gonna pay a little visit to Riley first..."

"Ahh... that should be fun..."

"For sure..."

"Take care of yourself, let me know how it goes..." he said as he stood and stuck out his hand.

Rawlins took it, saying quietly. "Thanks, Ed. Oh...you still got that pup?"

"Yep..."

"Save her for me..."

"Right..."

GUIDING the bay across the snow-covered bridge, Colt listened to the muffled sounds his mount's hooves made as they crossed the wooden structure. Gazing ahead, he noticed the ranch buildings were dark. Mumbling to himself, "Guess, I'll just have to wake some people up…"

Reining up in front of a hitch rail, he dismounted, looping the leather around the wood. Digging in his coat pocket he took the badge out and pinned it to his shirt. In a few steps he was at the door, inhaling a breath, his fist began banging on the ornate wood. He stopped, then resumed pounding. In a few moments he saw weak light bloom through the curtained windows and heard quick footsteps arriving, slowing then stopping on the other side, he took a step back.

The door flew open, spreading light onto the porch illuminating Rawlins. Tom's mouth dropped open when he recognized him. He asked grumpily, "What'da you want?"

Keeping his temper in check, Rawlins announced curtly, "We got business to discuss…" shoving his way past the sleepy-eyed Riley.

Frowning, Tom closed out the cold and strode to the front of Rawlins. "Yeah? What about?"

Unbuttoning his coat and pushing the material away, he saw Riley's eyes fixate on the badge then flick stormy eyes to his face. Colt motioned to a chair indicating for Tom to sit. "Have a seat… this might take a while…"

Tightening the sash on a plaid flannel robe, Tom stood his ground. "Say what ya got ta say, then git out…"

"Tom…what's going on…oh, hello Mister Rawlins…" as Ruth entered the room, looking at him, then her husband. "Tom, what's going on?"

Riley answered grouchily, "Go back to bed, Ruth…"

"Um…sorry to barge in on you like this, Miz Riley…" Colt apologized politely.

She nodded in response.

"…But your husband and I have some business to discuss…"

"Oh…at this time of the night?" she glanced at Tom.

"Yessum..."

Her eyes turned back to the tall man. "Have you seen Carlie Anne, Mister Rawlins? How's she doing?"

"I reckon she'll be alright, Ma'am..." he threw his gaze to Riley, "...been checking up on a few things."

Tom's eyes narrowed.

"Oh...I'll go make coffee..."

"None for me, Ma'am..."

"I need some..." she said over her shoulder as she disappeared from sight.

Watching her leave the room, Colt turned his attention to Riley, baiting him. "The Missus seems nice...how in the world did she end up with a scoundrel like you?"

"Shad-up...and get out!" He made a move towards the door.

"Not so fast...Riley. I ain't done, yet..."

Tom turned and waited.

"Peers to me...you straddling a thin line...Riley..."

"About what?"

"...Those two buffoons you hired. Telling them to burn down Carlie's home while she was in it. Then trying to kidnap and kill her..."

Riley chuckled, throwing a bluff. "Don't know where you get your information from, Mister...didn't hire anyone to kill her or burn her home." he lied. "Sides, why would I want to do that for? Her folks was good people..."

"So I've heard. But that fella in jail is singing another tune..."

"What fella?"

"...Kidnapping and attempted murder charge carries a heavy sentence..."

Riley blustered, "What the hell ya talking about?"

"I'm saying...since all this was...is your idea..."

"Like hell..."

"...You could be hanged along with Phillips..."

Tom's finger pointed at the door as he hissed like a rabid cat, "Get out!"

Striding towards the door, Colt buttoned up his coat as he sent a hard look back at Riley. "You've been warned..."

Spittle flew with fury when he shouted, "Get out!"

Opening the door a crack, Colt then turned half way around, "Oh...by the way...Evans is dead...Carlie Anne killed him and she took a chunk out of Phillips arm too, but he'll live..."

"Out!" he yelled.

Colt smiled as he stepped out and closed the door.

"Thomas Riley! What in the world have you done?"

"Shad-up, Ruth" as he savagely shoved her aside, making her drop the tray with filled cups of coffee, shattering them and splashing coffee all over the floor.

Tom stomped off to his room.

Ruth sat down on the settee and burst into tears.

45

When Rawlins finally reached the cabin in the wee hours of the morning, the light in the window beamed like a welcoming beacon to his tired eyes and body. He sat there a few moments thinking that he felt like he had arrived home. *Home?* The word startled him; why was he even having those kinds of thoughts? He was a drifter. Home to him in the past had been wherever he laid his head each night, mostly with a canopy of stars for a roof.

The bay blew, knocking him out of his musings. The horse was ready to be unsaddled, fed and under cover away from the cold.

Unsaddling the bay in the lean-to barn, he grained him. Closing the door softly between the cabin and barn, Colt walked over to his bed. Glancing at Carlie's bunk his heart jumped in his chest when he saw that it was empty. Casting his eyes quickly around the room, he saw her sound asleep in the rocker. He heaved a sigh of relief.

Tossing his things on the bed, he removed his coat and gun belt. Walking over to the fireplace, he came to stand in front of her, noticing her grandmother's blanket resting on her lap with her hands wrapped limply around her pistol.

Bending down, he placed more wood on the fire. As Colt straightened, his eyes tapered as he took stock of Carlie's appearance. Those ridiculously long lashes lay feathered against a pale backdrop, cheekbones more prominent since the last time he'd seen her. Tendrils of her hair were in disarray as usual. Except for being thinner, Carlie looked much the same.

For being such a ragamuffin and scatterbrained as hell, Colt had to admit the kid was daring and smart. Her folks had overprotected Carlie Anne and now for the very first time she had to stand on her own two feet, forcing the girl to do things she probably never thought she would have to do.

Colt gave a tired sigh as he carefully unwrapped her fingers from the grip of the pistol, placing it on the mantel. It was then his eye caught the splintered hole in the wood. He ran a finger across the rough edges as his gaze drifted back toward the sleeping girl. Colt rubbed his tired eyes, then allowed his gaze to wander back to the flames.

A noise alerted him as he witnessed her flying out of the rocker. The cover tangled her legs sent her sprawling. Carlie rolled over and crawled like a crab backwards until she was about twelve feet away.

Those bastards have scared the hell out of Carlie Anne... Colt realized.

Blinking and rubbing her eyes with the heel of her hand, Carlie recognized the man standing over her. She gradually rose. "You scared me, Mister Rawlins," she whispered.

"I'm sorry, I didn't mean to," he replied.

Picking up the blanket, Carlie swung it around her shoulders. "Yeah...well, you did," she said, pulling the blanket tighter around her ears. Her fists knotted within its folds, fixing a taut gaze on Colt Rawlins.

Ed was right, Carlie Anne did look like death warmed over. "Ed told me what happened," Colt said softly.

Carlie's eyes flicked over to the floor by her bunk.

211

"I'm sorry I wasn't here and you had to go through all of that by yourself," he said.

"Where were you? You disappeared into thin air…"

"Went to Missoula…"

Carlie's eyes popped.

"To see what I could find on Riley…"

"Did you?"

"Yeah…but I'm too tired to go into it right now…"

She looked away then her eyes flashed back to Rawlins. "I don't think I have ever been so frightened in my life," Carlie said as her eyes zeroed in on him more. "You ever been scared, Mister Rawlins?" she whispered. "So scared you can't breathe and your insides are like a block of ice? You ever been scared like that, Mister Rawlins?"

Nodding. "Many a time."

Carlie went on as if she hadn't heard him. "He called me a bitch. Am I a bitch, Mister Rawlins?" she asked.

He opened his mouth to reply then closed it, the girl had to get the fear out of her system.

She rushed on. "I mean the only time I've ever used the word was for a female dog or a wolf…" Carlie continued to rattle on without a break. "…I know the other meaning, it means, uh…it means a nasty woman, but I never thought of myself as nasty… Am I nasty, Mister Rawlins?"

He started to answer, but clamped his mouth shut as she took off again.

"I mean, I always thought I was pretty nice to folks, not nasty. Do you think I am nasty, Mister Rawlins, am I?" Carlie asked softly finally running out of steam.

Smiling, he answered, "No, I wouldn't call you that…"

"Oh…" she sighed in relief. "…That's nice to know."

Throwing another log on the fire, he moved away from the heat. Colt tucked thumbs in his hip pockets and gazed at the ragamuffin wrapped in her grandmother's blanket. "Guess that trick Harley taught you, cutting the lead of your bullets really works. Evans looked like a cannonball had gone through his gut," Colt said.

Her eyes came back into focus. "Was that his name?"

"Yeah, Luke Evans," Colt replied softly.

Her eyes flicked back to her bunk. Reliving that night, she spoke in even softer tones. "They came to take me somewhere and kill me," her eyes swept back to his face. "I've never killed anyone before...did you ever kill anyone, Mister Rawlins?" Not waiting for an answer, she hurried on. "...I killed a man, Mister Rawlins, well, almost two..." Carlie said.

"I know...I stopped by the sheriff's office and Ed filled me in..."

"Oh...I don't think I'm ever gonna use those bullets again..." she said coming up for a short burst of air, then rushed on. "... Mister Rawlins, does that mean I'm a killer?" Carlie asked quietly.

The kid was still in shock, the words bubbling up out of her like a spring.

"No, Honey, you're not a killer. Sometimes situations put us in circumstances we can't control, you acted in self-defense. You were trying to stay alive," Colt replied.

"Oh..." she exhaled softly. "...That's good to know."

Taking a few steps toward her Colt explained, "Sometimes we have to do things we're not proud of, but it's either that or ending up buried six feet under..."

Carlie barely heard him. "...The second one..."

Colt offered up. "Stu Phillips," he said

"Oh...well...this Phillips said Tom paid them only five hundred dollars to get rid of me. I, uh...I told him he'd gotten shanghaied..." Carlie trailed off.

Colt smiled, the kid had managed to hang on to her sense of humor despite all that had happened to her.

Carlie glanced up at him. "That's not very much money to pay to get rid of someone is it? I mean, well, it is and it isn't. I mean… if Tom was able to get rid of me at such a cheap cost?" Carlie stopped, then added, "Right?"

Colt nodded.

Carlie swallowed. "I see…" she whispered.

Rawlins kept watching those haunted eyes flick toward her bunk, then away again.

"Mister Rawlins, tomorrow when it's light, would you check and make sure I got all the red stains off the floor," her eyes brushed him once again. "I mean, I know I got the stains out, I scrubbed and scrubbed all night, but my mind says I didn't…and I just…I just want to be sure. If I didn't, I'll scrub them again," she said as eyes flicked again to her bunk.

Girl was teetering on the brink of collapsing, her nerves as taut as the strings on a fiddle. The shock of what she had to do was affecting her a lot more than I figured it would, Colt's mind said.

You would've been right proud of her son, she did mighty fine.

Colt glance up and around hearing the voice, his eyes traveling back to Carlie's face. *Did she hear Harley, too? By the look on her face, no. Harley, quit doing that to me!* His mind replied. *Now I'm the one going loco!*

That rusty laugh seemed to echo in his head.

Colt rolled his eyes at the voice coming from the rafters. Then his gaze came back to rest on Carlie. "Honey, we're both exhausted…" he said. "…I've been in the saddle for a week and you… well…you've had an experience that would tear anyone apart, especially a young girl."

"Woman," a tough voice replied.

"Well, all right, a woman," Colt reluctantly agreed.

Carlie moved in closer, then sagged against his body. She snuggled her face into his shirt, taking Rawlins by surprise.

"I'm glad you came back, Mister Rawlins, I'm really glad," she said, her voice muffled by his shirt.

Muscular arms enclosed the body engulfed in her grandmother's blanket. "Yeah, me too, Carlie, me too," he answered softly, enjoying the tight grip her arms had around his torso. He dropped a kiss onto the top of her head.

46

The noon meal was once again a quiet affair between Ruth and Tom Riley. At times he seemed a man possessed since he had begun this logging venture.

Sighing inwardly, she picked up the dirty dishes and then set them in the pan to soak. Gathering the corner of her apron she wrapped it around the pot handle. Walking back to the table she poured more coffee for Tom, then her own before setting the pot on the table and retaking her seat. Placing her forearms on the table in front of her, she lightly clasped her hands together while giving her husband a straight gaze. Taking a deep breath, she plunged into her question. "Tom, why are you so determined to run Carlie Anne off? I heard what was said the other night when Mister Rawlins was here, accomplice to murder and burning down her home, you'd go to jail, too or hanged. What's gotten into you?"

His swallow of coffee suddenly went down the wrong pipe hearing Ruth's words, sending him into a coughing fit. Able to breathe again, he blurted out, "Like...hell...I had nothing to do with it!"

"Why would you even *think* of doing something like that?" she accused him.

"Now…Ruth…you know I wouldn't go and do that…" he lied.

"…The Russells were good people…"

"…Dammit, Ruth…" he interrupted. "…I tol' you I had nothing to do with burning her house down!"

"Who'd you hire to scare her half to death and try to kill her?"

Angrily he rose, abruptly knocking over his chair. It clattered loudly against the planked flooring. "No…one…" Tom gritted through clenched teeth, his hands bunched into fists at his sides.

"Colt Rawlins don't seem to me to be someone who would lie…" Ruth warned.

Opening his mouth to retort, he slapped it shut when he heard the front door slam and a voice call out. "Mister Riley? We's got a big storm moving in…"

Stepping around the table, Tom looked over his shoulder at his wife. "Stay outta this Ruth, ain't none of your concern…" as he strode purposely to the front room.

She heard the voices hurriedly discussing the impending weather, then the door slammed again and all was quiet. Ruth sighed. Tom and she hadn't seen eye to eye for some time now, and if what Colt Rawlins' said was true…she wanted no part of her husband anymore.

LEANING AGAINST THE PORCH POST, Rawlins was keeping a steady eye on the slate-grey clouds that were building from the North-west, then flattening out becoming a storm wall.

His mind turned to Carlie Anne. She was trying so hard to deal with almost insurmountable odds, especially for a female. Most women would have given up, moved to town and try to snag a husband, but not Carlie Anne. She was going to stay and hang on to this lonesome piece of ground for as long as she could. Colt chewed thoughtfully on that idea for a moment.

Glancing at the grey wall in the sky, Rawlins had to admit someone up there must be protecting that little forest fairy. By all accounts, Carlie Anne Russell should've been dead by now. She had to be in God's hands, that's all there was to it. Sighing, he realized they needed to get a move on before the storm hit. Opening the door, he called out, "Carlie..."

❧

THE AIR around them had turned into a full-blown blizzard, with the wind gaining in intensity when Colt pulled in next to Carlie riding one of Harley's mules. Touching her arm to gain her attention, Rawlins pulled the scarf down from his face and leaned in close to her. He shouted against the wind, "That's about all we can do for now. We need to head back..."

Snow-flaked eyelashes peeked out above the scarf as she nodded in agreement. Turning the mule back towards the cabin, she followed Rawlins.

Both riders ducked their heads as they rode into the barn. Carlie gratefully slid off her mount and promptly stuck her gloved hands under her armpits to warm them.

Un-cinching the gear from his mount, he observed Carlie out of the corner of his eye. "Go on inside, get warmed up. I'll take care of your gear," he offered.

"I can take care of my own gear, Mister Rawlins," she said. Trying to make her fingers work the leather stiff with cold, a big hand closed over her small one.

"Here, I'll do that, you go on inside and get warmed up," Colt told her.

Carlie angrily swatted at his hand. "Go on leave me be, I'm not a baby. I can take care of my own gear..."

Rawlins backed off. "Why do you always have to be so pigheaded with me? I'm just trying to help you," he said, pulling the gear off his mule and placing it on a stall partition.

"I didn't ask you to come here," she said, lifting the saddle off her mule, throwing it on a barrel. "Harley did, and all you've done since you've been here is cause me trouble," removing the bridle then yanking a halter off the nail and hanging up the bridle.

Observing her, Colt rested his arms across his saddle. "You know, I could say the same about you..."

She aimed a dirty look in Rawlins' direction before picking up the scoop and digging into the feed bin. Silently, she added grain to each food box.

Rawlins broke the cold air with his quiet baritone. "Honey, Harley loved and cared about you very much," he began. "He had a gut feeling that Tom Riley was up to no good and he knew he wasn't going to be able to give you the protection or help that you needed. Riley is not someone you want to play games with, he's like a man with gold fever, greed driving him to act insane..." Colt explained.

"So..." Carlie said. "...That's got nothing to do with me."

Rawlins sighed. *Kid had a rock for that head of hers...* "It has everything to do with you..."

She lifted the feed bin lid, throwing the scoop inside and let it fall back down with a bang, emphasizing her next words. Sticking her gloved hands back under her armpits to warm them, she began, "Mister Rawlins...I have never had so many bad things happen to me since you showed up. You must've packed all that trouble in those saddle bags of yours and I'm tired of it," she said, heaving in cold air till her lungs hurt. "You frustrate the hell out of me, making sure I know how clumsy and useless I am at trying to run this ranch, and I'm tired of you always wearing that halo you think you got on your head," Carlie finished then added. "One of these days that halo is gonna slip and then you're gonna be just like the rest of us..." she said, giving him a dark look.

Colt cocked a brow. "Is that what this is all about?" he asked.

Carlie remained silent, her feet planted with hands under her armpits as she continued to give him a hard stare.

Rawlins rolled his eyes to the barn's rafters, then back down to her fur encased face. "Carlie Anne, ranch work is hard, much harder when you got weather like this, not to mention Riley creating more problems for you," he said. "There is no way you can handle all of it by yourself. That's why Harley contacted me," he added softly.

Carlie didn't move, but her eyes cast down to her boots as she spoke quietly. "I handled it just fine last year…"

"Last year, yes, but how about the long haul?" he asked. "What about all the years to come after? What about Riley? You're going to wear yourself out, making yourself sick, trying to stay two steps ahead of him," he said. "Riley is the sort that can outlast you, taking his time before he strikes again. What will you do then?" Colt asked.

A stubborn chin rose as defiant eyes glared back, "I'll fight,"

"With what?"

Eyes filled with anger. "Contrary to what you think of me, I'm not a blithering idiot, Mister Rawlins," she said.

An eyebrow rose as he returned hers with a steady gaze.

Carlie spun on her toes then, opening the door and entered the walkthrough, slamming it behind her.

Colt pinched the bridge of his nose then rubbed tired eyes. "Damn kid," he muttered. "Harley, if you wasn't already dead I'd drag her up to your place and dump her there for the winter," he said.

Rusty soft laughter filled the barn. *I spect you would son. I told ya she had a hard head.*

"Damn you, Harley! Why do you always get me into theses predicaments?" Colt fired back. "Or better yet, why do I *allow* you to sucker me into these situations?"

Ye always wuz partial to a pretty face.

Colt grumbled, "Shut-up Harley, just shut-up…" blowing out the lantern, he followed Carlie into the cabin.

Laughter twittered from the barn rafters.

47

Watching Carlie mope around the cabin the last few days, going out the door and coming back in, not interested in much of anything, he finally slapped the book shut he was reading announcing, "I think it's time we got a tree..."

She stopped her pacing and spun looking at him. "A tree? For what?"

"It's almost Christmas, ain't it?"

Shrugging, "Oh..."

Instead of being excited like he thought she would be, he watched her walk over to the rack holding their gear and pluck her woolies off the peg and step into them, buckling the belt strap and announcing, "I'm gonna check the stock...I need to see how Thor and Storm are doing...anyways..." As she slipped arms into her coat, jamming the fur cap on her head, she turned and disappeared into the walk through. He heard the door open and softly close. Colt sighed.

A few moments later through the window, he watched her ride Wallie up the hill to the ridge and then disappear. Turning, he absentmindedly scratched the stubble on his cheeks as he gazed around the room, thinking. *Now would be a good time to go get that pup...maybe it would cheer her up...*

Quickly, buckling his gun belt and gathering his things, Colt strode out to saddle his bay.

🦂

"HARLAN...YOU and Sweets roust yourselves outta them bunks, go saddle three harses..."

"Where's we goin'?"

"Gonna git rid of that Russell girl for good."

Sweets' eyebrows shot to his hairline.

Not moving, but narrowing his eyes at his boss, Harlan asked, "What's in it fer us?"

Tom spun. After thinking for a few moments, he replied, "I'll give each of you fifty bucks..."

"For being party ta a killin'? I don't think so..."

Looking at the other cowpoke, "Sweets?"

Throwing a quick glance at Harlan, Sweets shook his head. "Naw...I ain't looking ta git hanged for something stupid..."

Grinning Harlan offered up, "Looks to be, yer on yer own, Boss..."

Fury rose in Tom Riley's eyes. "All righty...if that's the way ya feel...pack your gear and git out."

The two cut a surprised look at each other.

"We want what's owed us..."

"Tell the Missus I fired you. Get what's owed you from her." With that Tom Riley stomped out slamming the bunkhouse door in his wake. Muttering, "Damn fools..."

🦂

IN THE BARN, Tom pried the lid off of a wooden box. He smiled as he stared at the rows of dynamite sticks. His eyes shone with a malice thinking of the soon to be end of Carlie Anne Russell and all the land he could take after her death.

4 8

Tom Riley dismounted, ground tying his horse on the backside of the girl's cabin. He listened. There were no human sounds he could discern coming from the log structure. The air was silent and cold. Normal wildlife sounds were muffled by the deep snow pack.

Reaching under his coat, he pulled out his pistol and stealthily took steps toward the porch. Tiptoeing across the wood, he leaned an ear next to the door. He didn't hear a sound. Taking a breath to fortify himself he shoved it open, hoping to surprise her. His eyes narrowed when he saw that no one was inside. Riley strode further into the room, glancing at the beds, then he spun and walked back out. Gazing towards the ridge, he noticed a well-used trail. Turning, he walked back to his mount, stepped into the saddle. He joined the trail on the hunt for Carlie Anne Russell.

REINING up in front of Ed's office, Ruth stepped stiffly down from the leather. Throwing the reins over the rail, she took the three steps up and opened his door.

Two sets of eyes glanced up in surprise.

"Why...Ruth! Mighty cold for you to be out riding today..."

Taking a huge breath, she announced. "I've left Tom."

Colt and Ed threw a quick gaze at each other before the sheriff replied. "Sorry to hear that..."

"I know he's behind this harassment of Carlie Anne..." her eyes settled on the tall man sipping coffee. "Mister Rawlins? I'm not sure, but I think he may have gone after her..." she switched her gaze back to Ed. "He fired two of our men today because they wouldn't go with him this morning..." she looked back at Rawlins, "I think she may be in danger..."

Straightening and setting his cup down on the desk, Colt asked, "When did you last see your husband, Miz Riley?"

She heaved in more air, "He went to the bunkhouse, then a few minutes later he stormed out and went into the barn. Shortly after that, he rode out. Then Harlan and Sweets came for their pay and told me why they were fired. Said he was gonna get rid of that Russell girl for good...is what they told me..." She looked at Colt, "He aims to kill her, Mister Rawlins..."

Ed whispered, "Damn...fool...."

Scooping the pup up and tucking her into his coat, Rawlins hurried to the door, opening it letting the brutal cold in.

"Get to her in time, Mister Rawlins, please..." Ruth pleaded.

"Thanks, Miz Riley, I'll try..."

"Hold up, I'm coming with you...Ruth, go to the house. I know Barb would love some company." Slipping into his heavy coat, he held the door open for her. "Mind if I take your horse?"

"Go ahead...just hand me my satchel..."

Doing so, Ed mounted quickly then urged the sorrel to catch up with Rawlins and his big bay.

ARRIVING from the east with Page, Colt studied the area. Everything seemed the same until they rounded the corral and saw the door to the cabin standing wide open. Colt's anger was evident when he exploded, "Aww...hell..."

Stepping out of the saddle, he took the pup out of his coat and set her down. She ran lickety-split through the door. He followed, his eyes looking for some kind of struggle...*Nothing...*

Following, Ed asked, "Anything?"

"Nope, either she didn't come back from checking the stock or Riley was here looking for her...I shut this door when I left to go get the pup."

Turning, Ed walked back thru the door and to his left. There he spotted men's boot tracks. "Hey Rawlins, come look at this."

When Colt arrived at his side, he pointed, "You make these?"

Eyes followed the tracks back behind the cabin then studied the trail they made in the snow now showing a set of hoof prints as they went by the porch. "Nope...that's gotta be Riley..." Colt pointed, "Carlie left towards the ridge there...and he's following her."

REINING Wallie up so he could have a breather, Carlie gazed at the beauty surrounding her. The snow pack was pristine in its whiteness, the sun glinting off it making it dazzle like millions of diamonds. The spruce, fir and pine limbs bent to the will of the snow. She breathed deeply of the sharp, cold air then exhaled, watching her breath become frozen fog then dissipate. Nudging the sorrel gently, the gelding began plowing through the belly deep snow.

FOLLOWING the trench that was plowed out by the girl's horse,

Tom Riley kept his mount moving slowly after her. Her trail was leading him right where he wanted her, the old mine. He smiled.

§

WALLIE STOPPED and nickered as Carlie studied the terrain, hoping for a glimpse of Thor, or the cattle, but saw nothing moving against the landscape. Patting his neck, she reassured him, puffs of fog highlighting her words, "It's alright, big boy...let's head towards the abandoned mine...see if some of the cattle took shelter there," nudging him with her heels.

The old mine was nestled in a steep draw, providing shelter from the snow and gnashing your teeth kind of winds that could drop temperatures to sixty below in nothing flat. Approaching the played-out mine, memories were dredged up from deep within her mind. She remembered Lone Wolf and her exploring it on many occasions. Carlie smiled faintly, she still missed him even after all these years and often wondered what had happened to her childhood friend. She sighed heartily, knowing that she would probably never find out.

Throwing a leg over the pommel, she hopped down. The snow wasn't as deep here but glancing around she saw the drifts the wind had made about twenty yards away, burying granite walls. If one didn't know the lay of the land, they would never suspect what was hidden underneath.

Refocusing on the snow, Carlie looked for hoof prints. She saw none of those, but many others; fox, squirrel, and an old print of a mountain lion. Walking in, she immediately felt warmer. Memories invaded her mind of when she and Lone Wolf had explored the tunnels in the dead mine. She smiled faintly as she touched an old timber support.

Hearing Wallie nicker, she turned and walked into the bright sunshine, expecting to see Thor.

She gasped in shock when she saw Tom Riley standing near her sorrel holding his rifle trained on her.

Her hands went immediately to her sides, but she had forgotten to put her gun belt on. Carlie gulped as her eyes flicked quickly to her rifle in its scabbard. She softly sucked in air for her deflated lungs trying to quell the feeling of doom.

Riley had her cornered good and no one would be able to rescue her now. Her mind began a series of flashing scenarios on how to save herself, but none of them felt good enough. Taking a deep breath, Carlie strode right up to Riley, trying to throw him off guard.

Eyes narrowed with scorn as he watched the girl with the ridiculous fur cap on her head wearing woolies walk towards him.

"You're a far piece from your land, Mister Riley...what brings you up here?"

His lopsided grin held a malice that sent the willies skittering down her back, suddenly making her feel chilled.

"You."

"Me? Why I'm honored, Mister Riley," she replied sarcastically.

"I come to collect my land..."

"Your land?"

"Yes."

Shaking her head, smiling, Carlie looked down at her snow-cover boots, then back up at him. Raising that stubborn chin with the dimple into the air, she squinted against the bright sunlight. "Over my dead body...Riley..." Immediately, she knew she had just made the situation worse. She kept a stern gaze on Riley hopefully hiding her insides knocking against her ribs like rocks in a barrel rolling downhill.

He chuckled. "That can be arranged..." as he cocked the lever back inserting a cartridge in the chamber of his rifle, pointing it at her chest from his hip.

She looked at the rifle aimed at her and took a deep breath, diving for Riley's knees. With the sudden impact of her body, his finger automatically pulled the trigger as his rifle fired harmlessly into the air. The sound vibrated across the granite escarpments. Carlie tried to scramble out of his reach. She didn't make it as he brought his rifle around and slammed the butt into her temple, sending her sprawling into the snow, out cold.

49

age and Rawlins jerked on their mounts' reins hearing the
rifle shot echo against the hills. No other sounds drifted
down to their ears, just numbing silence after that
one shot.

Peering up the track made by two other horses, Ed voiced,
"That came from about where the old mine is…" He glanced over
at Colt. "Carlie have a rifle with her?"

His heart in his throat, he just nodded to the sheriff. Colt
regretted that he had let Carlie Anne ride off by herself, but it was
too late now. Digging his heels into his bay's sides, he urged the
gelding forward through the deep track. He wished they could
move faster, but the belly deep snow hindered that even with a
plowed trail.

Ed followed behind him single file.

❧

PUSHING himself up out of the snow, Riley took a deep breath
staring at the still form of the Russell girl. Throwing his glance

towards the mouth of the mine, he grinned. Walking over, bending, he picked her up and slung her over his shoulder, not noticing that her fur cap had fallen off. He strode into the darkness ten yards or so and dumped her body on the packed dirt floor. Giving one more glance at her, he walked back out to his mount and opened his saddlebag. Retrieving a couple of sticks of dynamite and fuse, Riley entered the mine again. Studying the posts and beams, he settled on the two nearest the entrance, tucking the sticks behind each side post. After inserting the fuse in each end, he walked backwards trailing and wrapping the fuse line together. Reaching the exterior, he glanced over his shoulder judging the distance, length of fuse and his get-away time, Riley swept snow out of the way and laid the fuse down. His fingers dipped into his shirt pocket and scraped out a few matches. He stared into the tunnel one last time. "Sleep well, Dearie…"

Striking the matches against his leather chaps, the phosphorous flared. He stared at it for a moment then smiled as he bent down and lit the end of the fuse. Watching the sparks and flames begin following the fuse, he turned and ran, mounting quickly and dug his heels into the gelding hightailing it as fast as he could make the horse go.

HEARING THE HUGE KAABOOM, the sound sending echoes across the mountains, Colt reined up sharply, yelling, "Damn you, Riley!"

"How ya know it's Riley?"

"Carlie knows nuthin' about dynamite." He spurred his horse into a lope spraying snow as they rode hard towards the old mine.

THOR'S EARS pricked forward towards the loud noise that seemed to shake the ground beneath him. His nostrils flared catching the unusual scent the wind blew his way. Curious, he took off towards the direction of the noise.

&⃟

SAILING OFF THE SADDLE, he ran to the fresh mound of rock closing off the mine entrance. Colt bellowed, "Carlie! Carlie!" He heard nothing except his voice echoing across the hills.

Feeling something squirming inside his coat he looked down at a little black nose just a twitching. Reaching in he pulled the pup out and set her in the snow. She immediately put her nose to the ground and began sniffing; her tail wagging so hard it looked about to come off.

Colt began tossing the chunks of rock aside trying to clear an opening. Ed followed suit working alongside him.

The pup found Carlie's fur hat. Picking it up in her teeth she climbed the rock and dropped it in front of the two men and began barking.

They stopped their work to stare at her.

Picking it up, "That's Carlie's hat." Colt looked at the pup and gestured with it. "Where is she? You know where she is?"

He would have sworn that pup was grinning at him. "Is Carlie inside the mine?"

The pup yapped some more then whirled, climbing the rock sniffing. At the top of the mound she looked back at the men and kept barking, her tail wagging fast and furious.

"Would you lookie there...she's tracking Carlie's scent. How in the hell did that little squirt know to do that?"

Colt shrugged, "Do' no...but it's worth a shot." Looking at the pup, "You want us to dig there?"

A growl erupted into more frenzied yapping.

Both men climbed higher and began tossing rocks from where the pup indicated.

&❧

Exhaling a happy sigh, Tom Riley kept his horse at a constant plodding gate. For the first time in months he felt relief flood his body. Once he filed the paperwork he'd be the biggest landowner in the area and the richest, combining the Russells' prized stock with his along with the timber he could now scalp form the hillsides. He was going to be sitting mighty pretty a few months from now. Riley smiled thinking of how he had outwitted that stupid girl.

Catching something out of the corner of his left eye, his head swiveled. Eyes lit up as he watched the big black horse plow the snow like a steam engine, heading his way. He was a sight to see, mane and tail flowing as he loped through the snow.

Grinning, he released the rope from its leather strap and shook it out, whispering, "You're mine now too, ya black devil!" He waited as the stallion moved closer.

Thor slowed then stopped entirely outside the throwing length of the rope, warily eyeing the man twenty-five feet away. His nostrils flared. Instinct told him this man was his enemy.

Riley nudged his mount forward. The gelding nickered in protest. He knew he was no match for the big stallion. Tom kicked him harder in the ribs and slapped him hard across his rump making him move faster.

Thor shied to his right, still keeping out of range of the rope.

Kicking his mount again, urging him closer to the black, Riley shook out the rope and begun twirling it around his head then let it sail through the air. It hit the stallion across the withers.

Thor moved quickly back then stood quietly waiting, watching.

Jerking his horse's head roughly around and kicking the

gelding hard in the ribs, Riley closed the gap between himself and the black.

Thor snorted then lunged, whirling at the last second to hit the gelding broadside with his flank, kicking out his back legs. One hoof caught the gelding in its ribs as the other hit his shoulder. The horse stumbled doing a head dip and flipped over on his back, sending snow flying as he pinned his rider beneath twelve hundred pounds of squirming, squealing horseflesh.

🐾

SHEDDING their coats long ago due to the exertion of moving rock, Rawlins and Page suddenly heard a horse scream in the distance.

"What the dickens..."

"Sound travels far in this thin air..." Colt offered taking a deep breath. "Probably a big cat got itself a fresh meal..." he resumed pitching rock.

Page shook his head reaching for another small boulder.

The pup remained right there with the men, tail wagging and giving little yips as if she was encouraging them.

Colt smiled. Reaching over, he ruffled her ears, then grunted as he tried to dislodge a larger boulder.

🐾

SCRAMBLING TO GAIN ITS FOOTING, the gelding's hooves stumbled raking Riley as he struggled to rise. Bones cracked. He screamed in agony, those cries reaching across the hills then fell silent.

The gelding walked a few paces blowing and shaking, then hung his head and remained still.

Riley laid in the snow with his eyes closed trying to breathe. He became aware of the cold snow melting beneath him, soaking his coat and shirt beginning to chill him.

Thor knew the danger was over as he walked to the body and blew in his face.

Riley's eyes flew open as he stared at the black. "You bastard..." he croaked.

For an answer, Thor raised a leg and drove his hoof into the ribs of the man. More cracking noises were heard and a slight groan. The stallion turned and trotted away.

arlie stirred, and then an unfathomable pounding in her head seemed to drain every ounce of strength from her body. Her world turned black again.

TIREDLY ED SAT, watching Colt still frantically trying to remove boulders. Some of the larger ones they had used the horses to pull and roll out of the way after wrapping their lassos around them. "Gonna be dark soon..."

Stopping to catch his breath, Colt worked his way back down to Ed, glancing at the twilight lit sky edging closer to darkness. "Stars will give us light..." as he walked over to cleaner snow, scooping a hand full and putting it in his mouth to melt. Swallowing the water, he looked at the sheriff, "Can't remember how far the tunnels go or how much air she may have left...we gotta keep working..."

Ed blinked. "You been here before?"

Scooping another handful of snow, Colt nodded. "Long time ago..." as he slid his leather gloves over his hands.

"When?"

"Too many years ago...let's get back to work..." He climbed the mound where the pup sat patiently waiting.

Colt dug more debris away and shoved a boulder out of the way to reveal a gaping hole. He shouted excitedly, "Got it!" as he slipped down to his belly and peered into the black hole. "Carlie? Carlie...you hear me?"

When he slid back from the small entrance, the pup disappeared. "Hey!"

"That pup will find her...she's smarter then I figured."

"Hope you're right. I can't get through."

Inside, the pup began sniffing around and found Carlie lying still. As she began licking her hand, fingers twitched. She repeated the actions on her cheek. Carlie groaned. Her eyelids felt as if she had huge weights on them. The pup stepped up her endeavors to arouse the girl.

The silence killing him, Colt leaned into the hole and called out, "Carlie? Carlie...can you hear me?"

A leg moved.

The pup barked.

"Carlie?"

The pup yipped.

She stirred, rolling over on her back. The pup once again began licking her cheek, then barked again.

Colt was becoming frantic. He dug some more hoping to enlarge the hole. The debris was too packed. He called again, "Carlie! Answer me!"

Somewhere in her unconscious mind, Colt's voice registered.

The pup felt her movement and yipped again.

"Carlie! Dammit! I can't get in there...Carlie? You hear me?"

The pup licked her face again.

Carlie opened her eyes to tar-black darkness. Her hand brushed against her wet cheek.

A slight growl broke into frenzied barking.

"Carlie?"

Hearing Colt's voice, she whispered, "Mister Rawlins?" She struggled to sit up. Something kept dodging around her; she reached out her hand and felt the soft fur. It barked then the little body ran to the opening and yipped again.

Shifting to her knees, Carlie began crawling towards the sound. Her head was pounding so hard it was making her dizzy, forcing her to stop until the spell passed.

"Carlie! Answer me!"

Hearing that warm soothing baritone, Carlie wet her lips. "Mister Rawlins?" But it came out as a croak. Clearing her throat, she tried again. "Mister Rawlins..."

Hearing her voice Colt sighed with relief. "Carlie...over here..." turning to the sheriff, "You got a match on you?"

"I think so..." Digging in his shirt pocket, Ed pulled out two. Stepping on the rock pile he stretched and handed them to Colt.

Striking one against granite, the phosphorus flared. Scooting closer, he stuck his hand through the opening, calling out, "Carlie...over here..."

She glanced up at the brightness of the flame sticking out like a sore thumb in the pitch-blackness. She crawled towards it.

The pup was dancing around her yipping, running back and forth between her and the opening.

The flame suddenly died, leaving her world dark again. Carlie stifled a sob calling out, "Mister Rawlins?"

"I'm here, Half-pint...follow the pup..."

"I can't see..."

Striking the second match against rock, he pushed it into the opening. "Here...right here...follow the pup..."

"I'm trying..." she answered weakly.

"Dammit! Try harder!" Colt bellowed, shaking the match out when it burned his fingers.

She closed her eyes hearing his frustrated yell. Carlie crawled further towards his voice and the pup's excited yips. Reaching out, her hand felt the barrier the dynamite had created. Her mind flicked briefly to Tom Riley. She tossed him out of her head and pulled herself into a wobbly standing position. She hung on to the rock to balance her unsteady body. Glancing up, she could see the stars overhead. She heaved a sigh of relief. "Mister Rawlins?"

"Carlie...I can't come get you...can't make the hole any bigger. You've got to try and climb out..."

She nodded, even though she knew Colt couldn't see her actions. Movement alongside of her had her watching the pup scramble up and over the debris and scamper out of sight. Taking a deep breath and slowly exhaling, she mentally tried to put strength into her wobbly limbs.

The pup kept dancing near the hole giving occasional yips as if she was encouraging Carlie.

A burst of air exploded from Colt's lungs when he saw Carlie's arms and head slowly emerge from the mine. Reaching quickly, he grabbed her and pulled her the rest of the way out.

Ignoring her pounding head, Carlie flew into his arms, wrapping hers around his neck so tight he thought he would suffocate. He smiled, holding her securely against his chest listening to her sobs. "Here...now, it's all right...you're safe...I've got you..." Swinging her into his arms he slowly moved to the bottom of the shale debris setting her on a large boulder. Turning to Ed, "Get my canteen...will ya?"

"If it ain't frozen..." striding over and plucking it from the saddle horn shaking it as he walked back then handed it to Colt.

The pup had climbed into Carlie's lap and was licking away her salty tears. She wrapped her arms around the bundle of fur and buried her face in its body.

Unscrewing the cap, he pushed the canteen at Carlie, while he tucked stray tendrils of hair away from her face.

She winced even though his touch was gentle. She gratefully took the water and drank some of it, wiping her mouth with the sleeve of her dirty over-grown coat.

Colt's eyes narrowed when he saw the lump and swollen-shut right eye. Even in the darkness he could see the bruise forming. "Riley do that to you?"

She nodded, then took another sip of water. Her voice squeaked, "He came here to kill me...Mister Rawlins..."

Squatting in front of her, "You wanna tell me what happened?"

"I don't know...my head is killing me..."

Placing a hand on her shoulder, "Try..."

Glancing at Colt, she took a big breath, "I came up here to see if some of the cattle had sheltered inside the mine...they've done that before..." Carlie explained. "When I came out he was there with his rifle pointed at me..." she sipped more air into her lungs. "I dove at his legs, knocking him down..."

Colt smiled.

"...We tussled a bit then he slammed the rifle butt into my head..." she sucked in more air. "...And that's all I remember... until you came..." she finished softly.

"He blew up the entrance to the mine with dynamite..." Colt told her.

"Oh..."

Looking at the sheriff, "That's attempted murder, Ed..."

Nodding in agreement, the sheriff said, "The law will take care of Riley, Carlie Anne...he won't get away with this...I'll make sure of that."

Recognizing the voice, her head turned slowly towards the sheriff. "Mister Ed...where did you come from?"

"Been here the whole time...Ruth came into town, told us her suspicions and here we are..." he nodded at the dog. "If it t'weren't for that pup...

"Where'd it come from?"

"Uh...well...it was s'posed to be a surprise, but well...she's your Christmas present..." Colt revealed.

"Mister Rawlins..."

He cocked his head, smiling faintly, "Don't ya think it's time to drop the Mister and just call me Colt?"

She stared at him trying to comprehend what he said. Her head felt like a herd of buffalo was stampeding through it. She closed her eyes; all she wanted was to sleep in her nice warm bed for days.

Scooping her into his arms, "We need to get you home, Half-pint. I think you've had enough excitement for one day."

Laying her head against his broad shoulder, Carlie relaxed, closing her eyes. She realized she liked the comfort of his big strong arms holding her. She sighed softly.

He smiled hearing that, placing her on the leather.

Sitting straighter, she tried to peer through the darkness, looking all around. "Where's Waldo?"

The sheriff looked around, "Huh?" handing over her hat.

She took it saying, "Wallie..." Placing her elbow on the horn, Carlie rested her head in her palm. "My head hurts too much..."

Colt touched her thigh, "Need to get you home..." as he stuck a snow crusted boot in the stirrup.

"No...wait..." Dragging in more air, she sat straighter, stuck two fingers in her mouth and blew a shrill whistle.

A far-off nicker answered.

"That's him..." Carlie replied.

Picking up the pup, Colt handed her to Carlie, then climbed up behind her, adjusting himself behind the cantle. Looking at the sheriff, "Ed, you ready?"

Settling into his saddle, picking up the reins, "Yep..."

Nodding, "Let's go...then..." Urging his mount over to Wallie and taking his reins, Colt led the party through the star-lit snow away from the mine and towards home.

Carlie rested her back against Colt's warm, solid chest and closed her eyes.

C arlie Anne had recuperated from her ordeal with Riley, at least that's what she wanted everyone to believe, including him. But he knew it wasn't so. The light had gone out of her eyes and her chatterbox banter was gone.

She insisted that the pup was part Scottish terrier or full-blooded and that thrilled her to death because that had always been her favorite breed. Carlie named her Poppie and the two were inseparable.

The sheriff and Colt finally found Riley's body a week later. It was almost unrecognizable due to its mangled state. They left it where it lay buried under a pile of rocks.

The Riley Ranch was up for sale, but so far there were no takers. His logging business had fallen apart and the loggers left as did many of the cowhands. They had no loyalty to the brand. Ruth continued to live with the sheriff and his wife Barb. Riley's Empire was no more.

ॐ

STIRRING THE COALS, Colt threw two more logs on the fire, then walked over to the door. Opening it, he gazed at Carlie standing by the corral looking forlorn staring up at the millions of stars the clear skies had produced this night. Poppie was with her, sniffing around as usual.

Stepping back inside, he grabbed his heavy wool coat and slipped arms into the sleeves, then buttoned it. Heading back outside, he shut the door softly behind him and began the trek to where Carlie stood.

Hearing footsteps crunch behind her, Carlie looked over her shoulder. "Hey..."

"Hey yourself..." as he placed his forearms on the top rail, hands clasped lightly together looking at the stars above. "Beautiful, aren't they?"

She nodded, still remaining silent.

Puffs of warm breath accented the calm.

Cutting her a quizzical look, "You all right? Been awful quiet here lately..."

Shrugging, "I guess..."

Poppie came over to Colt placing two paws on his pants leg, greeting him. He reached down and scratched around her ears. Satisfied, she scampered into the corral.

Carlie began speaking softly, "A long time ago when Lone Wolf disappeared without a word..."

Colt's breath caught.

"Gramma brought me outside on a night like this..." as she took her arm and gestured to the clear star-lit sky. "I was very upset because he never bothered to let me know he was leaving... he just disappeared..."

His memory bank tried to retrieve the memories.

"...She would reach up into the sky and gather handfuls of stars and put them in my coat...she called them *My pocketful of stars...*" Carlie pulled open the tattered pocket gesturing with it. "She told me whenever I was missing Lone Wolf to take a few stars from my pocket and blow them in the direction of the wind and he would receive them..." She sighed, "I guess he never got them..."

Colt's heart gave a tug. Silently he reached up and grabbed a handful of stars and brushed them off into her pocket. "Oops... there's another..." as he brushed one remaining imaginary star off his fingertips. He repeated the process again, saying, "That should hold you for a while..."

"Thank you..." She stepped a few paces away from Colt with her back to him. "I believe in my childish way, I loved him..." she breathed deeply of the cold air. "And I guess in a way...I still love him...I miss him...I wish he was here..."

"He is..."

Whirling, Carlie gasped, staring at the tall man who'd rescued her a few weeks ago.

Colt grinned looking down at his boots then back at her. "A long time ago when I was a young buck, I became friends with a little girl. Her hair was the color of golden grasses and she talked faster than the singing waters of a stream..."

Carlie whispered, "*Hupia Baa'*" saying her name he had given her in Shoshone, Singing Water.

"She taught me the white man's words. Even though I was white, I had never heard them spoken. She taught me to write the white man's words and I taught her Shoshone..."

"*Takan bia'sia...*" she whispered his name.

"My Shoshone is a little rusty..." he admitted. "I left Grey Elk, not because I didn't want to stay, I did. But because I wasn't Shoshone. I was white and I needed to find myself and see if I did truly fit into a white man's world."

Carlie's mouth clapped shut as she continued to stare at her long-lost childhood friend now standing in front of her.

"I know nothing of my past except what Grey Elk told me...he bartered for me from some Pawnee and took me to raise as his own when I could barely walk."

"But...but you've gotten so big and tall..."

He chuckled. "I grew up and so did you, Carlie..." he continued, "I tried to block out all things Shoshone, including a beautiful little girl with golden hair and turn white again and I succeeded. Then I received a letter from Harley saying to come here, he needed my help. It took me awhile, but I finally remembered those times we spent together and I guess I loved that little girl, too and I've come to realize I still do..." He tilted his head at Carlie, "I guess you could say, I've come home...if you'll have me?"

"Oh...*Takan bia'sia*...I've missed you so much..." as she ran into his outstretched arms. He welcomed her, lifting her into his arms hugging her as if he would never let her go.

She wrapped her legs around his waist and her arms around his neck, squeezing tightly.

"You're choking me..."

Releasing her stranglehold on him, she pushed herself back. With her hands resting on his shoulders, she grinned impishly, teasing him. "You know...I've never been kissed by a man before..."

Cocking a brow, "That so?"

"Uh-huh..."

"Well...we might just have to do something about that...ya think?"

"Do you give free kissing lessons?"

He grinned, "I think that could be arranged..." as his hand slid behind her head cupping her neck pulling her to him.

Their lips brushed, hers tentative, his hungry as they explored each other.

Coming up for air, Colt let her slip from his arms to stand in the snow.

"Well...that was nice..." Carlie said simply.

He stared at her, "That all you can say about your first kiss?"

She cut him a sly glance, "I need more lessons..."

He threw back his head and laughed.

Carlie liked the sound of his deep baritone when he laughed.

Taking her arm, "Let's go decorate that tree that's taking up space...all right?"

Nodding, Carlie called to Poppie. The pup scampered ahead as two reunited long-lost friends walked back to the cabin, arm in arm.

52

ONE YEAR LATER

Wiping the excess grease off his hands with a rag after packing the buckboard's wheel hubs, Colt Rawlins leaned against the doorjamb of the barn glancing around the yard. His bay and Wallie were shuffling around in the corral with the mules. He watched Poppie slip under the rail and go sniff noses with Carlie's horse. Contented clucking noises from the chickens scratching around reached his ears. His eyes settled on his wife sitting on the steps of their new home, drawing as usual with her sketchpad on her knees. The drawing she had made of him lassoing a calf that she gave him that one Christmas at the cabin was now framed and hung over the mantle of the granite fireplace. It still amazed him how she captured every little detail so accurately. One thing was for sure, he'd see to it that she always had a *Pocketful of Stars*.

His eyes lifted to the hewn logs shining brightly in the sun. It had taken a while but with Carlie Anne's drawings and help from others, they had rebuilt the original home much like it was before Riley and his henchmen burned it, using the cut lumber Riley had stacked. No sense in letting good wood go to waste.

Colt had bought the Riley stock from Ruth, then hired her to cook and take care of the house. Carlie still couldn't cook and probably never would learn the knack of it. Too, Ruth was company for her when he was gone. Right now, Ruth was away for a week visiting friends, forcing Colt to do the majority of cooking.

He'd turned the lean-to portion of the barn into a makeshift bunkhouse and had hired a few of Riley's trustworthy hands to join *Three Pines Ranch*.

He and Carlie Anne were expecting their first child in a few months. She wasn't happy about foregoing her britches but relented and now wore dresses to accommodate her growing tummy.

His eyes lifted, gazing at the bright blue summer sky. *Well... Harley...ya happy?*

A rusty laugh echoed in Colt's mind. *Shor am...Ya wrastled my Half-pint and married her...gonna have a young'n of yer own...Hell Yeah! I'm happy!*

Colt chuckled hearing Harley's reply.

Well...son, my work is done here...reckon I'll be passin' on. It's time I go see my Katydid and little boy...But...I don't want ta haf ta come back and straighten out yer arse...ya hear me?

Who...me? Naw...

Again, a familiar laugh seemed to echo in Colt's mind. He whispered, "I'm gonna miss you, you old coot..."

The voice seemed faint in his mind when Harley replied, *See ya, son...*

"Bye...Harley..." and then it seemed the old man's presence just disappeared. Colt sighed, looking over at the house. His eyes widened as he saw roiling black smoke pouring out the kitchen windows. He yelled, "Carlie!"

She looked up from her drawing at him, a quizzical frown on her face. "What?"

Sprinting towards her, he pointed, "The kitchen's on fire... what the hell did you do?" as he took the steps sailing past her.

Carlie's mouth dropped open as her head swiveled seeing the smoke, "Oh...no..." dropping the pad and scurrying after her husband. When she arrived, she saw Colt pulling a tray of burnt to nubbins supposed to be biscuits out of the cook stove.

He gave her a disgusted look as he walked to the back porch and tossed them into the grass, then returned. The pan clattered on the tabletop as he tossed the towel and gave her a stern look.

Carlie's eyes filled and her lower lip trembled as she looked at him.

Colt's anger melted.

"I'm...sorry..."

Taking a finger, he crooked it, gesturing for her.

Walking around the table, Carlie went into his arms, her words muffled into his shirt. "I'm sorry..."

Colt sighed. "Just pray Ruth comes back a day early..."

Lifting her head, Carlie stared at him, then burst into laughter. He joined her.

After catching her breath, she reached up and cupped the back of his neck with her hand bringing his face closer to hers.

A dark brow cocked. "Well..."

Smiling eyes teased, "I need another kissing lesson..."

"I think that can be arranged..." wrapping his arms around her and pulling her in close, his lips took hers.

Carlie's mouth parted willingly as she returned the gesture kissing him thoroughly.

The End!!

NOTE FROM THE AUTHOR

Thank you for reading *Pocketful of Stars*, I hope you enjoyed reading it as much as I had fun writing it!

Please leave a review if you feel inclined to...

Until we meet again...Happy Trails!!

ABOUT THE AUTHOR

Author Juliette Douglas is shown with white thoroughbred stallion Arctic Bright View who played 'Silver' in the 2013 remake of **The Lone Ranger**. Both hail from Marshall County, Kentucky. (Photo by Lois Cunningham, Benton, KY)

SADDLE UP... LET'S RIDE!

Visit our websites:
http://juliettedouglas2016.wix.com/mysite
www.megsonfarms.com

Visit Juliette Douglas via Facebook.

facebook.com/author.juliette.douglas

Made in the USA
Columbia, SC
28 September 2024

42542550R00143